SPYCORP

ALEXANDER

DEEV

Novel by Alexander Deev.
Cover and design by Sasha Lend.
Photo credit: George Mayer

to contact the project visit
www.spycorp.co

WORD BY AUTHOR

The following story is a set of events that happened not so long ago. These events are known to me through the documents and the media files I acquired from an anonymous source. Those documents and files were used to create the written pieces that are the content of the novel. These pieces were intended to be as close to the documents acquired as possible. They precisely portray the events as these events happened. I also should note that as soon as I finished the novel, all initial sources were destroyed as it was my agreement with the giver. I also note that all names, dates, and other details able to help the identification of these events' participants were altered to protect my source. The rest is true.

ELISE

PART ONE

Oct, 29

Morning and Day

Private Audio Diary of Elise

by Elise

As I remember it, Martin was almost asleep, drifting in a smog of his dream. And it was a telephone call that made him totally awake. That part of his mind which was away from the real world entered the reality. Suddenly, shaken. While he was talking - unsteady hand, pressing an instrument to his ear - his face changed. That was something. Something on the other end of the line.

I worked for this doc film studio for a couple of years. We all here, or at least most of us, have some other jobs on the side. Our days it is not so easy to make your living making the non-fiction features. And for us, the industry does not provide a permanent current of orders and sales. TV channels big enough won't pay for anything you do and won't give you an order to do anything you can do.

Once, I decided to use the opportunity for such a job because for a young girl like me, without some highly positioned friends and relatives, and without a prominent inheritance, an occupation a bit closer to TV, or something that at least might seem to be a more creative kind of business, was more promising than some other opportunities I could choose from.

Though, I am not a kind of person who at any given moment in one's life is expecting the unbelievable to happen. To happen and to carry you away from the world of boring reality. But the bloody truth is that I as usually expected my next turn to be a little better than it was indeed. When you start dating someone, do not you expect this new person to be a little more interesting than your previous experiences? If you don't, we are different. That's for sure.

Me, I always seize an opportunity for a portion of sweet dreams about something better entering my life when beginning new relations with my new boyfriend. I'm not that kind of female who expects someone to marry her right on the spot and arrange the most perfect marriage ever with the most perfect kids, etc. Of course not. One may say I was not born in the nineteenth century. But maybe I hope for something that is more like an adventure. At least, one little adventure appearing out of the blue in a current of my ever boring life. And maybe he would be more fascinating than a usual person. A little smarter than the guys usually are. Just a little. And only then it all appears to be the same old crap. Nothing so special.

And maybe that is also the way I could feel about a new occupation. What if it is a new move forward? Something that can finally change my life previously scheduled with so many absolutely expected things to happen. My route in life and career was an endless line of different jobs which were so similar in meaning. I was extending the way of loser items on my employee list with things like the shop assistant and do-this-and-that girl. And I dreamed of traveling. To buy a ticket for an airplane and to take a place in a heavy machine ready to carry me and some hundred other people to another continent across the sea. And maybe I would like to be the only passenger who didn't care to buy the return ticket.

In my dreams, I never saw someone like Leo DiCaprio or James Franco, but so many times I saw myself leaving my hometown on a giant aircraft. It is not that I don't like handsome actors, just I didn't see them in my dreams so often as the steel wings breaking the clouds of pure white in the sky of crystal blue. And no matter, if you want to see some international celebrity, maybe you will need to cross the ocean for a beginning.

As a schoolgirl, I always was the best at geography knowing all capitals of all countries, because in my younger years I found some fun in studying the maps. Subconsciously I just wanted to get away from here and as far as possible. Someday, somewhere to Latin America, Australia, any distant and beautiful destination.

But instead, I was here in the tiny room which was something between office and store. A place Martin, who de facto became my closest chief, called the studio. But the studio was not filled with the art. Not the pieces of Da Vinci, Monet, and Modigliani, but tons of papers, photos enfolded in the yellow and red document cases together with some features by Michael Moore belonged to its shelves, which stood across two longer walls of a rectangular room.

And right then, I found myself standing near Martin who was sitting behind his monitor having a face of a man who was just unexpectedly struck. Expression of weird shock, excitement, and astonishment blended was frozen in his eyes. Some few seconds before, he was just talking on the phone, and now it was a different kind of Martin in front of me. Whether it was this someone on the other end of the conversation who made him feel so or something else, I will never have a chance to know. I was still standing with some papers he asked me to bring in my hands watching him unconsciously. I pretended I did not notice anything I was not supposed to notice. Here it is. I said and was going to show the diagrams of primal importance from the study he wanted to know about. But he was somewhere far away. And all Martin responded with was What? that he said in such unsure way that I didn't know whether I should've continued unfolding a summary of research contents. Or maybe I should've just left a pack of sheets filled with figures and researcher

explanations on his table and move away silently.
So... This showcase in view of the author actually explains why situation could take the form like this and to develop to the point when... I began slowly almost moved only by the inertia of my intention which previously was clear. But then I did not think it was a good time to talk on the subject. I'll better explain you this a bit later. I said. He responded with a sigh coming from so far away. Yeah... And by saying this he still was staring somewhere through the wall, his eyes wide open. And I slid away to be absolutely forgotten for some hours until I would be needed again for some please-bring-me-this errand.
After some minutes he picked up the notebook and pencil and left the room. I spent the rest of the day reading some stuff which could turn to be useful for Martin's next documentary film, drinking coffee and eating sandwiches. Alone. Thanks to my rapid metabolism which allows me to put as many sandwiches inside my stomach as I please, without thinking about what will happen to my skinny body constitution. Finally, it looks like I fished something out of this paper pile. Something that can be useful. And then satisfied, I went home.
This evening, I watched a couple of boring TV shows, read some book and spent some time dreaming about my future.
Recorded October 29, before going to bed. End of line.

Oct, 29
Morning
from Dictaphone Record
by Martin

I still do not know what it really was. And I expect the absolute essence of happening to be never revealed to my poor mind. Was it luck or misfortune? I only can say it was unusual. Sitting in front of a monitor, I was trying to gather all pieces of supposed documentary feature into a single shape. My stomach was in process with the breakfast I ate an hour earlier, and my brains were processing the pieces of video and the writing stuff while trying to overcome a state of sleepiness. I asked Elise whether she could find and bring me a folder with some papers I wanted to see in addition to what I saw on display.

And then it came. The thing was falling out of the blue sky. My old-fashioned office phone rang, and I almost instinctively picked up the instrument while continuing to view the lines of text and the photos covering a surface of my computer's monitor. That was the call of a lifetime.

I am a person who hardly perceives too many things emotionally. But about this matter... my thoughts and feelings mix in a turmoil state of mind I have.

Currently, I try to finish my new work as fast as I can, no matter that indeed there were moments when I regarded it like the oeuvre. And at some moment I thought that maybe I shouldn't hurry up too much, but to prepare the ground for it and wait for revelations and glimpses that should be developing momentum for the great work. I really don't think it is a crazy idea to think about a doc film as about the piece of art. I mean, at least, such thing can be one in theory. So, I thought maybe it was better just to collect some material and to concentrate on the work mentally.

Just some days ago I was asked to do some job. And now I'm obliged to make a film on the topic that isn't my primal interest. I say obliged, because I mean I didn't want to do it, especially borrowing time from my project number one. I mean, that looks to me like wasting time. But that was the order from the company which is one of the very few clients asking for our production. That means that we really depend on them. That means we depend on their cramped audience and the soap, cola and bouillon cube advertisers. That means if we - first of all me as director and author - don't make exactly what they ask for and when they ask, we'll go out of the industry. And I will need to find some other job to do in the case.

And so, in a state like this, I receive The Call. And

here comes the voice on the other side of the wire which shakes my life entirely. At the moment, I could not know it. I felt crazy and irritated from the very morning. But then I also sensed that this could be the most interesting.

A voice on the other end offered me to be provided with information of great importance. In the situation like that, there was too much of everything-for-you thing. And it was the voice itself that didn't sound natural to me. It was like it was produced by some vocal synthesizer or was computer-effect masked. Early in our conversation, I started to feel that there had to be something wrong with it. And most probably, it seemed to be some crazy joke. Since the day the telephone was once introduced by Mr. Bell to humanity, there was always a part of this humanity that played in the way like this to entertain themselves with such a silly game.

And step by step, as one phrase was added after another, the thing felt strange. At some moment, it didn't look funny at all, but really strange. Almost from the beginning, a guy who was on the other end of the line started to perform tricks that I am still not able to understand. He was telling me about things that no one except me could know. At least, I thought so before that moment. He was telling me about what I was doing yesterday and some days ago and also my numbers, passwords and all the most

intimate data things. How can anybody know what I use to open my e-mail? I've been hacked or something.
Nobody could know that much about me. I hardly can say that I have any close friends of mine. And I don't remember any stable personal relations - including these with women - in recent years. Now I think all this was done to make me agree to no matter what proposed. But when you propose to a journalist, a writer or any television man something really sensational, why would you play so much of a game then? Why almost threaten?
There are questions you can't answer. Especially, when there are other people's minds and the other people's plans involved. So, all I know I should get to the place at a time fixed to be ready to receive some sensational material which should be revealed through media, the requirements provided. And it was stressed that I should never tell anybody about details of this meeting.
I was so shocked that for some instants it seemed to me I did not know what to do then. When indeed deep inside I knew, of course. And then I noticed I was watched by Elise. As I understand, I looked strange and astonished. Possibly a little weird. And she looked at me in some peculiar way. I just forgot what I asked her about before and why she was standing right then and there, catching me in a state

like this. And finally, I was a little irritated about her. She was standing in front of me with her long unwashed hair hanging down. Gosh, why does not she try to be a little more of a woman? She is not that bad I should admit. Now I consider that subconsciously I chose to hire her among all of the opportunities - actually not a great variety of candidates - also because she had the most attractive looks. And she indeed can be a rather attractive girl. She is rather handsome. Sure she is. But maybe, some strange people like me tend to get together with other people who are a little strange too, somehow.

So, I cast an irritated glance at Elise after being not able to understand what she wanted from me. And then I rushed out of the room to prepare myself, alone, to get ready for the meeting that was so inevitable then. That seemed that the voice on the other end had the real power or either way represented it. So there were no ways out and no real escape then. Just wait for what will happen next. And just do what you can.

Some Notes on Documentary Films
from Dictaphone Record
by Martin

I do not know how it happened this way, but now I am supposed to make two docs when initially all the strength of my poor troubled mind was directed to the embodiment of one movie only. This one movie had to be something about international industry giants, modern conglomerates that control so much of human lives around the globe. In contemporary reality, it is so common when two or three corporations have almost the entire control over the industry. And so, this way or the other, they do influence the world. They change it in a particular way.

And this film should've had some rather pathetic title like Towers of Power or Babel Towers or Power Incorporated or something else dealing with towers and powers.

Architecture is all about some symbols. Why does any corporation in the city desire to erect a new skyscraping tower higher than any other one did before? Why they want their office to be placed higher than all other offices? They really want to dominate no matter what. What a peculiar reincarnation of primal biological motives inside a system of the corporate machinery. They want to be bigger and wider than others more than they want profits. Profits are just their instrument to get bigger. That is their food of the gods. People want the profits, but corporations do not. They just want to get bigger, no matter what their so much respected shareholders want.

That is the thing I was initially interested in. That was supposed to be something with the POV and at the same time embracing the entire human race in its scales.

But they asked me to do something else. What a nice case it is! I just encountered an incorporated strength of the giants about whom I wanted to tell the world into a shape of the network on which I depend and which is in some way or the other is another dominion of another international multi-conglomerate.

The film I was told to make is supposed to be about prostitution. That is quite a hot topic our days with all of this disputed state legalization and the human smuggling from Eastern Europe. That is such a big world embracing many levels from the bottom of bordellos to the top luxury of pro escort ladies providing their services to the rich people from privileged society. Yes, the topic is not bad for a doc. But that was quite irritating to be forced to do what I did not intend to. And why me? There is such a variety of TV people who can do it. It is true that some of my investigating documentaries connected in their issue to politics and crime achieved some modest success, but that won't help much in the matter.

When beginning a new thing ordered by the network, I would go through some usual dull ritual. I would call to one person representing them just to check out whether there are requirements about which I don't know. But usually, I always know about all the requirements. And the truth is that in this way I just report to them that their order is received and will be executed.

So, I picked up the instrument and dialed the number to connect to someone whom I know and about whom I had never cared and who knows me and who had never cared about me too.

So, what things exactly do you want me to discuss in the film? I asked somewhere in the middle of a dull talk. There should be something interesting. Find and show it. Show it in diversity. I mean in different kinds of it, from a low side of it to the top of it where the big money flow. That was the answer I received. Go and get it from down to up, from left to right.

Oct, 29
Morning
from Dictaphone Record
by Martin

The day when I was going to meet Mr. Shadow. At morning it was misty. Indeed, a mist covered an area for many blocks ahead from my place. As it was agreed, I was supposed to meet a stranger on the spot. Time and place set. I went to a corner where there were a few small shops and some cafe. There were a few people around. And in the fog like this, it even seemed that there were no people at all. I waited and then... I waited a little more. At some point, I began to think that I misunderstood the address or time. Or I thought it was some stupid joke indeed. And someone is cruelly laughing. Like I am still some insecure schoolboy. Actually, I felt quite nervous.

I tried to knock at the cafe window. No one seemed to be there too. I got no answer. But after several minutes more, I tried again. And that time, a person appeared. I mean a guy from a cafe. I tried to order some coffee. He tried to persuade me that they don't serve anything until they open. Rules, you know. I argued a little. And after some few attempts, I achieved success. The cafe guy managed to bring me some coffee in a plastic mug.

I decided it was enough. I finish the coffee, I go home, and the joke is over. I finished but hesitated. Maybe the coffee was really good, and I asked for one more cup. It took some time. I drank this second one. And at that moment I was positive about going back home to have some nap.

I went in the direction to a bus stop. And then when I turned to another street and started walking in another direction, I suddenly recognized something strange with a corner of my eye. I turned back. And I saw that there was a strangely dressed person. It wasn't an absolutely strange suit, but... He wore the gray coat and gray hat. The hat covered most of his face with a shadow.

I made a few unsure steps toward him. I stood there and almost tried to talk. I waited that he would talk first, probably. But instead... He just produced a wrap from under his coat. He held the folder in his hand for a while. I hesitated and then slowly I took the wrap from him. In all this mist he looked really like... Mr. Shadow. Like a guy from the comics strip who could be both the good and the evil. He didn't say anything. He just made a silence gesture. He crossed a lower part of his face with his index finger. And I didn't see his face. Just a sign of silence.

And in a mist, he was swept away by his quick sportsman-like stride. Now I am thinking about all this, and I don't know what it really means to me.

It's time to unwrap the mystery.

Oct, 30

Private Audio Diary of Elise

by Elise

Last night I had a strange dream. There was nothing strange about the images I received in it, but there was something strange about a feeling I had in it. And when I woke up, I felt uneasy for a while. I stood in the endless field of strawberries. Sun was high, the sky was blue, and there was nothing as the eye could see but strawberries. I felt I wanted to taste them. I reached out for the strawberries and took one. And then put it into my mouth. But that berry was tasteless. Disappointed, I took another one, but it also had no sweetness and no taste at all. Then suddenly, I understood that I was standing there in this endless field of strawberries being nude. I had no clothes on me and didn't feel shame. And for an instant, I felt like I wanted it. And then the dream was over.

When I woke up, I wondered what my subconsciousness wanted to tell me. And is there any message to be read or it's just another strange dream? My first thought was to take a morning shower. That had to be refreshing. I took my pajamas and my underwear off. Then I wondered why I did it in the bedroom, but not in the bathroom.

For a couple of seconds or so, I stood undressed there, feeling myself like when meditating and then directed to the bathroom's door. And the shower was refreshing and nice indeed. I felt like I entirely woke up after that.

Last evening Martin called me and told me he would be off the studio, said he would work in the field probably. And so, I arrived at the studio when it was past eleven o'clock. I spent some time sorting some useful files containing some useful information from folder to folder and ate another sandwich. After one and a half hour work, I decided that I would give myself a day vacation and maybe while walking through the city I would find a couple of new ideas for a new doc project nesting in my mind.

I went to a cinema to watch some rather mediocre but rather bearable Hollywood's blockbuster. And also I entertained myself with a walk through the park and made some little shopping, as little money in my possession does not permit me more. That was not so freaking great, but that was not the worst day of my life. At home, I spent my day's rest usually. A little of TV, some food, and some book. Right now I almost forgot to put my pajamas on. I wish myself the nice dreams.

Night, October 30. Going to bed, end of a line.

Oct, 30
from Dictaphone Record
by Martin

As I woke up this day, I tried to prolong my late morning activities as much as possible. Maybe it was subconscious. Because as soon as I finished my breakfast and tooth brushing, I was supposed to face the dangerous wrap containing I did not know what. What if inside there was some bomb mechanism hidden? And there was indeed a bomb of some kind. And there is not a thing in the world that can stop a modern journalist from being curious. Or better say sensational. In my view, a modern journalist is always a greedy person. It is just a kind of greed that differs. A dishonest journalist is greedy for money, and honest is greedy for information. Maybe, being honest means choosing priorities and holding back some of your desires, most of all.

When the time comes to do it, all you can is to do it. I took the wrap. Opened it. Inside there was no bomb. Indeed there was one. But it was made of data explosive.

Inside it, there was a big envelope with a word Instructions printed on it in big letters in its center. And below it, in little letters, there was a recommendation. You better follow this. I took the envelope and saw that it was lying on the top of many other envelopes of smaller size. I tore the instructions envelope and inside I found a couple of pages with what indeed happened to be instructions on how I should receive the information. And it also said what can happen to me if I don't do it in a recommended way. I don't want to say what it was supposed to happen to me if I do it deliberately and without following the instructions, but the rest of it, in general, consisted of the order in which I should open an envelope after an envelope. And it actually said that I should not go to the next stage until I am not done completely with the current information from a current envelope. So, each envelope bore the number and sometimes a title too. I found one with the digit one printed on it. I tore it and inside I found nothing but the USB flash drive. I tapped some other envelopes, and it looked like inside there was also nothing but the similar flash drive sticks.

Well, that should be a little container for big secrets. What was there? I thought maybe there was some unbeatable computer virus which would kill my laptop's digital sanity in a second as soon as I only launch the flash drive, no matter how strong my protection is. But the real virus of my life is not a digital one, but the virus of journalist's curiosity. What am I in this game? Am I a cat or a mouse in it? And do you remember what killed the cat actually?

As I plugged a dangerous flash drive in, I was sitting and gazing at the window on my monitor like being paralyzed for a minute or so. In total there were two files. One was the text file and one – a video. The text file consisted of instructions about what I should do first. And one of the first things was about an interview with some girl. Her full contact information and address were listed in the file. And if to talk about the video file, I think that is such a thing about which it would be completely true to say that seeing is believing, because that is the thing which is hard to describe in plain words. Well, in general, I would say the video consisted of some sort of secretly made records that were full of... well... They were full of sex.

Some Notes on the Subject of Prostitution from Dictaphone Record by Martin

Prostitution is a kind of human activity that is historically coined as the oldest profession in the world. But it is also true that many people still consider this activity to be absolutely unsuitable for the normal society. Many consider that thing should be out of decent society. They would prefer this profession to be in the shadow of the gray sector's economy. To be a dark part of social life. This opinion survives our days, when in many European countries - and around the world too – the prostitution gained legal status. And at the same time when almost no one is concerned about existence and global flourishing of the commercial porn industry. That is possible to note that in between the porn production and the prostitution there is a huge difference. At least that is what many people do believe. But is it really so? At least is it such a big difference across the entire range of comparison? What I mean... I mean that we may say that a porn actress may choose more. She can choose not to participate in a porn movie. She can choose it if she thinks there is something she does not want to do and if there is someone with whom she does not

want to do this. Or there are both these obstacles together. Also, it is true that hardly many porn stars list too many requirements from their side. Actually, it seems that a modern pornography feature - or something like a short video - is done in the very obscure frameworks, bearing not a lot of limitations, if it has any at all. So, most of the porn stars seem quite ready to perform everything they may be asked to perform. For a porn star, a video audience is the final consumer of a product. For a prostitute, it is a certain person with certain wishes. Well... at least, in theory. The difference between the real sex and the video is that a video should present as much as possible to make a person kinky and excited. When in reality all of that may be not needed that much. Though, of course, it varies. So, that is why a porn star may do everything for money, just to stay in business. If she asks for requirements, she may find herself to be not that much wanted for this specific kind of job. And also, at least, the VIP escort girls charge more than a regular porn star for one hour. I mean the porn stars do not always earn more cash.
To expand this idea - I had heard from one of my acquaintances, who is definitely more informed about the matter than me, that there are the escort girls who won't do absolutely anything you ask. They do have the requirements. And they may simply inform you on that before you start to do anything.

And most probably, that will be noted in the advertisement. In some part that can be called, uh, resume. That is how I suppose everything except the photos in the ad can be called. And also if a girl receives the clients privately at her place, she may theoretically choose people to whom she opens the private door. In this case, she may note in her advertisement that she has some face control. There is nothing to talk about forced prostitution, or about that kind of it that just comes from the severe poverty. It is an evident evil, but it is different when one chooses it consciously like when someone starts participating the porn production also without an external pressure but just having both the opportunity and the wish. Or at least having no reasons against this way of earning money.

Laws against prostitution are based on some moral code probably in bigger extent than on anything else. The stealing is immoral, but is there a law against it only because of its moral quality? Laws in the modern rational world are actually a system of governmental rule, but indeed they are part of economic one, because the economy, better say money, is what everyone including govt people is worried about. On the economic side, stealing is not good because when someone steals, he gets benefits not giving to society. It is a bad thing because it is not a fair exchange and there is nothing to do with morals. And a fair exchange is the principal element and also the symbol of contemporary democracy. Ten Commandments are not important that much anymore. Instead, we have one major one – Thou Shalt Exchange Fairly. And do it as much as possible. And that is why the stealing is not good. One should not take when he gives nothing. That is the very principal rule of capitalism. But prostitution is not stealing, it is an exchange, and in a legal mode, it is not a forced activity.

And is it true that prostitution should not be legal only due to some specific moral code of society that allows so many other things to happen, but cannot tolerate one item more? Or maybe it is just a question of official position. The government doesn't want to lose the support of the conservative part of society. When on the other side, they also won't issue laws that will be very severe to prostitutes. And frankly speaking, I almost sure that almost in any parliament there are enough of men - and possibly women too - who did not avoid an option provided by the elite escort call girls. And also there is a known case that explains the conventionality of the thing. It was in California. One nimble entrepreneur benefited from the porn studio where clients paid to be filmed. There were the rooms and the girls in the rooms who were contracted as actresses. And if some guy paid money, he could spend an hour in the room with a girl while it all was filmed on a camera placed in there. After that, a guy received a private copy for himself. So actually, it was nothing but another bordello, just with a particular option of filming the process. So, is it just a matter of calling the things with the names? Is it so important for authorities to have a legal but unjust reason to say that they don't support and promote such things?

And what would we say about girls who are indeed nothing but the latent prostitutes? Those girls who live with the men they maybe do not like at all, but who get laid with them just for the financial benefits of a mutual living. Are they better than the escort girls? Are they better only because they probably take more money and things for one night and have less of the sexual intercourse? At least, the escort girls name the certain prices for certain services. In this regard, they do not cheat themselves and the people around. A significant difference between the latent prostitutes and those who are called the prostitutes is in quantities of the money and the sexual acts they have, together with the option of pretending to be a regular person. Imagine some guy at a luxurious party telling his friends that this girl with him is his girlfriend and it doesn't matter that she sleeps with him only because of his money. Nonsense! The escort girls may pretend an orgasm in exchange for money, but not being your girlfriend.

Why pretending is so important in our society?
Prostitution coexisted alongside with the different moral codes in a variety of national cultures through the ages. In some cultures, there was a tradition coined by historians as the sacred prostitution. That means the girls who served in the temples could provide their bodies to the worshipers as some kind of sacred medium for connection to the divinity and also earn some offerings for the temple of their goddess. For example, as considered it was a common thing for Aphrodite's temple in Corinth. But why then in so many ages the society did not find a proper place for this kind of activity?
In 1949, the United Nations issued a convention against prostitution, but to a current day, it is less than the hundred countries of the world that ratified it. And a list of those who refused to sign it includes the US, Germany, and many others. On the other side, there are still a few countries that legalized the matter taking it under control, like any other kind of business.
The Netherlands is the country especially famous for its liberal attitude towards everything. But the truth is that in the Netherlands the legal industry of prostitution has a value of something like 800 million dollars when in Switzerland a similar legalized sector of the economy has an estimation of approximately 3.5 billion dollars. And that means

even a more significant disproportion when comparing the outcomes of industry per capita as Switzerland is less populated than the Netherlands. Not saying, that Germany's legal sector is over 18 billion. And it is not saying about estimations of the illegal sectors in some other countries that are even more than that. All the world value both legal and illegal is stated by some sources to be around 185 billion dollars. The problem is that the governments of the world cannot stop this and that means that a considerable portion of this money comes into the hands of criminal syndicates around the globe. And that is very easy to suggest that this money is used for the people smuggling, drugs trafficking, and buying weapons.

Who wins in this war? And why the governments let these huge sums flow out of their views? And what if our society is somehow based on the lies more than on the true facts? But maybe, this antagonism between a big part of the society and the prostitution industry is somehow based on something that cannot be erased from the genes of humanity? Maybe there is something that keeps this latent conflict on the stage, no matter what? As usual, there are still more questions than answers to be found.

Oct, 31
from Dictaphone Record
by Martin

Then it was time to find the girl. Actually, I already knew a big lot about her from a file. Pile of data telling what her height and weight are, and what her other physical measurements are. Also, I knew where she works, what company had hired her, what her career was and what her career is, and there was also a little on what her career can be in future. I knew about her parents and origins in general. I knew, of course, all of her contact data including address and phone number. And there also was a lot of other stuff about her of smaller interest. But maybe it is just my old-fashioned journalist's habit – to find at least more than one source on the same subject, to have it a little in stereo.

When you try to find someone's traces on the web, and for this purpose, you start going through social networks, you can easily find a lot of people with the same name. Especially if this name is not a rare one, as it was in my case. But to be able to find the actual social pages of Sue - or Susan, that is her first name - I just filled in a little more specific information including education, age, and hometown. And that was not indeed that hard after all. To my disappointment - or was it a disappointment? - social pages did not prove to be a comprehensive source on her, as she rarely used them. Me, I think if someone does not use the social media too much, then there can be two most common explanations. First is that for this person, a computer is not his or her pet friend. And second is that real life is too bright for this person and then there is no need for a virtual living that much.

And in general, I found not a lot of new facts. And most of what I found was only a confirmation of some info from the file. And on the web, there was just a little part of data on her if compared to the file. There was only one little peculiar thing to add to her image. She once posed as Playboy magazine model. And of course, I could not stand the temptation to find the photo shoot on one of the internet pages. I had experienced only a little weak thought telling me that it was possibly not a correct thing to do. To try to know how a person looks without clothes just before you are going to meet her. But that little thought was weak for sure, and it vanished earlier than I was able to recognize it. In the end, she knew what she was doing. To pose nude for a periodical issue means that some other people will be able to see it, I suppose. Her photo shoot appeared in one of the Latin American editions. She gained a desirable title of Playmate of the month. The photo shoot itself was quite a usual one for this sort of magazines. The sunny ocean side served as location. And the girl was barely nude on almost all of the photographs. On some photographs, she had white jeans on. The best photo was probably that one where her silhouette stood against the sunset so that she presented something like some statue on the background of the scarlet sky. On this picture, her figure was dark against the sun. And she stretched herself up like some strangely beautiful plant. Was it sexy? Yes, for sure. There was also something like a mixture of interview and personal data. Personal data was a usual data, of course. Height, weight, and the size of her breasts. Plus she answered some questions. All it was written in Spanish and my knowledge of this language to which Cervantes and Lope de Vega belonged is quite limited. Despite this fact, with use of a web translator, I got information in general. There was nothing that seemed to be very useful, only some specific facts of her bio and some her particular preferences. For example, she said that once she was deeply in love with a woman and also that she adores her ex-boyfriends and she is crazy about oral sex. That all did not contribute to her personal image too much but probably had some effect on me. Probably that was just because a girl is pretty and that is the thing which usually influences the perception of a lonely man.

Well... I had some summary on her, but could not imagine what she would be in reality. I knew that she is a pretty blonde girl. She is baby-faced. Though not too much. Childish smile, beautiful breasts, thin waist. And she is not tall. Also, she had a few little tattoos. And one of them, for example, presented a name Lolita written in some old typewriter letters on the side of her palm. And also it looked like she prefers to be considered sexy, imaginative and probably even a little kinky. I mean, she is a girl who cares about what people think about her looks. And perhaps she just wants the people to think about her looks. In our days, physical exhibitionism is not enough for people. They would also like to take off mentally. But all that did not tell me what she was indeed.

After completing a brief profile, I went outside to search for more details in the field. The simplest way to find out more was to see the girl sometime after her working hours and at the same time to see what place where she is employed looks like. I didn't want to encounter her at her apartment's door, because I believe that the people, when they meet you for the first time, are more collaborative in public places, but less in their private place or near it. So, this way there could be more chances to fix a possible interview. I am involved in quite a strange matter now. And so, I need to know her side of the story as she is one of the principals in it.

As I arrived at the place, I encountered another tower of power. It was a tall glass-and-stone building, where another mighty faceless corporation nested. And somewhere in between a tenth and a fifteenth floor, a blonde girl with a pretty face was executing her primitive tasks as one of the thousands of office employees, who were placed on an almost lowest grade of career pyramid and who spend usual 38 hours a week for the sake of the firm's existence.

My first idea was to go the easiest way. At the reception desk, I gave a name and occupation of the person I was searching for. I simply asked whether I could talk to her. To my surprise, I did not get what I wanted. A girl at reception was not able to find anyone with this name. She told me, in case I had no appointment, I better had to go off.

It was almost the end of a working day, and five minutes after a reception desk proved to be useless, I stood outside, thinking how I would try to find her next time. Then suddenly, I recognized something with the corner of my eye, and that was something that seemed subconsciously important. It was a girl. It was the girl, and she was walking toward me. I saw a face which was now so much familiar to me. She walked past me, and I turned, watching her back for an instant. Then I hurriedly cast a name Susan from behind her, but a girl did not turn around and kept going away. I was almost disappointed and almost ready to run for her. After an instant more, I almost screamed Sue in one desperate syllable. She turned back and looked at me without big puzzlement. I made a step forward, and she suddenly smiled her childish smile.

I think I would like to talk to you. I told her. Then I explained that I am a journalist and I make some film and if she doesn't see any problem with it, I would like to interview her. She agreed almost immediately, and we fixed when and where we would meet. When I was going to bed this day, I didn't think about problems concerning current documentary filmmaking, but mostly about how the girl, who wasn't exactly perfect and maybe didn't look entirely like a superwoman from the Hollywood blockbuster, was indeed very pretty. She was indeed nicely pretty when even all of her clothes were on.

Nov, 2
Morning and Day
Private Audio Diary of Elise
by Elise

That was the day when I did not want to go somewhere and to do something. Maybe I just felt melancholic, and so, it was a feeling that all I could do today was to be lazy or to be sleepy. Actually, it was supposed to be vacant. But a day before, Martin asked me to appear at the studio to provide some help. He said there was something he would like me to watch with him together. He said he was not quite sure about what it was on the video record he had.

When I arrived at the studio, Martin did not wait until I would prepare another cup of coffee for myself. He asked me to come closer to his monitor. What he had shown to me was some security kind of footage. Black-and-white video with a viewpoint a little from above. You can't see faces in general, and you don't hear any sound because actually, there is no any sound. As it looked, a location was some office. That was a usual office. And footage represented some very long - as I could judge by the timeline of player - combination of some episodes of a usual office life featuring mostly two girls. As it was evident by their clothing and figures, that were the same two girls almost in every part of the footage. Their faces were not clear, but after some time they started to seem recognizable. I still was not sure that I could identify any of them if I would meet any of the two on the street, but at least in this security footage, it seems I could identify them from the others. The one was blonde, and another had a darker hair and was taller. A taller one looked to be a little more of a leader in their couple. At least, it subconsciously seemed to be so from their body language. What I thought about was whether they always use hidden cameras to watch how employees work at the office. It is one thing to watch for thieves in the supermarkets and another - to control every manager in the corporate building. And my second thought was about what the girls were doing.

And what Martin actually asked me was - What do you think they are doing? Do you see something except usual things? What I saw was that they were talking, passing to each other some papers. Sometimes the one could cast a short glance at the other. I didn't see anything except usual things. That is probably what any two do to each other when they are familiar, and they share working space. I am not telepathic or something. So, I hardly can declare something sure looking at some people exchanging glances as part of some plot-free silent BW movie. In a silent movie with Chaplin, they at least show the words on a black screen to make a viewer know what the hell is going on. And at least in a typical silent movie, there are some jokes like someone falling after stepping on a banana skin. I saw nothing exceptional or specific, and I was puzzled about where Martin took this footage from. And what purpose he followed with this I didn't know. Can it help to make some documentary film? Maybe that will be the first ever black-and-white silent documentary. And then it may make a revolution on the next Cannes film festival. I suppose critics will piss with the boiled liquid out of pure excitement.

And finally, after a couple of hours in which we tried to see something in this footage, Martin informed me that he made an appointment for an interview and if I don't mind, he would like me to be present on the spot at the day. I did not mind, and so I will meet the interviewee too, in a couple of days from now.

And now I am going to sleep, so – end of a line.

Nov, 5

Susan's Interview One

from Dictaphone Record

by Martin and Elise

Martin: What we are going to talk about is an extraordinary case. We talked about it with you on the phone yesterday. And as you remarked yourself, it is not easy to believe that all of this is quite true. And now as you agreed to talk to me not concealing any facts, I'm going to ask you once more the same question as yesterday. Are you really ready to talk about all of this?

Susan: Yes. I'm ready... Absolutely.

M.: As I told you before, if there are any reasons for it, for example, if you are afraid that someone may use this information against you somehow or if there is any personal threat to you or to someone who has a relation to you, you may decide to tell not everything. But in this case, we just need to set the limits of our talks.

S.: Well... No. I don't think there is something... threatening. I don't think there is something to hide from people. Absolutely so. And I didn't commit any sort of crime in my life. I suppose... I think that if anybody on any TV show would ask me, I am ready to tell the entire story. All the true. I mean I would tell it to any open media source without any problems.

M.: Sure?

S.: It's OK. You may just ask.

M.: And one more thing. I asked my friend to support me in this interview. Her name is Elise. What I mean, she may add some additional focus for things. Don't you mind this?

Elise: So? Can I stay, Susan?

S.: Sure. And you may call me Sue.

M.: Then, let's begin. First things first. And what I'm going to ask you, in the beginning, is – when and how did it all start?

S.: You mean... When did it begin?

M.: Exactly. I mean, when it was that moment when you might say you felt your life began to change. Just tell the first line of the story.

S.: Well. It all began as I suppose... when Jane appeared. When Jane appeared in my life and at our office.

M.: And who is Jane?

S.: Jane is a girl who worked with me. She is not from our town. As I know, she lived in the other city. She worked for our company for some years, and when she moved from her hometown, she got a place in our city.

M.: Can you describe her? What was she like? Tell us something about her personality.

S.: Jane - If I would try to describe her in a single word - I think I would just spell her name. Jane [soft laughter]. Well, when I saw her for the first time, my only thought was that she is a pretty woman. Maybe it is better to say that she is almost striking... beautiful. No. She is. Striking beauty. Jane is a little taller than me. And she has red hair. And she is very good-looking.

M.: What were your relations when she just appeared at your office?

S.: From the very beginning, we did well. And after a week I would say we made friends. Yes, I think we were friends on a second week after we met. We were doing some similar stuff at the office. And after the first week, uh, we always spent coffee breaks together. We mostly were chatting about different things. I found out that Jane was not only good-looking but also a lovely, smart, and well-humored person. She was a fantastic company. She was fun.

S.: And then, one day, she told me some story. I could believe it or not. As I wish. She said it was my choice to believe it or not because a story was, no matter, an interesting one. Just she kinda tells me I better do not tell it some other people, at least as a true story. She tells me that there is some funny, unusual work she has on the side. There is some Agency that does not advertise its services too much. It is some kind of private entertainment company - a nice little company. And it helps people to diversify, to widen one's sexual life. But actually, it is nothing like an escort agency. It is just different.

M.: But then, what did the Agency offer to customers?

S.: It offered some different things. It offered some sort of private entertainment. It was not necessary for someone from the Agency to make love to customer... That could be different. Me, I am not that conscious about prostitution. It is quite a regular thing in our society. Just me, myself, I am not sure I can do it for money. Of course, I like sex like anybody else, but it is a bit different [laughter]. But I don't have anything against the sex workers. Sure. As Jane told me, the difference is that they try to give an adventure to a person. Some kind of sexy adventure, if you want. The major principle is that they organize it all only when they know well enough what the person really wants. Yes. That's the thing. But the scenario should be somehow unexpected for her or for him. And yes, there is a scenario. It is an important part of it. I mean how they do it. There is the scenario, and it is prepared according to this person's unrealized desires.

E.: So, do I understand it correctly? There is some kind of stage show?

S.: Well, no. It is not like a stage show. Maybe in something. A person is involved in some story, adventure. And the Agency makes this person feel good in the way.

M.: Person? – You mean a customer?

S.: No. Actually, not. This person is almost never the customer. I mean it is not the one placing the order. Services... are ordered by someone who knows this person well, who is close to him or her somehow. This one helps us to know about a person. In some exceptional cases this person – the Lead Hero...

M.: Lead Hero?

S.: That is how this person is called. The Lead Hero. It is just another specific term to make a long story short. So, this LH is almost never the one who contracts the Agency personally. It is this way only in some rare, exceptional cases. It is possible, but it is not a rule.

M.: All these things, did Jane tell about them all at once?

S.: No. I actually revealed it all after, in process. I mean, she told some general things. I was a bit intrigued by it. I did not know why she told it to me. Of course, she was always able to entertain me with her stories during a break and after hours, when we met in some cafe or at a nightclub.

M.: And what did happen next?

S.: She asked whether I wanted to fill the vacancy in the Agency.

M.: She did it the same day as she told you... the

story?

S.: No. She did it after a couple of days. She said there would be nothing tricky, nothing I was not able to do. And she said for the first time I would not need to do something special. And also she said that they would teach me everything I needed to know when indeed there was not a lot of it. And also she said if I didn't like it, I could quit at any moment. She said I was possibly a good fit for them. I didn't know what to answer. Usually, if she took me somewhere to do something funny, I would agree immediately, because it is always a nice time with Jane. I mean she knows how to have fun. But in this case, I was not sure. For a couple of days, I was considering her proposition, and then I just decided to see what it was like. I mean, to see the place and what it was. I was not that sure I would agree. Though, Jane was always the most persuasive person. She easily can persuade anybody.

Nov, 5

Evening

Private Audio Diary of Elise

by Elise

When Martin said that there would be an interview this evening, I did not know who would be our guest. I only knew that her name was Susan. Martin asked me whether I could stay for one more hour at the studio. We supposed to record an interview with someone. When this someone arrived, I had a feeling that I probably saw her somewhere before. And then I understood that it was that blonde girl from a strange videotape. I mean... there was nothing strange about the videotape, but it was strange that the footage seemed so useless. I thought maybe then I would be able to understand at least a little what it all was about. And then when I saw a girl, at least I knew her looks clearly. But that isn't much. I was actually unprepared for an interview. She entered the door and at first exposed some little indecisiveness when interrupting her way through the room. Then she laughed and tried to look really self-assured and made a few quick motions approaching a stool. As she was sitting there... At the first moment that made me think that she was probably infantile, maybe a little infantile, but not too much. Though maybe it was her looks that made me feel so. She is not very tall, and her face is a little childish you may say.

As I wasn't prepared to take an active part in the interview, I thought maybe Martin would like me to be present just to have some kind of witness. Or something. Maybe he needed to have someone else there in the room to break a possible intimacy. I mean... to be not tet-a-tet with this girl. And most probably these both reasons applied for my presence. An interview isn't anything like a date. So, when you happen to talk with a young blonde girl who likes to talk about sex, there should be some additional requirements. At least there should be someone else present. Better a woman. Despite the fact that I still can't clearly understand what fun it can be in this matter for me, I became curious about some of the things. As Martin sometimes uses to say - and I would quote him not because he is a great philosopher, but only because this time the phrase really fits in – journalism is probably a kind of illness. On my side, I would add that it is an illness of brain and sometimes a strange one. And first of all, I became interested in what we will reveal in the next chapter of the Blondish Tale. Let's call it that for a while. And also I am curious about what is the degree of stupidity - or probably, smartness - of our leading character. Just to practice my ability to

recognize the human qualities. My intuition. Kinda. As Martin said, we will meet her again after a few days. I think I will have a chance to know. And also I remember how Martin asked her whether I could be present. And the blonde doll took a short pause, and her eyes widened a little. And then she permitted it, and she was looking at me in some way. Call me Sue. She said so after a pause still having this gaze. My intuition gave me a hint at the moment. What I think about it now is that the girl is definitely bisexual.
The fifth of November, end of a line.

Description of Video One
from Dictaphone Record
by Martin

I interviewed Susan for the first time. Despite the fact that I previously had plans for a couple of projects more, now I felt almost entirely engaged with this one. Let's tell the world about Susan because Mr. Shadow wants it so much. And who am I? Am I more than an instrument in this matter? I ask myself again and again in recent days. But now I am too much interested in the truth, about the essence of this story. Who? Why? – are the two questions keeping to twist in my mind. And also the plot itself seems to be very intriguing. Quite spicy. In some way.

And then it was time to follow the next line from my personal instructions. And they told me that before interviewing Sue again, it was time to play another video. I got ready and launched a flash drive. Instructions prescribed that I can't copy files provided to me on my computer and that I should disable any internet connection before watching them, in case I watch them on a device able for a web connection.

What did I see in this video? I don't know. I mean I am not really able to tell precisely. Video had two parts. In the first one, a location was some apartment. In the beginning, two female figures appeared. I almost immediately supposed it was Sue and Jane. They were dressed differently for sure, but still could be quite recognizable in comparison to the office footage featuring them. They stood with their backs to a camera angle. And the camera was placed somewhere close to the ceiling as it seemed because a point of view was from above. For few instants, they stood rather close to each other and watched through window glass. Then as it seemed by her gesture, Jane asked Susan to come closer. Sue was still standing apart from her. And then she was watching her. Then Sue came closer. And Jane held out her hand and pointed to something across the street probably. Then they kept watching there. And they were talking a little. For a while. Then Jane disappeared from the view and reappeared again having something long and cylindrical in her hand. It was hard to tell what it exactly was, it could be some sort of bat or something else, but as she put a thinner end of it to her face, I understood that it was a spyglass or some sort of portable telescope removed from a tripod. She was looking at the other side of the street. And after a couple of seconds, she gave the tube to Susan. Sue took it slowly like being not sure about it. She cast a flashing glance at the internal side of the room. And then she also began looking through a spyglass at the other side of a street. For at least five minutes they kept watching this way, exchanging their observer instrument with each other. And after that, Susan looked at an internal side of the room for one more time. This time she did it more certainly. Her gaze was longer and was surely directed at some spot. It seemed that Jane somehow provoked it with some words she said because after a while she also looked in this direction. And only then I noticed that.

There was something else inside the room. And this something was hidden inside the dark spot of the shadow. And the angle of the camera also hid it as the camera was more focused on another side of room's space. I tried to identify what it was. And it is more correct to say – who it was. All I could see. As it seemed to me... This video footage isn't clear that much, I say again. Well, it was two legs. Appearing from the dark. Someone was sitting in the corner. And that was a woman as I supposed looking at forms of her legs and design of shoes on them. It was difficult to identify anything even about her shoes, but at least they seemed to be a female pair of shoes. With that little to be seen, this figure looked mysterious, powerful and challenging. What was her part in it? Was she the Lead Hero? How could I tell about it when I even didn't know what was going on?! When you don't know the play, you can't say

what role one of the actors has in it. Do I tell something that looks to be so evident? Next thing that happened was that Jane came closer to a mysterious figure comfortably sitting in the dark. At this moment Susan moved aside in the frame. And then she stood leaning against the wall in the right part of a picture. It was her figure that was visible clearly enough then, but not her face. But from her pose, as she touched the wall with the palms of her hands and bent her legs slowly moving down in softly sliding motion, that all looked rather sexy, even in the sight of the uncertain picture.
Then Jane gave a spyglass to a dark figure in the corner, and it looks like the woman used it to look at something that probably was still happening on the other side of the street. Jane sat down on the floor near the armchair in which a dark female figure was sitting. And then for the rest of time in this part of video nothing happened. All three stayed at their places, and as they were all in some distance from the center of the room's space on which camera was focused, it all looked like some abandoned chess board with the last figures standing in the endgame. That was all in the first half, but there was the second one. And I am not able now to tell what connection is between them.
In this second half, there were two new characters. An episode begins with an image of a girl sitting on a

bed in an apartment. She wears jeans, probably, some light unbuttoned jacket and blouse under it. Her hair is falling on her shoulders. She sits keeping her back straight like some good pupil in the class. She sits immovably for some period. Like a frozen sculpture of a good pupil. Then she stands and walks away from the room. After a short period of time she comes back, and as she opens the door and steps through a threshold, another girl appears too. At this moment she holds a hand of this other girl lightly. As it looks, this second girl wears some similar clothes. The only exception is a jacket. The first girl comes back to the bed and places herself on it in the same manner as she did when being alone. She sits with her back straight. At the same time, the second girl makes a couple of steps after door. For an instant, they watch each other in a frame of the frozen picture. Then the second girl makes a couple of confident steps toward the first one and then goes down on her knees. She starts kissing her hands and her neck and at this moment the first girl bends back a little. Then she takes off her jacket and puts it away in rapid motion, and this girl that stands on her knees continues to kiss her neck with her palms placed on a surface of the bed. Then the first girl unbuttons and takes off her blouse. They waste some time to take it off together with her bra. And then the previous image of kissing reappears with a difference that the girl sitting on the bed is topless and active one covers more of her body with her caresses. She mostly concentrates on her partner's belly, but time after time she rises still standing on her knees and moves up to reach the breasts. And breasts are good... They have nice shapes. And they are a little bigger than an average size of a young girl. Then she stands and makes a couple of short steps back, while another girl still rests on the bed. Half-lying, fixedly watching her partner. They both stared at each other, keeping a short distance.

And the active girl then starts to undress. She takes off everything. Shoes, blouse, jeans, and finally her bra and briefs. She even makes some soft dancing motions like someone trying to repeat after strip-dancer. When she is barely nude, she stands still with her legs a little apart and hands placed on her sides. It looks like she gives an opportunity for the other girl to see her well-shaped body. Fifteen seconds after that, she comes to a girl on the bed making a couple of steps backward. She stands on her knees again and takes her partner's jeans off together with her underpants. She kisses her legs. At that moment, finally, a passive girl entirely lies on the bed, spreading her hands wide. Then the active one stands and climbs on the bed placing one of her hands on its soft surface. She moves down, now placing her body over the body of her partner and starts kissing and caressing her. She goes a little up and down covering the girl's neck and the girl's breasts with her caresses. Then she comes down from the bed, now standing on her knees on the floor again. She looks at the face of a girl holding her legs at the same time. And after some pause, she bends, and her face becomes unseen as she hides it in between her partner's legs.

At this moment a video interrupts, and there is nothing else. I don't know how exactly two of its parts are connected. There should be some clue to tell it. I suppose in the second part there is probably nothing that can give any link. I only can tell that, actually, I forgot about one peculiar thing about the second part of the footage. In the room where two girls met there were big picture windows too.

Some Notes on Attractiveness of Voyeurism and Peeping
from Dictaphone Record
by Martin

What makes voyeurism so attractive? Maybe it is the feeling of having some power to break barriers that the others don't want you to break. That may give a person some position that may look to him as a position of some moderate dominance. And possibly, it is not a privilege over those who are watched, but even more over those who would like to watch, but who can't join the voyeur being not a part of the club.

I don't know what exactly it can be that makes it so exciting about secret voyeurism for others, because me, myself, I would prefer if someone would know. I would like if someone would willingly perform some sexy trick for me like a striptease or something else, maybe even of a more peculiar nature. I mean, it is really nice when someone wants to please you. But what is it when someone doesn't? And how can you know for sure that someone would be not offended in a case when it all would be discovered somehow? The thing is that the real voyeurs might be not interested in the evident exhibitionists at all. That is why some analysts may classify voyeurism as some

paraphilia.
It is an interesting question. How many people would reject an opportunity for watching someone in some intimate moments, if having the opportunity and knowing there will be no punishment? Modern times evidently provide us with too many reality shows that are too popular to deny the fact that the people like to watch other people doing things. And that may have deep roots. As we know from the legends, particularly from this about Lady Godiva, sometimes even a punishment won't stop a person from it. Peeping Tom is probably only a fictional character, but it doesn't matter in the case. People believe that such a person could exist. I mean, that if people believe that a person could cast a glance at the noble women as she rode nude on the horse through the street, even under punishment of death, then it means that the people do believe it is possible for a person to behave in this manner. At least partly. And if it is possible to behave so under strictest punishment, then, of course, many would do it when feeling themselves safe. And also would we like to watch someone noble or no matter whom? Maybe a lot of people would like to watch the celebrities and rich ladies and gentlemen of contemporary in their most intimate moments as they replaced the kings and queens for us. Is it a subconscious desire to destroy their advantage over

others and to share their benefits by the gift of secret knowledge? It is difficult to answer these questions.
Actually, before modern reality shows, there was Playboy magazine that was extremely popular in times before the world wide web as it was a unique chance to see photos of pretty women undressed. They were not of a noble origin, but they were good-looking. And the Lady from Coventry also was supposed to be very pretty as she was a wife of a powerful man. Maybe there is something about possession. Her husband had power, he possessed the lives of people in the land and also her beauty. But when she at least, in theory, provided others with a chance to see her nude, she broke her husband's dominion. She manifested her own right of possession.
So, when we talk about why people like to watch, there is a similar question on another side. Many stars seem to want to be exposed or even involved in a sex scandal as it potentially means more of stardom. People today who want to become stars perceive many such spicy elements as a regular part of celebrity life. The truth is that they also understand many other quite uncomfortable things about stardom like this. In this way, you may say that they want it. Some of them indeed will become stars. That means they will accept it as a part of the contract and on another side may even consider

many forms of celebrity exhibitionism desirable. And in this case, poor Tom may be regarded not only as a victim but also as a necessary element or even a sort of lover. It is considered that Cleopatra kept executing her lovers just after a single night of love. But there is no evidence that she had no pleasure those nights. So, maybe if we return to the image of the Lady of Coventry, we may suppose that she should've expected that someone would watch no matter. And that is what gives a spice to a situation. Actually, for me personally, Cleopatra and Godiva are two different characters. I would prefer the initial version of the legend. I mean one without Peeping Tom as this character appeared in folklore later and made this story more vulgar. Godiva probably is not a person who wanted to kill someone. She wanted to liberate poor people from the excessive power of her cruel husband. And at the same time, she found a peculiar way to break free from him with the help of her sexual attractiveness. She manifested her sexuality. And it was strong enough to direct the power in the entire city. Regarded this way she could have an own motivation for the ride. Yes, it doesn't diminish her merit. But still, it means she had it. And it's interesting that in this case, we can't say who is watching whom. In some meaning. Lady has still more power than a supposed citizen. So, it looks like good voyeurism is impossible without good exhibitionism. Two sides - voyeur and showman are nothing without each other. Like in any interaction, the pleasure of the other improves the experience.

Maybe the right question about that is not - what is so attractive about the voyeurism? But it is - what is so sexually attractive about the voyeurism? Remember Freud. He once said, at least as it is considered, that culture is repressive to the sexual nature of human beings. And the culture and the civilization probably began as soon as Adam and Eve put on the skins of animals as they were exiled from the Eden. Do we try to reveal more of nature into the others and in ourselves sometimes? Or maybe we are just always searching for the Sacred Garden from which the human race was once exiled?

I don't know... It looks like today I am not able to say something really worthy. I don't know why people do it, but what I know for sure is that the people do it. And they do it quite often.

Nov, 7

Susan's Interview Two

from Dictaphone Record

by Martin and Elise

Martin: We stopped at the moment when you decided, as you called it, to see what the place was. Right?

Susan: Huh... yep.

M.: Now, I would like you to tell me what the next thing in this story was. Did you come to see the place?

S.: Yes, I did. I told Jane I would like to see it and then maybe to decide if possible, of course. I always expected some fun whenever we went to some new place with Jane no matter was it another shop where I never bought a new T-shirt before or another art gallery. Or something. So, a couple of days after she said I could join, I decided I could look at it, at least. And a couple of days later, Jane led me there. After hours we left the building together, and there was a big expensive car waiting for us. We went outside the city, in some suburb area where there were mostly villas and big houses. We stopped in front of a luxurious villa. It was a big and beautiful house. What I thought when I saw it - I didn't remember that before I ever visited such a house. And that should be very nice to be at the party at such place... Yep... It is luxurious and pretty [soft laughter]. Yes, I think that was exactly what I thought about it. When we were out of the car, we crossed a little garden. There were a little garden and a big pool. Two great things I immediately noticed. Then we directed to the entrance, and Jane told me that I should remember about keeping secrets. Remember we keep secrets carefully here. She said something like this. When I was inside, I felt myself to be a small person. There was too much of space inside. It was something like a two-story foyer. Jane led me to some nice room where there was a sofa, and we sat there. Then she came out and returned with some cocktails. She said we needed to wait until the Head - it's a ruling person - would arrive. She said it would be soon. And we actually spent some time pleasantly. We were talking the nice talks and drinking the nice cocktails.

During this time I made an acquaintance with one girl who worked there. She was very nice-looking and well-humored. She was not very tall and with a pretty face. Her name was Ann. Jane told me that Ann was a person who worked with clients. She brings papers to sign and all of that. She performs some necessary legal thing. And stuff like this. As Jane said, usually she didn't perform any role.

M.: What does it mean - a role? Did Jane tell you

something about how the Agency worked then?
S.: That was exactly what she explained to me while we were waiting. She explained that the first rule is that it all should be secret, at least for some time, the second rule - she said - that it undoubtedly should be secret [giggle]. She also told me that it isn't a person involved in the game who places the order for it. The client should be someone familiar with this person and who wants to entertain this person. It's like making a pretty secret gift, well, something like that.
Elise: Excuse me. I'm going to interrupt you. You said there were cocktails. Did you drink a lot? Do you think there could be something unusual mixed in them?
S.: No... I think they were the usual cocktails.
M.: Go on. You were explaining how the contract is signed. What were the other special features of the Agency?
S.: What was special? Uh... There was a specific system of terms like Lead Hero, Scenario, Players, and other things.
M.: And what does Players mean?
S.: Player means a person who helps to make it all. It is someone from the Agency who entertains the Lead Hero.
M.: So, that Lead Hero is a principal person in all of this?
S.: Yes, it is possible to say so. Lead Hero is our

center of attention. It is his pleasure which is the most important.

M.: And Ann? Was she the player?

S.: As I understood, usually she wasn't, but she could have some minor part sometimes. At least that was what Jane told me.

M.: You were telling about your first day in the Agency. We interrupted you when Ann arrived, and you were drinking cocktails. Go on. Would you tell us what happened then?

S.: Then... Ann, she was not drinking with us. Jane said Ann always stays one hundred percent sober, no matter what. I thought she was joking. While we were waiting, I saw another player, I mean another one besides Jane. I wasn't sure that she is a player, but then I understood it was so, after some time. She just flashed to me when a door to another room was open for a moment. It was one second, but I saw her. She was gorgeous, a woman – not a girl... And then the Head of the Agency appeared. I was sitting alone on the sofa with a soft drink in my hand. And Jane returned from another part of the house and told me that if I didn't change my mind she, the mistress, would see me. As I understood then, the leader of the group was a woman too. Well, then Jane showed me where her cabinet was. I opened a door and went in. I was a bit afraid and excited at the same time. It was a room without windows. I think it is an important detail, somehow. I saw her for the first time, at that moment she was sitting at her table, and she was reading something. She was unaware. Like she didn't notice my presence. She was a tall woman. And she wore some kind of official costume. Behind her, there was a shelf with a lot of folders on it. Another thing I immediately noticed was their logo across the wall. It was a line of big unusual letters. It read Venus Agency. That is, as I understood, their name. For some time it was like she did not know that I existed at all. But then she moved her head and looked at me directly. That glance of her made me feel differently. She had beautiful green eyes. And there was something strict about how she looked. Maybe it was her costume. And also maybe some serious manner in which she behaved. As I remember she was always wearing such things and behaving this way. So, she actually made an impression like a high-class teacher from a very prestigious school. Yeah. You never had a feeling that you knew more than she did. Then we had a little talk, and I actually didn't get any new information. There was probably nothing that Jane didn't tell me before. Maybe only it was told more formally. So, it didn't add new things for that day, but just I got some respect for her. That was the thing she made you feel. No doubt. The respect for her. She had some kind of internal strength, I think.

She said there was a new order they had, and they would start working on it next week. And as it was an easy job and it fitted for a newcomer, I could fit in if I wanted. And then I could decide whether I would like to work with them more permanently as she explained. And also one more time she asked me no matter what to keep it secret. She said it had to be all kept an absolute secret at least for a couple of months. It is the interest of their clients, and that is very important. In this way.

M.: And what was your answer? Did you agree?

S.: I agreed, but it took another couple of days to do so. She gave me her phone number and told me at what hours I could call. And so I telephoned her. And I said I was ready to start. It was a special moment in my life, I suppose. I was a bit worried. But also excited, again. That day I talked to Jane about it. And she relaxed me.

M.: Did you feel you could trust her?

S.: Yes, sure. She is a lovely person.

M.: Did you feel it like you could confess any of your secrets to her? Was it that much?

S.: Well, I think it was. She is the best friend I ever had. She is the one you can trust.

E.: And then?

M.: Did you and Jane come somewhere to visit the client or probably a Lead Hero as you call it?

S.: No, we did not. I mean not that time. That time

we came to the house again. To this luxurious mansion which was the Venus Agency's home place. I adored their residence again as I remember. And as I was more relaxed that time, I just enjoyed its rooms and interiors. We just came here to discuss how it all would be. We, those who were supposed to take part, were told what to do and when. I was also briefed about simplest terms of their activities, despite the fact that Jane had already explained all that stuff to me. In this game [laughter] – it was the first one for me, and they call it the game - my role according to the scenario was simple. In general, I had to be present and... I just was needed to make a proper group. So, as there was nothing so complicated, I relaxed a bit, but not too much as I still couldn't imagine how it would be. I actually could imagine it as they explained to me what we were going to do. But I mean... I could not feel it, you know. I suppose one can't feel it before it happens. That's for sure. So, as I got it. What we did there in the mansion was some sort of rehearsal.

M.: Rehearsal? You mean you staged it? And what did you rehearse?

S.: It was - as I told before - what we should've done then, when we would be there, at the place. They actually call the place a ground. It's another term. There were five of us at the mansion that time. That included me, Jane, Ann, a girl whose name was

Sally, and Jess. Jess is the name of the head girl. I didn't tell you her name before. Jess acted as the Lead Hero. She took the place of this person, I mean.

M.: And did you know who would be the Lead Hero in that case?

S.: No, I didn't. I was told it was a secret and no one but Jess knew about it.

M.: Do I understand it right? Jess was not supposed to participate on the spot when it would be done... for real?

S.: Yes, it was this way. She just impersonated the LH. And others were learning their roles. It was interesting that Ann was supposed to take part.

M.: Would you tell us about what happened when you actually met the Lead Hero?

S.: It was the next day. We, I mean myself and Jane, arrived at some private apartment. It was a good one and placed in a prestigious area of the city. And in the first moments, I was a bit afraid that there was no one here. Maybe I felt myself like a burglar. But then I've noticed.

M.: What was it you noticed?

S.: There was another person, another one besides Jane and me. I think it was a woman. I only could judge by her legs.

E.: What do you mean only by legs?

S.: All I saw of her were her legs. She was sitting in the dark corner of the room, being deep in the darkness and all I could see were her legs and a little of her silhouette, but it was very uncertain. Only her legs came from the dark seen clearly. And I suppose so because of shapes and shoes. I am sure it was a woman though.

M.: You say it was a woman? Go on. What was the next thing you were doing?

S.: The next thing was that Jane came out to another room and then after a few moments returned with a telescopic tube. She gave it to me and asked me whether I would like to watch what happened outside. She asked me whether I thought there could be something interesting somewhere in this area of the city. She said that there was possibly something interesting very close to us, but we didn't know. Maybe it is just across the street. And with these words, she gave me the tube. I took it and looked through it across the street. At first, I pretended that I was searching freely for something I didn't know what. Then I looked straight at the windows of the building which stood right across the street. And there I saw Ann sitting on the bed in a room where the windows were as big as in apartment where we were. I then gave a tube back to Jane. And I was kinda telling her. Yes, there is something interesting, indeed. That was kinda signal. That meant that I saw Ann and that she was ready. Then Jane started watching through the tube. And then she asked. Do you want to know what happens now? But she said it not to me. She said it to this woman in the dark. And then she also added. It is interesting, indeed. Then the woman who sat in a chair found a voice. It was surprising to me. Almost like I thought she was mute. She just said. Tell me. That was all she said. And then Jane began to describe her the things she saw. Things that were happening on the other side of the street. And at that time Sally also appeared in a room in this building that stood against the building where we were. She joined Ann, and they began to do things planned, as we rehearsed it.

E.: And what was that?

S.: They caressed each other... They made love... in general.

M.: And Jane was telling you about it?

S.: Yes, she was describing everything they did. As Sally was kissing Ann and what spots... She told us about how they undressed each other and other things [giggle]. And then she gave the woman a tube, and she was watching girls for the rest of time. As Jane did so, she sat down on the floor. Close to her. I am not sure, but to me, it seemed like her hand went down her belly and she was... something like caressing herself. I am not sure, but it seemed so. I suppose... When we began this thing, I was a little uncertain, but as it progressed I felt more relaxed. And finally, I actually felt quite excited.

Nov, 7
Evening
Private Audio Diary of Elise
by Elise

It was a weird thing. The second interview with Sue... with Susan was even stranger than the first one. The girl was even more talkative this time. She told us a story that is indeed unusual one. And again I ask myself why Martin decided to have me near when making such an interview. This time I really became a witness of some intimate story. And it is true that if Martin listened to this alone, he would be in a complicated position. Or maybe he would be in a position from Kama Sutra? Uh... And in this case, it is also a complicated position for a journalist if to talk about ethics of the profession. If any ethics of journalism had ever existed in the real world, of course, but not only in some knightly codex that some professors should compose with the help of students in some universities. Ooff. That was something that I didn't expect to happen. It was like working on TV for one of the shows devoted to sex, like being an assistant for another reality.

Again... she readily told us about her adventures. But this time they were more interesting or just more peculiar. It is remarkable that she told us about what

was exciting for her in this affair. As I know, this interview wasn't the last one with the girl. And I expect even more of her unusual tales to come. I expect she won't come when telling us it all. I hope so. After we finished with an interview, Martin told me that he had something to say and to show me. He said he had some records confirming what the girl had told us. He said that I should keep it all in secret until we release the documentary film about these events. He also said that if I wanted to watch the videos, he would let me, but he wouldn't let me copy it because it was a part of an agreement between him and the person who provided this evidence to him. That video, as I understood in brief, is something like surveillance footage. Close in style. Actually, I am not the person who will tell the others something that will make everybody think I am crazy and kinky. And what about that video... I'll probably watch it if there will be a need for it, but not this time.
Now I am going to sleep and hope I will have normal dreams tonight. End of line.

Terminology Description Provided to Susan
Paper Document
from Archive of Martin

The AGENCY – is a group of people collaborating under principles described in the code of the Agency called in short the Code. The main aim of the group is a high-class luxury level entertainment that is provided on the terms of an agreement between the Agency and the client. Structure of the Agency is one-leveled in its hierarchy except for the Head who is chosen by the other members including the players and the other persons of general assistance. Head is one who bears more responsibility for organization and activities of the Agency.

The CODE – is a collection of principles that are primal rules for all activities of the Agency. The Code defines the mission of the Agency. Major principles are: (a) absolute secrecy of activities, (b) joy of the Lead Hero as the most important aim of any actions executed in the complex, (c) the absolute physical and informational safety for any participant on both sides, (d) prohibition of any methods requiring a crime or any law-breaking, the actions that lead to any health damage or any financial damage or any other kind of damage to the group or a person, (e) others.

The TECHNOLOGY – is a full complex of all methods and skills that can be used by the Agency in the process of its activity.

The CLIENT – is a person who places the order for entertaining the Lead Hero. This person provides an insight including information which client will decide possible to provide and which is essential for an understanding the Lead Hero's map of preferences, the Lead Hero's map of sexual desires and similar. By doing so, the client takes responsibility for providing this information which may appear to be personal for the Lead Hero.

The LEAD HERO – is a person who is familiar to the client and who is a major object for complex of actions. He is led through the events that are part of the complex and according to an approved scenario. It is important that the Lead Hero has no information on what will happen to him, but all, what will happen, is to be designed for his pleasure. No harm and no damage should be introduced to the

Lead Hero during the actions. And thus, it is the responsibility of client and people of the Agency.

The PLAYER / ACTOR / ACTRESS – is a person involved in performing a role which includes doings to please the Lead Hero.

The GAME – is complex of approved events performed according to the scenario, happening as a result of the single order.

The SCENARIO – is an order for the appearance of the events that are contents of the complex of the actions. The scenario aims to define the events in a certain way. That is to please the Lead Hero on the maximum level. The scenario is created on the basis of sexual preferences map and on the basis of understanding person's RFR and PFR.

The COMPLEX OF ACTIONS – is a sum of all events and doings by players/actors of the Agency during the realization of the scenario.

The ROLE – is a personal position in the complex of the actions for a specific player of the Agency in a current of realization of the approved scenario.

The INSIGHT – is a complex of information provided to the Agency by the client on the terms of full accordance between the client and the Agency and on the terms of assistance from the client to the Agency. Insight is crucial for creating the sexual preferences map of the Lead Hero. Insight may include oral descriptions received from the client, sources of digital media, photographs, and paper (including books, magazines and other) sources relating to preferences of the Lead Hero. Insight is used only for the aims of SPM and is not used for any other purposes. Agency does not store the insight after terminating the current complex of actions. Nothing of the insight can be provided to any third side. Complete terms for using the insight are described in the particular part of the Code devoted to this matter.

The SEXUAL PREFERENCES MAP / SPM – is a complex of personal preferences of the Lead Hero that defines what methods and actions can contribute to achieving the major aim. SPM is formed on the basis of insight and the understanding general human behavior and psychology. SPM determines the scenario and the complex of the actions. SPM includes the desire objects, the desire actions, and the desire places together with other elements.

The DESIRE OBJECT – is an image of a person who is sexually attractive for the Lead Hero. It may represent a personalized object from his or her supposed sexual fantasies.

The DESIRE ACTION – is action desired by the Lead Hero as one of the best possible ways of achieving the pleasure.

The DESIRE PLACE – is a place which is supposed to be one of the best places for reaching the pleasure.

The REALITY RATE / RFR / REALITY-FANTASY ADJUSTMENT LEVEL – is a level defined as the proportion of person's possible actions in reality in conditions of absolute availability to the person's actions in fantasy. RFR is defined in the range from zero to one (or in the range from 0% to 100%). That means that if the person's RFR is zero, he or she would like to do nothing from his or her fantasies despite having such fantasies. And another way he or she would like to do everything from his or her fantasies if his or her rate is defined as 1 (or 100%). Right determination of person's RFR helps to adjust his or her fantasies to what he or she would like to do in reality.

The POSSIBILITY RATE / PFR / POSSIBILITY-FANTASY ADJUSTMENT LEVEL – is a level defined as the proportion of the volume of what is possible to perform regarding the sources available to the Agency to all the actions desired by the person in his or her fantasies. PFR is defined in the range from zero to one (or in the range from 0% to 100%).

The FULL REALITY RATE / FRFR / PRFR – is a mathematical result gained as multiplication of RFR and PFR or proportion of what is possible and wanted by a person in reality to what is wanted by a person in fantasies. Rate is defined from 0 to 1 (or 0% to 100%).

The COMPENSATION RATE / CR (FRFR) – is an inverse number to FRFR. It determines what actions value should be added to deliver the full pleasure achievement.

The FULL PLEASURE ACHIEVEMENT LEVEL / FPAL – is a mark defined as a level in which the person is satisfied with the actions and elements of the scenario. Each element of the scenario depending on its specifics, a perception of the person and the position in time contributes its marginal value to the pleasure achieving. A scenario is balanced when FPAL is close to 100%.

The PLEASURE – feeling of absolute joy, happiness, and general emotional elevation together with the extensive production of endorphins in an organism.

Nov, 7
Evening
from Dictaphone Record
by Martin

Today we had one more interview with Susan. This one was bigger than the previous. And information appeared to be even more specific than before. The girl told us that they engaged some other person in the act of voyeurism and by this, she explained a connection between two parts of the video I watched before doing an interview. She also told us that all of this was rehearsed. I just unfolded another envelope with more of secret files in it. And there I found a video file that possibly proves this fact. Girls in this video do the same things as in previous one, but it happens in another place, and there is a tall dark-haired woman instead of the woman in the dark. And also they do the same things, repeating acts many times, memorizing. As they do it all, the dark-haired woman, who I suppose is the head girl, about whom Susan told us, directs their actions. At least it looks so. It is hard to say exactly what they do as there is no audio track attached to the footage and you can't hear what they are talking about. But I think she directs them. She looks to be very sure and a bit bossy with all these motions she makes. She has some manner. She is pointing to something, sometimes. She's telling them what to do as it looks. I mean she looks like a leader. Also except new video files, I entertained myself with a description of some terms about which Susan told us. These are the terms they use in the Agency in the process of work. That is a particular science slang, I should admit. That was especially funny to learn about these rates – RFR, RFRF and others like these. And also I finally learned what the pleasure is. That is very useful to know. ... Absolute joy ... emotional elevation ... production of endorphins. The government says we need to increase high-tech production in next years and that is one of the priorities for the nation. But it looks like they don't know anything about the increase of endorphins production. And it isn't listed among what they think to be the national priorities.

When the interview was over, I asked Elise whether she would like to stay to see some additional material connected to the facts we investigated. She said she needed to go home. I don't blame her because we stayed some couple hours after hours. I just asked in case. We agreed with Susan on our next interview. It will take place as soon as tomorrow. She told me that her story was still a long one to tell. I am not surprised about this as I know exactly how many unopened envelopes with other people's secrets I have. It is a long story to tell. So, I'm glad that the girl is so friendly with us and she is ready to give us as many interviews as we will ask from her. I wonder about her enthusiasm. Does she feel herself a little like in a TV show? Does she feel it can give her the fifteen seconds of fame? There is a very known and battered idea. It says that everyone thinks he has a story worth to write a book about, worth to make a film. And she probably thinks that her story is a special one. More fantastic than the stories of others. Actually, it is possible that the girl is right. No matter whether it is a truth or a tale.

Nov, 8

Susan's Interview Three

from Dictaphone Record

by Martin and Elise

Martin: After you were allowed to participate as a player - if I call it right - in the Agency's activities for the first time, how soon it was you returned there?

Susan: That was quite soon, in a couple of days. After that, we were often at the place.

M.: We?

S.: I mean Jane and me.

M.: Oh, yes, of course. Please, continue. You went there a couple of days later and then... did you start to prepare for the next thing? I mean, a next game.

S.: In some way. But actually, no. We were learning. True. It was more about having fun for me. It was like some pretty cool leisure. I was mentally relaxing after a dull work I am doing.

M.: But when your next time came? Was there any next time?

S.: Yes, there was. It was in a little more than a week.

M.: But in this week you visited the Agency's house several times?

S.: Yes, at least three times. I think.

M.: But what were you doing if you were not preparing for the... next thing?

S.: We prepared for the next thing too. But more it was - I would say... Actually, I was spending my time in a great company. And I've learned a lot of useful things there.
M.: Things? Sex things?
S.: Yes, mostly about sex. It changed my understanding of the matter really seriously. Jess read us a couple of interesting lectures, and I learned some practical things too.
M.: You mean it was like some school?
S.: Someway. Kinda. It was the academy to me. I would call it the Academy of the Venus [giggle]. In general, you know, Jess was indeed like some teacher. She told us about the history of eroticism in art... And about human perception of it through the centuries in general. She also told us about concepts of sex in different historical and ethnic cultures and some other very interesting things. Gosh, she is very smart. She is. Yeah.
M.: Can you tell us about the technology used by the Agency? What about all these terms and these rates? I mean, reality-fantasy and others alike. Seems quite weird.
S.: You know?!
M.: Yes, I have a paper, this one. I received it from the same source that told me about you. Don't ask me who it is, because it is a secret, but I just have this paper, and I was told I had to talk to you.

S.: Oh, really?!
M.: And... what about these terms and rates?
S.: Yes. Jess explained us it all. When I first saw it, I was a bit puzzled. But Jess is one who knows how to explain everything in a few words. Well, reality-fantasy rate and possibility-fantasy rate, that means... that means that we should estimate how much it is possible. What we can afford from person's wish list. You need to know what the person dreams about. And if we can't do it all, we should try to compensate it with something. Maybe to do something that has... a value to it. An example can be when a person dreams of making love with elves...
E.: With Elves?
S.: Yeah. But we can't give it, kinda. But maybe we can arrange that this person will have a sexy adventure featuring someone dressed as elf or we should propose something that will do well to a person who as we know have fantasies about elves. I mean that we kinda know what this person's fantasies are. We should use it to please a person, adequately estimating our sources, our possibilities. Jess says it is all the same, no matter whether it is industrial production, some services or some filmmaking. It is the same in any production. I mean our unlimited wishes and real possibilities. And stuff.
M.: Oh... Got it.

E.: And you said about art. I mean that you learned there about eroticism in art. What was that you learned? I mean at least can you tell us what authors you had discussed?
S.: Authors? Well. There were guys like... Velasquez, Botticelli, Helmut Newton and also this one - forgot the name - Collier. And there were many others.
M.: So, it was the art you discussed in these lessons? If it is possible to call it lessons, of course.
S.: Not only this. We also discussed the types of sexual fantasies. It all was learned by me during the first week. There were other things next week too. And it all was fascinating [giggle]. Fantasies, as Jess told us, are as different and complicated as the people who have them. Every person has some very private set of own fantasies because it is part of her unique individuality. Jess explained to us why it is important to remember about a personal side of the question every time you deal with person's intimate part of mentality. But no matter, as we should have some practical view about our doings, we should classify people's fantasies. And then there is still a question of proper choice among classified items when you deal with individual, but not with the mass of people. And also, there are some most common fantasies people enjoy. There are fantasies when one would like to pretend to be a teacher or a student - it is called the school fantasies no matter what kind of

school it is, secondary school, college, university or even an imaginary school. If you want an example, it can be a school of sex. Or some kind of the magic academy, it doesn't matter. There is sports type, and it is when a person would like to have sex with sportsmen or sportswomen or to have it in some athletic or training... way. There are different types of S&M fantasies, of course. And in this case, you should know what a person would like to be – submissive, dominant or both, and what extent. And there are also some physical and emotional aspects of perception. A person may like only some soft spanking or a more hardcore thing. A person may like something hard. Or to be punished more morally than physically. In some cases, a person may even enjoy punishment and humiliation in the presence of someone else. And it is crucial that this third one would be present as it makes humiliation a more real thing. I learned that. It is because, for some people, it is an excellent way to relax and to let another one to do things to her or his body. To receive more pleasure you need to relax as completely as possible and take off your control and your defense. When a person takes off clothes, it is not for sure that the defense is off too. And it also may be a useful thing as some people enjoy to make love with someone whom they feel to be strong and powerful. It is a very animal way. I mean a natural thing. And the other way, a person may like to dominate someone just to feel himself or herself more confident and sure and then more relaxed too. And also, preferences about clothes, costumes may differ. There are many things like this. Many guys like a woman to be dressed in sexy policewoman dress. Others prefer a lot of black latex. S&M is very common type today as I know. In general, Jess said you could make a picture of people's mass preferences through an understanding of what is typical for porn films today. She said it is even not because porn industry exactly knows what people want. But it is because people's tastes and demands are defined by porn as they start to watch it in very young years and it affects their secret sexual desires very much. It kinda affects their fantasies.

And one of the most important things I've learned about the fantasies is that the person's reality perception may be different from what he dreams about. Yes... And it's OK. Some woman may dream about rape, but it doesn't mean she would really like it in reality. Actually, one can't really dream about rape, because what one dreams about is a pleasurable and desirable thing. And rape is an unwanted thing. It is some misssterming... It is an issue of terms. Mixture of terms. It is not a rape this woman dreams about, but a specific kind of sexual intercourse. I mean sex in some specific conditions.

And it is a wanted one. And there are a lot of such things too. You should adjust the desired to the reality, I mean. And stuff like this.
And also, Jess gave us a separate lecture on the celebrity fantasies. She said it doesn't matter that the people don't fantasize about it too much, though they do, of course. And it is not true that they do it very rarely. People don't fantasize a lot about stars as they feel it is almost impossible to make love to a star, but high status is something that was always of a high sexual attractiveness for any tribe or group of people. She said it is something of nature for people. She explained to us why exactly Freud would agree with her theory, her understanding of it.
M.: And why?
S.: It is because... it is at the core of people's mentality. It has biological roots. And something. People gathered in tribes like animals gathered in the flocks to have additional opportunities which can be provided by society. And so, someone who is on top of the group is always more desirable. That is why, no matter how much the people have it in mind, they most probably would like it. Stardom is a very sexy thing [giggle]. The problem is that it is not so easy to turn a celebrity fantasy into action.
M.: Well. And that was all that happened that week?
S.: No. I also spent some time in their library on the advice of Jess. They kept there a lot of different sex

manuals from ancient ones of China and India to contemporary ones. I read seldom, but I read a couple of books there. Jess told me that the manuals have too many things about anatomy sometimes. And it isn't about what we dream about, but such things can be useful. It can be useful, I mean if you comprehend it properly. You just should learn not to learn only the technology of it. I mean you should perceive it all rather spontaneously like some kid exploring a new area. It is the best way to do it like a kid. And that was one more new thing to me...

Actually that day I saw a new girl. Her name was Barbara. Barbara was a fantastic beauty. I saw her only couple of times during all those days. She had impressive looks. Heavy breasts and hips that were perfectly rounded. And she seemed quite curvy when her waist was proportionally perfect at the same time. I mean it was quite a slim waist. She was probably a little taller than average woman's height. She always had some scent of superiority around her. She didn't talk too much and was mostly introverted. And she wore - as I understood it - luxury clothes only. She was an awesome thing. I felt real envy about her.

And the final thing for me that day at the mansion was a visit to a room of Jess again. She said that she would give me... some kind of homework. Time after time. She got out from her chair and stretched out her hand to a shelf behind her where there were a lot of folders. She started to choose one of them moving her palm over them. I don't know, maybe this one or maybe that. That was the very interesting case indeed. She was saying. Something like this. And then she picked up some folder accidentally, I think, and gave it to me. She told me I should've investigated it. She said exactly this word - investigate. She told me I should've read and watched what was in there and properly analyzed it on the basis of what I've learned in the Agency and then I was supposed to give her my full report and my opinion on it. As I almost physically felt there had to be something very unusual and she said that it wasn't an urgent matter, I decided that I would probably open that folder sometime later.

Nov, 8
Evening
Private Audio Diary of Elise
by Elise

That was another interview with Susan. And it was kinky. Again. I would say the girl told us about some of her sexual education if in this case, I can call it this. Some people are proud of their university education if they went to something like Yale, Cambridge or Oxford. This time it seems we found a blonde who is proud of something much more specific. Maybe I am just exaggerating it all. Yes, I most probably do. A little. But the girl is really thinking she is telling us a wonderful story. Interesting one. It is an unusual story if only at least half of it is true. Otherwise, it is usual unusual lies. The most interesting - at least to me, because I wouldn't say for Martin - was that the girl possessed some knowledge about fine art. And it is even more interesting that she possessed this knowledge thanks to this extravagant Agency. Gosh! Before, I knew about Velasquez and that he painted a nude Venus who looks in the mirror and her hip is sexily attacking viewer's attention, but I didn't know who Collier is. I didn't tell it to anybody. I exactly mean those two who were in the studio's room except me.

It's not a big shame. When I was at home, and when I ate enough, I was still hiding my secret little shame. Just for me, it looks like a shame to know less than some talkative sex-addicted blonde who likes to show off. And then I launched my computer to open Wikipedia to reveal who this Collier was. And John Collier was an outstanding Pre-Raphaelite artist who painted some fine portraits. He actually created pictures featuring nude beauties like Lady Godiva. As I saw the artwork, I was almost astonished. I even have a feeling that I would like to visit Herbert Art gallery where this picture should hang. Just to see it. There is a very fine delicate girl who is nude and sits on a horse. She looks very fragile, and that isn't how you would imagine the past masters to paint the noblewoman of early middle ages. At least, I finally learned something new about beautiful things with a little help of this blonde girl, despite the fact that most of what she brings to the seashore of my mind is like some garbage that needlessly floated from far away. I will try to think more about the Lady Godiva and Pre-Raphaelites, but not about things I am irritated about. Relax Elise, honey. Wish I have a good night's sleep.
End of line.

Some Notes on Sexual Attractiveness of Tennis Players
from Dictaphone Record
by Martin

It is a lovely, but also specific question – why do tennis players seem to be so incredibly attractive to so many people of the western civilization? In a wide range of sportswomen, tennis players are the patented sexual objects. And magazines like Playboy are fighting to get the famous WTA person to their covers. And they succeed in this complicated matter only in rare cases. A possible reason for this is that the contemporary pro tennis players are so famous and so wealthy that Playboy hardly can add anything of worth to this richness and stardom. To make some real tennis pro pose for a men's magazine, one should have some great luck with it. It is undoubtedly easier to undress some pro photo model of highest level than some tennis woman of the same ranking. Models accept it as a part of their profession. But why tennis? If I would mentally go through the top beauty list of those who play shielded under the Women Tennis Association, I would not find more of pretty women than there are in other competitions. The fact of course, that there are some impressive items on this list. And maybe I don't know everybody.

There are other kinds of sports that, as it looks to me, definitely have a higher concentration of beauties, in percentage terms. Of course, my TV sports viewer experience doesn't make me the leading expert in any sports statistics. But it is also true that like many other people who have some at least limited interest in sporting competitions, I notice pretty girls, their athletic efforts, and their fitting uniforms. And so, my very private opinion is that the tennis isn't the number one sport by the concentration of beauties. I would prefer to give this position to a free gymnastics. Maybe what makes them less attractive is that they often wear quite similar uniforms and a heavy makeup together with the fact that they don't win those million prizes as tennis players do. But talking about looks only, that seems to be quite evident to me that the world of free gymnastics is full of small, pretty and plastic young women.

There is also such a kind of sporting activity as figure skating. Probably there are as many beauties as in free gymnastics. And there are still more of pretty girls than in tennis if we talk about percentages and concentrations. These two sports should be very close to the maximum level as I suppose. Can a tennis player go to the site of competition dressed in policewoman costume decorated with a lot of rhinestones? And a figure skater can. In a matter of costumes, figure skating represents the leader of attractiveness. When of course, it is for sure that the tennis uniforms are one of the advantages for the WTA girls. But no matter figure skaters seem to be not less attractive. And again there is maybe a fact of their lower earnings. Actually, in addition to a list of beautiful sports, I would add snowboarding. And when tennis girls are advantageous with their clothes, then snowboarders are not so. They actually wear masks. Their goggles hide half of the face. And their equipment hides entire figure. That is the case when uniforms are not fitting, and you don't know how good-looking a girl is. But if regarded in a more casual suit, some of the snowboard women are very attractive. And they are indeed very flexible same way as girls in gymnastics and figure skating. I think movements in snowboarding may be very close to those in some dance. Actually, I suppose that it all may be connected to the estrogen levels somehow. What I mean is that the estrogen makes women more good-looking. It makes their features smoother. Sure, coaches don't select for prettier girls. They need results, but not looks. But some sports require more of flexibility, and others require more of strength. Strength is stimulated by the testosterone that is opposite to the estrogen. And flexibility is another quality that depends on the estrogen. That is why good looks together with a general female attractiveness go well with flexibility. For instance, pro dancers were always attractive in this way. But again, these sports with flexible women are less lucky on the side of incomes if compared to the WTA stars, I would repeat it. But is it only money? When playing tennis like a pro, a woman may earn as much as a man which is a rare, if not a unique case in the world sports. And the popularity of female competition isn't lower than this of men's tour.

But still, when we talk about tennis, some things may look as downsides. If we talk about its sexuality. It is considered that the men adore female players to scream that loud. But I would say that not all of the men do. And an example is me. Usually, it isn't very feminine. I believe it is a rather rude and maybe even a stupid association of this screaming with sounds that a woman releases during sexual intercourse. And in this way that is subconsciously - more correct to say almost subconsciously - linked to the success in the intimate part of life. If a woman screams this way when you do that kind of thing to her, then you are a great lover. That should be a logic. But I still don't think it is as attractive as it may be rude. I may like a woman to be loud in the process. But I hardly would like her to be that loud. Imagine someone screaming right to your ear a hundred decibels Oh-Yes scream. A result of few such orgasms may be some stage of deafness. You will be lucky to have your ears sound. I believe it is a very fine thing when a woman breathes out. Softly. Or some very delicate whispering sounds of ecstasy. It is only my own taste, but no matter I just can't get why those loud tennis screams are so great to others. Maybe there is some animal side in it. I mean there someone may see a force of an animal. Human females don't behave like this at any other place, but tennis court. And sport is something like a very civilized fight of human animals. All that physical tension and toughness. Male and female species are fighting to prove their superiority in rights of prolonging their genetic lines. Would Freud agree with this? Actually, he didn't know about genetics in a modern way, but he knew the rest of it. And even without knowledge of genetics, an entire thing stays to be the same.

Modern women's tennis becomes more and more athletic. A hard first strike that blows the ball at speed above hundred miles per hour. And muscular shoulders. That is among things that the one needs today to win the Grand Slam tournament. What I mean is that a woman needs more of unfeminine complexion to win WTA titles of contemporary. Free gymnastics won't do such thing to a body of a woman. It will develop flexibility, but not some elements of muscular strength and visible muscular heaviness that previously was more common to the male athletes.

But maybe the core of its sexual attractiveness doesn't come to us from a world of pro sport. Maybe it is somehow something else. I made a short investigation. Methods were primitive but available. And I learned that a sexual appeal of tennis woman probably appears on stage at earlier times. Times that were before pro tennis became that profitable. This fact is easily supported by many films and books that were created many years ago when tennis wasn't that pro. For example, one may remember how Dolores Haze's perverted step-father adored her tennis skills, despite the fact that the girl preferred some other activities. Tennis reentered Olympic competitions in 1988 during the Seoul games. That was the year when someone - it was Steffi Graf - was able to collect all annual Grand Slam titles in singles. After that, the competition was too tough to allow that to happen. This year, Olympics were surely a professional event. Previously tennis was in the games because the games were an amateur event and as early as in 1930 it was out of them. Then tennis was too amateur until 1988. But even before 1988, the filmmakers of different size could use tennis girls as a sexy addition to their stories. I believe that the tennis sex appeal appears earlier

than 1988. Probably after World war II just before the sexual revolution. Somehow even before the revolution.
And what did make tennis so sexy? I think the first right question is – who played it? Tennis was out of Olympic games not only due to the lack of professionalism but also because few countries were playing it. There were US, UK, New Zealand, and Australia. First winners of Grand Slams appeared from these nations. And why wasn't the tennis as widespread as football, for instance, another game that originated from Great Britain? In general, football needs one ball to make twenty-two persons play. But tennis is a different thing. It needs rackets able to withstand a tough clash with a tennis ball. And so these rackets need hard and expensive strings. Plus, there should be the net and the surface. What more of people played in the fifties? I suppose it was badminton. It needs some less expensive rackets. Someone just took a net from a garage and stuck its sharpened pillars into soft ground. Tennis was played by rich people. Young girls from richer families going to universities and wearing short white skirts in times when society wouldn't allow a young lady to wear such skirt in another case. But tennis just required it.
Their higher social status was what made them so attractive. Poor dockers and fishermen were in use

of boxing. But tennis was for girls and boys who went to colleges, and at those times it was quite a prosperity, if compared to an average situation, if your kids went to a good college. Remember that Gatsby couldn't go to university in his young years? And it is the purest belief that the people young but already prosperous are the best situated in life for any joys, including sexual amusements. And tennis is a thing that seems best suited for high society. Do you remember where David Larrabee from the original Sabrina 1954 movie preferred to seduce girls with the help of a bottle filled with expensive champagne? Higher social status has its sexual charm for most of the people. Especially in a society where everyone is crazy about one thing only which name is money. I actually mean – money is so grand for our civilization and our time, and maybe for any era of our civilization too. And there is also their tennis short skirts. They were allowed to wear them before Mary Quant introduced a miniskirt to western society in 1964. Isn't that a perk of a kind? Yes, miniskirt in a way was known to ancient periods of history, but not in this meaning. Then it meant the sexual revolution. Liberation of the woman and all the things like that. And that is where the sexual tennis appeal comes from. The scent of higher and more relaxed society together with uniforms revealing more of flesh. And here it is - the image of a clean, rich girl with a perfect pack of classic uniforms.

But doesn't it mean that we don't have such ladies today? Hardly. I believe that the women walking through the city after visiting the fitness center, wearing their fitting and revealing sports clothes, are the real tennis girls of our days.

Description of Video Two from Dictaphone Record by Martin

We did another interview with Susan. She told us some more facts. Story proceeds. I noticed that Elise was softer to Susan this time. She provoked her with some questions again, but she had a softer tone of her voice. She probably gets used to our principal witness and to her stories too. And my entire professional life now is floating from one meeting with Susan to another. I wouldn't say that this blonde girl is one who surprises me with her outstanding smarts, but I also wouldn't say that she irritates me with something or that I dislike her somehow. She doesn't make an impression of a bad girl or any kind of criminal. It isn't a villain kind of looks. You hardly can believe so. This smile and this behavior don't go with it. And what a kind of a doll face. It may make an impression of some moderate naivete. Like she is still a child in some way. Would she be able to carry some big responsibility in a case? But would such responsibility happen to a girl like this? Maybe that is why she wouldn't be elected a president. Type of a person who will never be able to be a big shot from a multinational company.

No need to talk about her anymore. I am going to

make a description of one more video file. A memory stick is plugged in, and I open the folder. Let's see what we have now in there. The video begins with a scene in some living room, and the camera angle is again from above. It is possibly some hotel room, as I can see dinner served in there. There is a woman whose face I can't see. I see only back of her neck. She has a ponytail. She sits, and her left leg rests on a right one. She is moving her leg a little, probably being bored and waiting. She takes a book from the table. She takes it in a brusque movement of a hand. She turns a couple of pages, and it seems like she reads, but not for a long time. She probably reads just a page or two. She closes the book fiercely and puts it back on the table. I don't know what book it is. I can't recognize a title printed on it as the resolution doesn't allow seeing much of detail. Then she stands up and comes to a tray with dinner. She doesn't take meal itself, but just a cluster of grapes. She eats grapes then sitting in the chair again. I suppose I better fast-forward the video as nothing happens. For fifteen minutes more she sits on a chair and only moves her leg a little sometimes.

The next happening of this video is that another woman enters the frame. It looks like it's Jane. Most probably her. She sits on the sofa against the woman. It is most probable that they are talking. Jane eats something from a tray. Then she reaches for her bag. As she comes into view, she puts her bag near on the sofa, and there is something. That thing is a little too big to be completely hidden in the little bag. She takes it out – that is some magazine, I suppose. Yes, it's a magazine. She shows it to a woman while talking to her at the same time. She points to the cover. And then she passes the magazine to the woman. The woman, as it looks, opens it and goes through its contents. Turning pages she slows her movements finding probably some article that seems interesting to her. Then as it looks, they discuss this article with Jane. Or maybe it is coincidence, and they actually talk about something else. And then there is nothing of interest for five minutes on in the footage. I mean they just talk and don't do something new. And then it just interrupts. Looks like nothing really happened.

Next part of the video seems to be more promising from the very beginning. It does so because its location is a more unusual one. It isn't a place that private as an apartment or a hotel room. It is a tennis court. That's indoor one, but still, it should be something more like a public place, I guess. A woman dressed for sports appears. She has shorts and t-shirt on. She wears a ponytail. And probably it is the same lady that was in a previous part of the video. I wouldn't tell that this time a camera angle is positioned that high from above. But that's thanks to the wideness of space there. This one who fixed the cameras for surveillance preferred to put them close to a ceiling, probably to see everything in any case, because the otherwise some object or person could get in a way, partly closing a view. She stays there like waiting for something or someone. Then she disappears from a view. And then she returns having a racket and couple of tennis balls with her. And then she practices her serve. She hits to no one because there is no one to play with her on the other side at the moment. But after some time another person appears. It looks to me that it is Susan. At least it is how I can judge from her complexion and hair. I suppose it is she. She has sports clothes too, but they are different from those of a woman. She has something more like a classic female tennis player outfit. She wears some light white tennis miniskirt and a light shirt. She goes to the opposite side of the court, and they start to play tennis. They do it for a while. And then Susan goes to the other side. She goes closer to a woman, and they sit on the bench talking about something. As Susan goes closer to a camera, it makes me feel surer that it is her. Though her face is still vague, her shapes are better recognizable now.

They sit on a bench for some five minutes. And... nothing really happens during these moments. And then one more person appears on the stage. It is another woman who also wears a classic tennis outfit. She has same miniskirt and a polo shirt with a revealing cut. She has beautiful forms. They are not too big. But that's what Playboy would like. She has D-sized breasts, I suppose, and they seem ready to jump out from her uniform. Her rounded hips seem to be heavy, and at the same time, her waist is surely outlined. And she has a ponytail too. And that is the common feature for all the three now. And these fitting uniforms including minimalist skirt suit her perfectly. She goes to the center of the court and stays there. She stands with her back against the net. Actually, it isn't her back exactly. What is pressing against the net is her hips. She puts her hands wide apart. This way she has her hands spread over the net behind her. And she leans back a little. Then she says something. It is evident that she talks to the two on the bench. At this moment Susan seems to make some comment to her friend as she turns her face to her and tells something with a slightly intimate air about it.

Five seconds later the two stand up and pace slowly toward the new girl. When they approach her, Susan exchanges a couple of short phrases with her. And then she says something to her friend, to a dark-haired woman who is not in a white tennis dress. As she stands with her face to camera, I understand that she wears some sort of mask. It covers her eyes only.

And it is black and probably designed like some extravagant piece of a lingerie set. An instant later, busty blonde goes down on her knees. When she stands on her knees, she raises her head to look Susan in the face. Susan receives this glance looking her in the face too. Susan then puts a palm on her head and tells her something. I become more and more curious about what they are talking to each other now. Her next doing is that she makes a blonde lose her ponytail. And then she touches the top of blonde lady's head softly, and her hand moves down to run smoothly over blonde's cheek. She does it all with her free hand and with her other hand, she holds a racket. It seems like Susan smiles when doing this. She tells to a woman on knees something again. The dark-haired woman stands near, in distance of one step to a woman standing on her knees and is watching all that happening. They freeze in their positions for few seconds. Susan stands on a left side. The dark-haired lady stands on a right side. And busty blond is in the middle between them. And they all still hold their rackets in their hands. Susan has a piece of equipment in her left hand. And dark-haired woman symmetrically in a right hand. And luxurious blonde also holds a racket in her right hand. Her grip is tighter than that of other two. Girls standing and watching her from above are holding their athletic weapons just slightly

touching them with the tips of their fingers. And tension at that moment seems to be as strong as the straightness of strings in their rackets. As I know in critical moments of the game even the best Wilson strings can let player down tearing apart after a hit of a tennis ball going at speed above hundred miles per hour. That may crush indeed.
And then the Busty Blonde - I suppose I can give her this name just for my own use, not that I think her to be a caricature person, but just... Busty says something to Susan. That seems to move her somehow as she goes out of her frozen state. And entire trio now loses the sense of modernistic sculpture composition which I would entitle a contemporary tennis school for girls. Susan tells Busty Blonde something. And she stands up. Probably that was what the girl told her to do. To stand up. Blonde moves. And at that moment she releases her racket from her tight grip and let it lay on the court's floor. At this moment the dark-haired woman is leaning against the net and rests on it slightly supporting her body this way. She seems to touch a net with the tips of her fingers. Now I think I should somehow invent a system that will help me to give names to some people whose real names I don't know. That will be more ethical than to call the ladies Busty Blondes or something else like this. I return to describing what happens in the video. Next

happening develops events with a sparkle of its strong momentum. Susan tears a white polo shirt on the blonde who stands now supporting herself against the net too. It is remarkable that the woman had no any bra under her shirt. The dark-haired woman doesn't take part in the action. She just watches it all with evident interest.

As Busty Blonde loses her polo shirt, or it is better to say that her polo shirt turns into pieces of tissue on the floor, she turns her back to the camera. At this moment Susan presses her racket stronger in her right arm. Blonde bends over the net, now making her hips look toward the camera with all the blossoming flesh they have. And now it becomes evident how little her tennis skirt is. Susan puts Blonde's miniskirt up, and it looks like she has no underwear at all. And next thing Susan does - she makes a rapid motion with her racket toward beautiful rounded and bare hips of Blonde. She spanks her with her racket. She makes a dozen of spanking motions. At first, Blonde reacts almost with no response, but then she makes soft movements. She moves her body. And Susan moves her lips. A couple of words to Blonde. And the woman, now topless, goes down and now stands on her knees again. The dark-haired woman pulls a little closer now. She almost seems to have an intention to take a more active part in the action. Susan repeats her

caresses over hairs and cheeks of the Blonde. She makes a little addition. She, as it seems, puts her thumb into the mouth of Busty Blonde. She keeps to tell her something. She caresses her moving fingers a little lower than her neck. Then Susan talks to a dark-haired lady in the mask. The woman in the mask moves a little closer and takes a back of Blonde's head, pulling her hairs. Her grip seems to be soft. Busty Blonde's head moves a little backward, and her face rises for a little bit up. The woman in the mask keeps it this way for a while and then loosens her grip and starts to caress Blonde's hair.
Susan says something and puts her racket from her left hand to the right one. She seems to give her racket to Blonde, but Blonde doesn't take it. Susan moves racket closer to her face and then... and then Blonde starts to kiss and to leak a handle of it. At least that is what it seems to be. I can be wrong. Susan takes a racket away from her for a while and then she puts its handle in between her breasts. And then she moves it a little up and down. Then she again gives it to her to kiss and to leak. And just a while later she puts the handle into her mouth. She seems to make inside-out motions. She says something to a dark-haired woman in the mask. And the woman undresses. She takes everything off. She takes everything except her little black mask. As she has her lingerie on, it takes some time to do so. She

does it without hurry. Still, she keeps watching what Susan does to the Blonde. For her, it takes around two minutes to undress. And she finished. Susan keeps repeating all of her tennis-racket-handle tricks for some time. The dark-haired woman sits down and then half-lies in a free but elegant pose like the Venus of Velasquez spreading her long legs on the floor in the direction of a camera. She keeps watching from a short distance without any single motion added.

Susan stops to do the handle tricks to Blonde and says something probably to both women now. She comes back a little, and it looks like she gives some space for them. Blonde lies down. She lies with her back against the floor, and her body is parallel to a tennis net. Susan comes closer and kneels down near her. It looks like she rips off her skirt and Blonde is completely naked now. Susan puts her hand in between Blonde's legs. She goes with her palms across the legs. And then she touches Blonde's pussy. At least it seems so. When she reaches it, Blonde moves and puts her legs a little apart. Susan says something to the dark-haired woman, and she rises. Now she is close to Busty Blonde's head. Actually, Blonde's head now is in between her legs. An instant later she... sits on her face. At this moment Susan presses her palm against Blonde's pussy. They keep their positions while repeating their moderate motions for a couple of minutes. And then this triple composition collapses. Susan stands up and undresses, and now all three of them are barely nude. At this moment a dark-haired woman bends to form a classic sixty-nine position. Susan is undressed. She sits close to them. And now she starts to caress them both softly repeating their rhythm. A thing that happens after can be described as chaotic combinations of female bodies. They touch each other. They kiss each other, and they do a lot of pleasing things to each other until they seem to be a little exhausted.

They lay on the tennis floor like some three parts that are leftover of something bigger than just experienced destruction, falling into separate pieces. A result of an internal explosion. They remain almost immovable for a minute or so. Susan becomes the first person to break this breathless immobility. She partly rises, lifting only an upper side of her body. And her head rests on her palm for a while. And then she stands up. Few instants later the other two follow her example. They seem to talk like friends. Susan becomes more cheerful, giving her usual portion of childish smiles. Then they get dressed. And then nothing of great significance happens.

This video has one more file attached to it. And it is, of course, another piece of surveillance footage. It is longer than previous one, but I will try to define its essential contents in fewer words. I think this video may have real importance for understanding what really happened in a preceding video chapter. In this video, similar things happen. Same as in the tennis sex video. The difference is that all that happens in another place. Actually, it doesn't happen on the tennis ground. It happens in some room. And there is Susan and a beautiful blonde with impressive forms, and there is this bossy dark-haired woman whom I expect to be the Agency's head-girl. She seems to direct them. And also there is some other blonde instead of the woman in the mask from the first tennis video. This footage is long because it is a composition made of many parts. In every such part, they perform all things Susan and the Blonde did in the tennis video. They repeat an entire story alternating it a little. And alternation is mostly about some details. In the first part Susan uses her laughter more often, and also she spanks her companion too softly. She shows some indecisiveness. She doesn't seem to be that sure about things she does, but her every next time is more confident. The tall woman seems to teach her. Most of the times they do it all dressed. They only imitate things. And... they just mark all these things they are supposed to do with their motions. And in the final parts, they do it with all the undressing.

And that looks like the first sex tennis video.

Now I know that I have something that should look incredibly interesting to the broad audience. But why someone powerful should have so much intention to expose it all through me? I wonder, and I don't know. I still don't know a thing about what the hell is going on. I hardly believe that someone mighty wants me just to make another reality show. Something that will make the audience go so freaking mad one more time. Or is it just a stupid joke? Too late for a joke. I now really think that for a joke it is too much. Why would someone treat me? Why would this someone give me a treat together with all these tricks? There is something. As I don't see the exact scale of the game, I can't imagine what the value it has in total. I see only some piece of it not knowing how little this piece is. And even this piece is under a dark glass of secrecy. Somehow I even become more afraid for my life. It is true that the sex and death closely intertwine in the eternal circle of life. And so, when I encounter so much of sex, I start to grow a subconscious fear inside me. At this moment I suppose that most probably the clue for understanding the matter is the names of persons involved. That can be a matter of blackmail or something like this. But if that's a right guess, then what should I do? Helping blackmail - together with uncovering the private life of people - is one of the worst possible sins for a journalist. Thou shalt not blackmail, Martin. Gosh, I hope to keep my reputation in a proper state or at least my life in any state close to normal. It isn't a great sign for mental sanity. Thinking about future in this manner now. Somebody, please save me, because I feel a scent of death together with the excitement of sex. And it is the most striking combination indeed. Someone who can put cameras in so many places, what links and ability this one has?..

All second part seems to be a rehearsal. I remember myself being in school theater and - with the exception that we did nothing sexual and we didn't undress - if someone would shoot us, that may look quite similar to that. I wonder what it could be if in college I were a part of some amateur theater company that possessed some pretty girls as part of its cast. What would I feel then? Strange fantasies today. But it's not a right question at all. My senses can make it all complicated. The interesting question is – what did the dark-haired woman in the mask felt on this tennis court in a moment their trio finally collapsed into separate pieces? When their beautiful human bodies were producing hot steam? I wish I knew. I wish I would. I just can't get rid of this feeling. All that matter nests in me deeper with every next second.

Nov, 12

Private Audio Diary of Elise

by Elise

Life goes in its usual way. That means it is rather boring. Blonde sex-thunder, this talkative blonde didn't visit my life for a couple of days. And it looks like Martin won't arrange another shocking erotic revelation for tomorrow. It seems he even returned to his previous projects. Themes which they involve are not so sexy as it seems. But a month ago he considered them to be interesting stuff. He gave me a couple of tasks. I should collect some information mostly from open sources on the activity of top corporations of the contemporary business world. But actually, I don't think it is for long. I don't believe curious blond will let us free. I can't know it, but I feel it for sure at the same instant. When I went home after our recent interview, my guts told me that when I was sitting in a subway car. And my guts don't lie to me.

Today was a rather usual day. I collected the information required and this time when I was explaining to Martin my notes he listened to me. I think that in his interest to powerful corporations there can be something personal. I don't know exactly, but maybe that can be some regret for own life of a person who wasn't born in a wealthy family. And so he tries to understand the ways of power in this world that put in a system may become a serious barrier on a way of making a career of the great and famous journalist. I mean that is what it can be. I am not sure about it.

At home, I felt a little depressed and went into a mood that usually produces dreams about going away one day and starting a new better life full of emotions and revelations. I thought about big aircraft with silver wings again. I even composed a silly little poem.

Oh, silver-winged bird for you I pray,
Oh, will you please just take me far away
Somewhere where I would like to stay,
To lands of dreams, to fairy-tale,
Oh, will you please one day?
And I try to earn the right
For one, the most desired flight.

It isn't cool that I compose rhythmical lines. That means I am not that well if to talk about mental state. But maybe it is quite usual to me – to get a little depressed time after time. I'm looking forward to tomorrow, hope it will be better. I'm yawning, and I'm going to bed.

End of line.

SUSAN

PART TWO

Nov, 15

Susan's Interview Four

from Dictaphone Record

by Martin and Elise

Susan: What should I talk about today?
Elise: You start an interview with a question.
S.: Yep [laughter].
E.: Just tell us what happened then. Tell us about your next time you took part in... those things.
Martin: Yes, I think that will be OK.
S.: Well, It was about a week after my first time.
M.: That time - was it really different then?
S.: Yes, that was very much different. Jess said that my first time was only an introduction and if I was not afraid... And if I had no any reason to prevent my active status within Agency, then I could join their team on a more permanent basis, but in this case, I had to learn more. Still, learn something new. She said it wasn't the trouble if I had no time for that all and I would prefer to drop an opportunity. And she said I could refuse without giving any particular reason because it was absolutely OK then. It is because this activity is rather specific and they understand and stuff like this. That's what she said then.
M.: But... you didn't choose to drop the opportunity?

S.: I chose to stay. I mean I just decided to see more of it. It wasn't that bad. It was a pretty nice thing to do. I should say that no matter how specific that was I don't remember myself having such... fun at work. That was quite an experience to me. And that time, an entire thing had to be a significant challenge to me because Jess told me that would be a full cycle.

E.: Full cycle? What do you mean?

S.: That means as I understood - that I would participate all things they usually do to set the game. I went from beginning to completion. I got full access to staging and other things. I kinda participated in the creation of the scenario. Creation of all of its elements. And it was especially special that I participated in the insight part of it.

M.: What is the insight part?

S.: Insight part – it is such stage of game-setting. It is... It is when we collect information about Lead Hero. But actually, it is more complicated. I can't explain it so correctly as Jess would do. But I think you need to understand what the Lead Hero would like and what would be too risky with the person. I think you know what I mean. Insight means that we collect everything that can be useful to draw the person's preferences. To outline her wishes. They kinda call it maps. That can be his or her favorite movies, favorite books or anything like this.

M.: This time there was an insight?

S.: Yes.
M.: And how did it happen in details? I mean, what exactly did you do?
S.: We knew some things about our supposed Lead Hero from the client. But it still needed some research. Jess made it clear that I would be one of those who would handle the matter. She said I would go there to do it. There was Jane too. Also, she thought maybe that would be right to send someone else because I hadn't any experience. But then she decided against it. She considered two of us would do.
E.: You said you would go there. You mean that is how you called collecting and analyzing the data or what? What was it exactly?
S.: No. That means that we went to an apartment belonging to an object of investigation.
E.: Excuse me!? But doesn't it mean breaking limits of some very personal space? I mean, that might be quite illegal. You can't go to someone's apartment without some permission. Or what was it?
S.: It wasn't like this. We had permission. It was agreed.
E.: Did you see any paper that gave you a right to enter one's apartment and search in it for something?
S.: No. But it was agreed. I am sure.
M.: Elise tries to say that if you had no permission

from the actual owner of an apartment, then that could be considered illegal. There is a law prohibiting intervention to personal life. That is very important indeed. We don't want you to tell something that may hurt you. Me, I wish you all the good. I don't want you to get in trouble. See. And we even can delete a part of an interview if it will be needed as it isn't our aim to make you a criminal. We don't want you to have trouble.

S.: No, you don't understand. That was absolutely OK. The client owned the apartment. They just shared it with the person who was our Lead Hero at that time. It's OK, no trouble [giggle].

M.: Oh, it's... good then.

E.: Go on. Just tell us how it was. You know, Martin and I... We are sometimes too much concerned about the ethical side of our profession. Forget about it. We are your friends. Just tell us your story. Just describe as many things as you remember.

S.: It's nice. [giggle].

M.: It's late, and we got tired a little as it seems. Girls, would you like some coffee?

S.: Oh, it's very nice of you.

E.: And me too.

M.: I'll bring some.

E.: You do well. You're a good interviewee. Just if something goes in a wrong way - tell us. We can have some sort of agreement, you know.

S.: Everything's fine [laughter]. You guys are professional guys. And I just will do as you tell me. I will answer any questions. There's no trouble about it. It's totally OK. I said I am going to tell an entire story. And I'm ready.

E.: It's not going to be the smallest of our works. We'll need to do much, really. But I think we will make a film that every TV channel would like to buy. I believe it can be our biggest success.

S.: Really?

E.: I'm not pretty sure, but it's possible. There are things the audience will like.

M.: Here. Your coffee.

S.: Oh, I adore cappuccino.

M.: When we stopped, you were telling us that you were to get some insight.

S.: Yes. We - Jane and me - went to an apartment where we could find some additional evidence of our investigated person's sexual preferences. Jane insisted that we would wear the leather jackets. That's the pretty clothes. And wearing something similar would make us look like a team. When we were inside, we also wore the gloves to be careful. We didn't turn it all inside-out, of course. We only looked at some things that were present there. When we were going to the place at night, I was hoping that a client would meet us there as it was his apartment. It was an unusual experience for me. And I didn't feel totally relaxed, despite the fact Jane was with me. She was able to make me sure about things in most of the cases because she is a great girl who knows how to handle anything properly. But no matter, you know, it was terrifying just a bit [laughter]. Jane told me that a person couldn't be present with us that night because a person didn't want to be exposed. Too careful in a way.

M.: You said that it was his apartment. Was this person a husband to the Lead Hero or lover, or friend? Did you know anything about him?

S.: Actually, no. We didn't know anything. I think Jess knew more. I suppose. And maybe Ann did too. Maybe she at least met this person. But one could be somehow in a mask or something. We didn't know a thing, for sure. I didn't know whether it was a man or woman.

M.: But in the apartment that was shared by this person with the Lead Hero, there could be some private things.

S.: Yes, but it was their love nest. Inside this little apartment, there were things they shared. And as we knew, their sexual preferences were quite similar. Maybe even they did become similar while they were together. In some way. So, as I understand, we could search the apartment without any risk of revealing someone's identity.

M.: And things you found there - were they useful?

S.: When we were going back to the Agency that night, I thought that we found almost nothing that would really help us to create a map of personal preferences, but Jess told us that the information we gave her was quite useful. Actually, we just told her about what we did see in there. I thought that it could be useful to take some photographs. And I was ready to use my phone for this purpose, but Jane told me it was against our principles. It isn't something that was absolutely prohibited. But it is better to say that it is not. Well, it is not ethical, or something. Uh... we just saw it and told what we saw to the other girls. That is how it was. We found some stuff there. There were a lot of erotic films. Some were only softcore. Some were evidently porn films. We also saw some posters of celebrities and sportswomen on the walls. Not a lot, but there were some. We also found some costumes from sex-shop, and I told Jess that this could be very useful as we could make a scenario involving characters they liked. But Jess said that it was most probably better to introduce something new to a person, but that had to be something a person would like, of course.

M.: That helped to create the image then?

S.: Yes, it did. We then began to think what story to use. And Jess proposed from the very beginning that it would be a celebrity sex fantasy. She said that was what we got from analysis of all data and things on person's preferences we had. When we commenced making suggestions for a scenario, for its outline, I said that maybe that would be fun if that would be a fantasy featuring photographer. Something like a famous photographer seducing a model during the production. Jess said that this idea wasn't bad. But maybe it wasn't what we needed in the case. As it turned out, most of the outline was invented by Jane. And Jess made some few but important remarks.

E.: As I understand, you just sat there and made a plan for it. How much time did it take? A couple of hours? Or more?

S.: No, actually we sat there for a whole day. It took some time. It was two days after we returned from an apartment with our additional insight information. We were returning to the question of scenario during the day. It was quite a usual day at the Agency. But we always returned to it and discussed, I can say. And finally, we had something everyone agreed with.

M.: What was it? What was the outline?

S.: In the process, we decided to add some sports element to the game. I mean that had to be something like an episode from person's sporting life. Something like this. That was Jess's concept. She said we evidently had information that the sport was what turned our person on. She liked fitness, and she believed that the people who do sports are not just healthier. They are also sexier. And we knew that she was spending a lot of time doing sports and fitness to keep in shape. We considered that she no matter never regarded the sports as something that can be fun. At least, it can be fun inside the sexual fantasy. Jess explained that reversing something rather serious into a game can be most effective. That is why people have a fantasy about sex with a school teacher. School is very dull usually and turning it inside-out seems most desirable for people. And sport is something that needs the discipline and training, and many other things like this. That is why we decided to introduce such thing to her. A sport like something absolutely entertaining. Previously it was like work for her because, as we understood, she was a person who thinks about it like about her daily duty. A person like her thinks that if she won't keep in shape, she won't make a good career and won't look attractive. And so she needs to do it like some work. But a game is what also can be found in the core of the sports. That is the exact phrase as Jess told it to me. And that was how we created an outline for the future action. That was supposed to be a story involving celebrity who likes sports.

E.: Celebrity? What do you mean? But it isn't so easy to persuade a celebrity to take part in such things. Is

Agency so powerful it can get anyone and anybody for its activities?

S.: No, it wasn't this way. It just meant that one of the girls would act a celebrity part. It is more important to bring the scent of celebrity and stardom than the celebrity itself. That was what the person should've felt. And no matter, deep inside, the person understands that it's only a game. But it won't prevent anybody from having fun. I mean, we just needed to present someone as a celebrity. And it was that superb lady. Barbara took this part. She really looks that great. She is luxurious. I suppose she was a perfect candidate for the thing.

E.: How did you achieve this? Effect of stardom. It isn't that easy. What did you do? Hired a limousine and other expensive stuff? I mean, you need a lot of things to present someone like a superstar, and these things are quite expensive. And if you don't, then the entire thing may look like a fake.

S.: Yes, you're right. You kinda start to get it. We discussed this during setting. I think you could be useful if you would be one of us. I really think so. You give some right ideas [soft laughter]. You see... well, that was very important that the principal part of the action took place at the sports center. And at the sports center, everyone wears sports uniforms. And that means there is no big difference in between rich woman and woman belonging to a middle-class

society.
M.: But you still needed to make the object feel... a scent of celebrity, you call it.
S.: Yes. And that is why we needed to make one, but a very efficient thing. It hadn't to be too expensive. But somehow it had to be effective. And that was a magazine.
E.: Magazine?
S.: Yes. That was a magazine. We made a copy of the magazine with photographs of Barbara on its pages. And this way my idea about photo shoot appeared to be useful. When of course, it was useful in another way. We started from choosing the name for the magazine. There were some options like the Shoot, the Luxury... the Bounty Hunter. But then we decided to concentrate on the photo shoot first. What we came to was that Barbara would present something like contemporary Barbarella.
E.: What is Barbarella?
S.: It's such an old sci-fi film. There is a very sexy girl who struggles with her enemies to save the galaxy. She is the Queen of the Galaxy. And her name is Barbarella. And that is what we decided our Barbara had to be. It was very well, you see. I mean, Barbara and Barbarella [giggle]. And she was something like a spacewoman, superwoman, celebrity and a little bit of a cool video game character blended into one. In this photo shoot, she was floating in zero gravity and

wearing some pretty white space costumes. She was impressive and very erotic. And then that was why we named a magazine the Futuro. Futuro means future, and that's very good to place the spacewoman on a cover of the magazine with a name like this.

M.: But it wasn't a real magazine?

S.: Yeah, exactly. It was a single copy of a magazine that never existed before and would never exist after that. But it all looked very natural for a glamorous magazine. It was full of contents. We even made all contents inside to make it a real thing. And photo shoot was great. It was produced with the use of chromakey and computer graphics in a professional studio. It cost some money, but its cost wasn't enormous. We also added some contents, of course. We just took some classic sci-fi stories and articles from other magazines. It wasn't difficult. It just took some time. But it was fun.

E.: And how did you use it? I understand that you needed to persuade your object that some girl was a star when she wasn't.

S.: We didn't need to persuade her. We just needed to give it some scent of star-life.

E.: And?

S.: Well, there were two parts of the action. The story was divided to make a person feel it all proper way. I learned then that the sex doesn't begin in a bedroom

or on the spot where people do it. It begins a way earlier. Many things that happen before define how great it will be.
M.: And... What happened in a first part of the story?
S.: Before going to a major part, Jane met an object and spent some time with her. And at some moment she offhandedly showed that great magazine she just bought. That's it. That is how she gave her a feeling of Barbara's star image. That just made her feel so. Girl on pages of such great magazine always feels like a star.
E.: Forgive me for interrupting, but you said Jane and her, they spent some time together. Do you mean they made love?
S.: No, they didn't. It wasn't prescribed in this part of the action. The aim was to give this feeling to an object, but nothing else. It just took some time, because it should've been smooth. No special attention.
M.: It was only a preparation?
S.: Yes, and it was especially OK as our object was a woman who liked it to happen softly and in rather slow motion [giggle]. Well, you know, some people would prefer to get all on the spot, immediately. And you can say that our object was somehow absolutely different to it.
E.: And major part was something that happened after that?

S.: It happened two days later at the sports center where there were tennis courts. That meant we still had time for rehearsals if we would decide to change something. And rehearsals were very useful to me [giggle]. In the beginning, it wasn't easy.
M.: What do you mean?
S.: I mean I wasn't doing everything right. And bit by bit I learned to do it. Our idea was that our object would meet Barbara, who should've seemed to be a star to her, on the indoor tennis court. Maybe that would be better outdoors, but that was a bit risky. Someone could see it. And there were problems about it. Jess told us that the Lead Hero was worried about exposing her identity and most probably she would wear a mask. What I thought was that I hardly saw a person wearing a mask in the situation like that. It supposed to be quite a private thing after all. And also we decided there had to be an element of soft submission. Jess told us some signs showed that the LH would like it. So, a beginning of the story was that Barbara appears on the court and tells me that she lost her recent match and I punish her for that... Like this. Actually, the beginning is very important. We call it debut. At this period of a game, person explores the setting, and that is why it is so important. It influences the entire experience. Well, I should've punished her and there was a moment when I should've spanked Barbara with a tennis

racket and when we began to rehearse it, I was too careful with her. It was a natural thing because Barbara has that beautiful delicate body and her buttocks are very delicate too [giggle]. I couldn't imagine that I could do such things to her. Rehearsals made me spank her properly. I mean, Jess told me that I did it too lightly and if I thought that it would be too painful for Barbara she could spank me to make me see that it could look more realistic, but still not being really painful. She has a sense of humor, that Jess. She said it was just a game. And Barbara isn't really fond of BDSM indeed. And we would never do something to someone who doesn't want it. I just had to do it almost playfully. But it also had to seem more realistic. And when I really understood it wasn't pain and got used, I learned to do it right. So, I mean, rehearsals were useful, despite the fact I failed to do it perfectly. I still was making some quite rough mistakes. There was a moment when I should've told it. Now, it's time to be punished. You know the rules in our school. Something like this, I mean. Girls told me that a phrase shouldn't be exactly like on paper, but it should come from the heart and fit in an entire story. And I had to tell it to Barbara and then start spanking her, but instead, I became paralyzed. It is one thing to rehearse, and another is to do it in reality. It was Barbara who saved me. She became a victim ready for punishment. And she said. I am ready to any punishment I deserve. You should not have mercy. As she said it, I got excited, and it wasn't easy to keep being a tough tennis coach because I should've kept my character in this shape. I shouldn't smile and shouldn't get soft. It wasn't easy for me. And pause that happened before words of Barbara seemed to be an eternal one. Maybe it was only five seconds, but I was afraid that it was too long. And it wasn't an only mistake I made. I forgot about the balls. I totally forgot.

E.: Balls?

S.: [Long laughter] I mean tennis balls, of course. Well, you see, after I spanked Barbie I had to give her exercise. I should have told her that she lost those matches because... she was not one thing with her racket. She does not feel it right. And also that she should learn to be united with her racket. And she should have a proper grip. I should've told that she should've held it lightly and tight at the same time. And feel it. And then I should've shown her how to hold a racket and let her do it and also put it into her mouth and in between her breast telling her these things again. I mean those same words about how to hold a racket properly. And also I should've taken a couple of tennis balls and held it in my hand and then I had to give them to Barbie. I mean I should've held them in my palm and pressed them. And then I order that Barbara does the same. But I just forgot that I should've had the balls in my pocket. Before Barbara appeared on the court, I played tennis a little with this woman who was our object. She was looking hot, and she came in a mask, and it made me feel uneasy. And I was one to one with her. And I even had a tiny panic feeling deep inside, thinking about what it could be if Barbara wouldn't come and I would need to do it all alone. And so, I forgot that I should've kept a couple of balls with me. I let them fly over the net to the other side of the court and forgot about them. Gosh! But it all turned out to be alright. Barbara was great, and I relaxed. I understood that she could support me if I would do something wrong. And I kinda had my confidence back at some moment. And also when we returned to the Agency's mansion, she gave a good report on me. She told girls that on the first try I was the best thing possible. So, it went rather smooth. Just, you know, those balls and the racket were important as a symbol of sex. Jess told me that it was nothing like some phallic symbol. It was more like a symbol of sexy action. Interaction. Racket and balls meant stardom and richness belonging to the world of tennis elite. Maybe it was supposed to mean richness and comfort of people from the elite tennis club. Some stuff like this. That's what it was indeed. There was actually one funny thing. At some instant, I had to tear Barbara's clothes. And when I first heard about it, I asked whether we could change our plan a little, because I was sure that I wouldn't be able to do it. But Jess explained that the clothes could be made of such fragile tissue that everyone can tear it apart easily. And we even tore one set of the clothes on Barbara during one of the rehearsals. Usually, we rehearsed it technically. Only pretending to do all the stuff. And that time we did everything almost like in a real situation. I mean, there were all the words and all the doings. And I tore her uniforms. We also visited the place where all should've happened. I mean, we visited what is called a staging site or a ground. And as soon as we arrived there, I was worried that no matter how long we rehearsed, the real thing could turn to be different. I was worried about the fact that we should've done it on the court's floor. I thought it should be quite uncomfortable. 'Cause the floor isn't like a warm bed. It might be cold and hard. When I told about it to Jess, she explained that she considered this. She said we would be able to use tissues of our clothes, but actually, there was no reason to worry, because the floor wouldn't be cold as a place was heated in the evening. And the most important, as she said, that it is not about regular comfort, but it is about new sensations. It is about doing the things in another way than usually. And, I think, it did work well. It was a lot of new sensations. And it was really unusual.

Nov, 15

Private Audio Diary of Elise

by Elise

We got one more interview with Susan. I wonder how many times I will enter this phrase at the beginning of my daily record. I think, now I feel easier about her. Maybe because now it seems I know her better and because we're no matter supposed to spend some amount of time together. But it is also true that I still don't feel I agree with her. I mean it isn't her words I don't agree, but her feelings. The way she tells us her story is something. I feel like talking with a child sometimes. She seems to be a person who never suffers depression. What a happy kid! It seems to me that she improved her speech. And at the same time, she becomes more descriptive. What a-facts she got!
Maybe she got relaxed, or maybe I got used. She speaks about many things like some kid who heard how adults are talking. I mean, she uses terms, especially these pseudo-scientific ones learned from the Agency. She heard many things from someone else. And now she accents she knows. But maybe that is what makes me feel relaxed about her. She seems to be just a funny kid who believes in her own fantasies.
Yes, and about fantasies, Martin told me that no matter how strange all her stories seem to be, he has

proof for them. I think I should watch those videos. I just don't want to do it now. I wonder if I would tell something like this to someone, would this someone believe at least half of it. I think you really should have serious proof for such stories to make someone believe. And you need to like telling your stories to people. But the truth is probably not that important as we taught to think about it. People mostly believe in what they want to believe. Human society is built on its normality. And that means that everything that most of the people do often is considered to be normal. And people lie too often. A lie is quite normal then. And then in such kind of society, the truth is only a vague conception. And what is the truth?

Yawn and end of a line.

Scenario Provided to Susan
Paper Document
from Archive of Martin

Title: Starlit Tennis.
Supposed parts: Tennis Academy Coach (Coach), Tennis Academy Student (Student), Friend.
Object's roles: Voyeur, Assistant.
Elements: Sports Fantasy, Celebrity Fantasy, Soft Submission, and Dominance.
Part specifics: The Coach is tough. It is a person of great life experience. A student is a little lightheaded. She totally respects the Coach and has no moral strength to resist superiority of the Coach. The central line of Coach's part is a soft dominance. The central line of Student's part is readiness for submission. Friend's part doesn't require any specific elements.
Notes from the Object's preferences analysis: Object is interested in celebrity life. Celebrity element is desirable for the Object. The analysis shows that some elements of soft BDSM won't hurt the Object's perception of the action. Object believes that doing sports improves a person's life in all aspects. Object prefers women despite the fact she had experience with the men. And there is no proof that she complains about these experiences. The analysis shows that there is a high probability that her

preference to women is based on a belief that for her it would be better to build the relations with a woman than with a man, but she doesn't find sex with the men dissatisfying and unwanted. That means she is not exactly a lesbian.

Setting

Required: Fake magazine, tennis rackets, tennis balls, and equipment.

Stage sites: Hotel room, indoor tennis court.

Story and remarks

Part One: Friend and Object spend some time in a hotel room, and during their chatting, the Friend shows a fake magazine to the Object. It is crucial that the Friend wouldn't hurry and would spend enough time with the Object. A magazine should be demonstrated in an offhand manner like something that is not so important, but the Object should not have a chance to avoid watching it. The aim of this action is to give the scent of celebrity to the Student in the mind of the Object. Performing this task is entirely laid upon the actress who takes a part of the Friend.

Part Two: The Coach and the Object meet on the indoor tennis court. Student appears. She goes to the center of the court to attract most of the attention. She declares that she lost her match again. She should talk with the soft feeling of guilt in her voice. She may talk with pauses in her speech that should accent a lack of self-confidence. After finishing the phrase, she may direct her glance to the floor in order to show a feeling of guilt. That will prepare the Object for the following part in the action. Coach explains to the Student that she should be punished. The Coach shouldn't tell how the Student will be punished, but instead, Coach should note that she knows what will happen next. The Coach may use phrases: You know what the rules are in our academy; You know what you should do then; You know what happens to those who lose; similar phrases. Coach shows to the Object *how girls are punished in our tennis academy.* She may make a remark indicating that the Object will see it now. The Student should go down on knees showing that she is ready for punishment. The Coach should let the Student's hair down. That symbolizes her changed status. Coach orders the Student to prepare for the punishment (spanking). Student goes to the net and supporting herself with it bends over it giving her buttocks to the Coach. Coach puts the Student's skirt up, revealing her hips. At this moment the Object sees that the Student has no underpants. Coach spanks the Student with a tennis racket. Coach tells the Student that she is not good enough to wear the uniforms of their academy. Coach tells her that she should win more matches. After telling this, Coach tears the Student's clothes. The Student becomes nude. Coach tells the Student that she should earn her right to wear her uniforms. Coach tells the Student that until she is not good enough, she cannot wear clothes with the badge of their tennis academy. The Coach may give this speech before tearing the clothes of Student, in the process of it, after it or during all three stages. The Coach may use phrases like: You do not deserve your uniforms; You have to improve quality of your performance; similar phrases. After finishing the *punishment* act of the game, Coach resumes *teaching*. The Coach should explain to the Student what she should learn in order to show a better performance. Coach explains that she should entirely feel her racket, balls, and the court itself. Coach also explains that she should learn to be *one item* with her equipment or she won't be able to be good enough and that she should learn to hold her racket in a proper way. To make the Student learn this, the Coach gives her examples of exercises designed to improve these elements of sporting abilities. Coach shows to the Student how to hold the handle of a tennis racket and how to hold the balls. Coach demonstrates the different extents of pressure and tightness. Student repeats after her. Coach puts the handle of a tennis racket to the mouth of Student, puts it in between her breasts and moves it over her body. Coach explains that this should help the Student to feel her *instrument of victory* stronger. Also, the Coach may ask Student to lay her nude body on the floor, telling her that this is a proper way to feel the court. During the *teaching* act, Coach may use phrases like: Feel it; Try to feel it with your entire body; You should learn to give yourself to it; similar phrases. In addition, the Coach may use the phrase: If you want to win the match, to win the title, to win the hearts and minds of the audience, you should hold the balls tighter. During the *teaching* act, tennis should become associated with the pleasure of sex. That should make a next stage more desirable for the Object. Exercises during the *teaching* act should symbolize the movements of sexual pleasure. It is not necessary to associate them with pleasing the male genital parts, but that could be understood like it both directly and subconsciously. That may add some spicy element to the action considering the gender preferences of the Object. After completion of the *punishment* and *teaching* acts, the final act begins. In between the *punishment* and *teaching* acts or after completion of both, Coach may arrange a face-sitting or any other position comfortable for the Student to perform cunnilingus. That can be presented as one more punishment for the Student. The Coach may use phrases like: Do you think you are punished?; It looks like that for a bad girl like you it is not enough; I believe you should have more of it; similar phrases. Reaching an orgasm during this interaction is not recommended as it should happen in the final act. Final act may be and recommended to be spontaneous as it will help to release the Object's desire. No specific recommendations are made about the final act except its free development.

Participation of the Object: Despite the fact that the Object was deeply investigated, her ability for openness during the sexual interaction is not made clear. It is recommended that the Object's involvement in the action may differ from voyeurism to active participation. It is a responsibility of the actress performing the Coach's part to decide how intense at any given moment involvement of the Object should be. Actress performing the Coach should stimulate the Object to involve in interaction by asking her *to help* with the Student and by this to delegate some of the prescribed actions to the Object if the Object is ready for such actions. Actress performing the Coach should decide whether the Object is ready or not. Participation of the Object in the final act is strictly recommended. Both actresses should do their best to make the Object ready for the final act. At the moment of its beginning, the Object should feel free to participate in it. Involvement should happen by the will of the Object. Actress

performing the Coach should not give the orders to the Object, but only some recommendations and requests. The Object should be treated with full respect. It is recommended to use slow rhythmical caresses to excite the Object. Object's excitement should develop slowly and smoothly.
The rest is improvisation.

Nov, 18
from Dictaphone Record
by Martin

I am waiting for what will happen next. I try to work on my project devoted to an influence of international corporations on our life. When of course, Susan takes more and more of my attention. Her stories are too interesting indeed. Maybe I just need to find someone for lovemaking. I spend too much time working these days, and my personal life doesn't show any signs of existence. I hope that will not interfere with my intention to make a couple of good documentaries in next several months.

Elise went to another city for a couple of days. She will be back to the end of this week. She is a good girl. Doesn't matter that I never told her that, and doesn't matter that I will never tell her that. Probably. I just know she is. At this period of time, I will try to understand how much important she is for my professional work. I should feel what I miss without her. She is out for a short vacation and to meet her family, but she promised she would continue some work. She said she would read a couple of useful sources and would give me a report later. And meanwhile, I'll continue talks with Susan. I'm gonna get another interview. I read another revealing paper showing how girls prepared for one of their games. I couldn't expect that someone could do it so seriously. I suppose when they make porn films they may use less of paper to write the story. I don't know how it all can be so serious. Maybe just clients of the Agency pay huge money for it. And I wonder where they get such clients with such money. No, I know that the really rich people exist. It is just interesting to know how they get any of their clients. I still don't clearly understand what hides beneath all these sexy games. But I suppose it can be something very cruel or dangerous if it isn't just my paranoia talking to me.

If it isn't what it all seems. And it's possible because I don't believe that someone gave me all of this stuff just to tell exciting stories. That means it can be a very serious affair, most probably involving the big money and interests of powerful people. Those who sit above us in their government buildings and on the upper floors of skyscrapers in their big offices with a panorama view. They always wanted to manipulate the media in order to get even more of power. Am I pawn in the game? Can I drop it? And do I really have a choice?

Nov, 21
Susan's Interview Five
from Dictaphone Record
by Martin

Martin: I am alone tonight. Elise went to visit her family. That is why I will interview you one to one this evening. Are you ready?
Susan: [soft laughter] Sure. Do you want to ask something particular?
M.: No, I think we will talk about same things as before. I just want to know about the next chapter of your story. And I also have some new questions to you.
S.: OK.
M.: During our previous meetings, you said you could leave the Agency at any moment, and you didn't decide what you would choose. After that tennis thing, did you leave? Or did you stay?
S.: I decided to have more of it. It wasn't bad, not at all. It was entertaining, and those girls kept me a great company.
M.: Can you tell me what were the most important events that happened to you in the Agency during the week after the tennis story?
S.: I just kept learning new things, and Jess gave me a new homework.

M.: New homework? You mean you made the previous one, and Jess gave you one more task?
S.: Not exactly. I didn't complete a previous task. Jess said it's OK. She said there was no need to hurry. I just forgot to open that folder and didn't check out what was inside.
M.: You mean that folder she gave you to learn from?
S.: Uh-huh.
M.: Were you not curious?
S.: I was, but... I just had much fun at the time. And I had a work to do. That's all.
M.: Did you know what was inside?
S.: Yes, I knew. There were papers and other things about one of the Agency's cases. I had to read it and to watch it. To know how they work. It was like an example, you know.
M.: And new homework task, what was it?
S.: It was about inventing fantasies. Jess told me that in Agency I should've learned to create interesting fantasies that would please other people. She said it would be better if it was something pleasing to me too, because it isn't so easy to know what is good for others, but if it is nice for you, then it is most probably can be nice to someone else.
M.: And how exactly it should've been? You wrote some story down?
S.: Actually, no. Maybe it could be not so good if I would write it. Jess asked me to prepare the story

and tell it to her [giggle].
M.: Forgive me, but does it mean you... you made things together? I mean, did it mean to perform the action from your fantasy? Was it like staging your own scenario?
S.: No. It was different. Jess said that it was an exercise of dreaming. It meant I should've learned to create a good story inside my mind. And I should be able to imagine all of the things in my mind. And fantasy should be good enough to impress someone other, to excite someone other only with its idea. Not with its flesh, but with its soul. Flesh means the embodiment of it when it's coming to reality. The soul is its essence and its idea. Well, and it was important to be able to tell an interesting story that the others would like. Something with a cool idea. And that is why I had to tell it to Jess in her cabinet witching her in the eye. And she said that to emphasize the quality of exercise I had to tell her a fantasy featuring both of us, not only me but her too.
M.: That should be quite an experience.
S.: [laughter] Yeah... you know, it was supposed to make me learn a creative part of it. That's because in Agency you tell your version for a scenario to others without using any props and sets. And that means you should be able to express yourself freely and to be able to tell it so others can see what good things are in it. That's what it was.

M.: And did you do it? Did you tell the story to her?

S.: Yes, I did it the next day. She gave me the minimum amount of time to complete. And she said that this had to be a private fantasy. She meant that I had to invent without anybody's help. That should develop my ability, and I should develop my ability, but not someone other's ability. She said it wasn't to check whether I was good at it or not. It was to develop my skill because she said she knew that I was good. And she even said that I was exceptionally good. It was pleasing, you know. She also said that actually, almost everyone is good about sexy things. Maybe not exceptionally good, but rather good, because it is given to us by nature. We just should develop it. We should reopen it because our society makes its best to stop natural things in us. That is what Freud and other guys like him were talking about. And she said I had to make it in twenty-four hours in order to improve my genuine ability to dream and to fantasize. You can trim it all then. I mean, change some details. You can improve something. But the core of it should immediately appear because it should be a natural idea. In some way. It should come from your feelings, from your heart. You know, what I learned, thanks to Jess, is that in sex you should use your heart too, not only... well. That means that the more senses you use, the bigger pleasure you perceive. And that is why you need to use your heart and your imagination too. And that was a new homework to me. And I kinda got top marks for it next day. Jess said my imagination was OK.

M.: I just had a little doubt, because you haven't done previous homework immediately, as you said. I just thought maybe you are the one who doesn't like to do homework. And when you were a student, were you receiving the top marks for homework? Did you allow yourself to forget about homework often?

S.: Actually, I was preparing my homework well. Usually. I don't wanna say I was the best pupil. I just was rather good at some subjects. But, at least, I didn't miss the lessons, and usually, I did homework. There was a couple of times when I forgot to do it or maybe left tasks undone on purpose [giggle].

M.: So, it's not you – a bad girl?

S.: Well... I don't think I am bad [laughter]. Actually, there is nothing bad about being a bad girl. In some way. It can be very nice to be a good bad girl if you understand. I mean, in the Agency most of the girls were something like the good bad girls. All were but Ann. Ann is just a good good-girl. And bad girls were really good too [giggle].

M.: But then bad is good. Is not it a paradox?

S.: Paradox? No, it isn't. It isn't because such badness can be not about being really bad, but about being cool and interesting to others. And cool is the great thing.

M.: We are going a little too far this way. It is really pleasing to talk to you about different things.

S.: Thanks.

M.: But actually it is late, and I would like to make a focus on our most important matter. Well, you said your homework was about fantasy. It can be very private, but if it's possible, can you give some specifications?

S.: Specifications? You mean to tell more about it?

M.: Yes, I mean more details. It can be useful information. Possibly, it may show something to me.

S.: Well, fantasy was a school type. About teacher and school girl. And detention. I think Jess could be such perfect strict teacher, you know. She fits for it. I told it to Jess this way. But the truth is that I just used one of my private fantasies. Fantasy I didn't share before, one that was reoccurring in my mind time after time those days. Sometimes I fantasized that there were Jess and Barbara with me. Other times it could be only Jess. And also it could be other girls taking parts of teacher and some other schoolgirl. In few cases, I fantasized that there was this woman in mask with us. She impressed me indeed. She wore a mask, and I didn't see her entire face. But I saw most of what you need to see. You know. She was gorgeous about everything. And her body is terrific. She really looks like someone who is a little crazy about fitness and sports. I fantasized about her. A couple of times. And in these dreams of mine, she also was a strict but sexy teacher treating me in a cold manner. I think someone who is really hot, this one can keep being cold on the surface sometimes and that still can be wonderful.

M.: Actually, I don't remember myself talking with someone about what she fantasizes about. It is for the first time in my whole career.

S.: There is always something happening for the first time. I believe it is a rule of life. That is how we discover the world [laughter].

M.: And, excuse me, it means that you fantasized about being a schoolgirl?

S.: Uh-huh. I think I can be a wonderful sexy schoolgirl. I am sure of performing this character. That definitely fits me more than tennis academy trainer for sure [laughter]. And that is why I chose it. I believe that if some men's magazine will do a photo shoot featuring me and I will be a schoolgirl in it, then it will be a great photo shoot.

M.: You like doing photos?

S.: Yes. Why not!?

M.: Did you ever try to make a model career? You are a good-looking young girl, and you say you like photo art. It isn't easy to become a pro model, but our days almost everyone has the opportunity to try. And in such cases, girls usually try something about it.

S.: Well, you know, I was on pages of Playboy. Once, I was traveling. I went to the Caribbean islands. And there I met a photographer who wanted to make a photo shoot with me. I agreed almost immediately. He was very persuasive. He said he wouldn't give me a lot of money, but he said I would look great on photos. And it was a photo shoot made on the seaside. There was a beach, and sun, and waves...

M.: I saw it. It isn't that I made a really deep investigation about you. I hope you understand that I made some brief profile on you just in order to ask the better questions to you, to make an interview better. It is a usual thing. In such cases. And, you know, the photo shoot is an excellent one.

S.: [laughter] Really? Oh, you know, you may go as deep as you need about me. It's no problem because I told it before - you may ask anything you need. I trust you like a pro. And actually what is on the internet. It's no matter public. It's OK. And do you really think that photo shoot was great?

M.: Definitely. One of the best seaside photo shoots I ever saw in men's magazine. Waves and beach were great, and you were even better.

S.: [laughter] I know. It was published in Latin America. And then after some time - as I know - in one of European Playboy's issues. But it was not published in our country. I don't know why.

M.: I saw it on the internet. And after that, did you try career?
S.: I tried, but maybe I didn't try too hard. I talked to some people, and they told me I'm not what the industry may need. They didn't tell it this way, roughly. But that was what I understood from their words. I just heard a subtext of it, because you know, they always refuse in a way you understand it, but they tell it so politely. Or almost politely, I would say. As I understood, the models today are tall and slim, and flat, and very cold, you know. And I am not tall enough, and my body is not that good to promote all the stuff. Brands and fragrances. Well, I don't think I can become a pro model really. If only something unexpected will happen to me, then who knows... [giggle]. But I no matter participated in a few more nice photo shoots. And at least I like photos. I like photo art.
M.: Do you share your photo sets through social networks? Do you have an Instagram account?
S.: Well, no. I'm not a very active user. And I don't have an Instagram account. I probably will launch a page, just maybe later. Do you think I should?
M.: Maybe, if you feel like it. Many girls seem to be crazy about it. You can also do it. And probably, you will become one of these pretty ladies who have millions of followers.
S.: Thanks. I think I should try. And do you use it?

M.: No, I don't, but I don't make a lot of photographs. I am more of a writer than photographer. Do you prefer to communicate with friends through different media?
S.: You know actually, I don't have a lot of friends. I mean close friends. I mean, a number is less than thousand. I prefer to talk and to communicate in reality, somewhere in the club. I like cool parties. I don't know. Maybe I like being in some great place. To me, sitting in front of the monitor at home isn't like being in a great place. I like having fun in real. There is nothing wrong with sitting in front of computer's monitor, but it is just different. I would say that I prefer to watch a person in the eye. And there are phones and other things. And I use the internet like everybody else. I use Skype and other things sometimes.
M.: If you don't mind, if it's not a very private question, who are your friends? I just would like to know what they are like. Please don't think I ask strange questions. Just... who? Do you keep relations with girls from your school, for example?
S.: Girls from school? No, I don't. There are not a lot of girls on a list of my friends. There are some. But I keep relations with some of my ex-boyfriends. Most of them are good guys. And there are some girls from my job and couple of girls I met at club parties. Mostly, I try to keep coolest people on my lists.

M.: OK. I should say, this evening it is a second unusual thing happening. It is our fifth interview, and only now I finally start to learn something about your personality. During previous interviews, all that I revealed about you except those facts that have a relation to our investigation is what kind of coffee you like. So, maybe I should ask a couple of questions to know you better. Will it be true to say that you are the person open to communication?

S.: Yes, it's true. I'm always open to people. That's the sort of a person I am. And about coffee, I would like to have a cup of coffee right now, if you don't mind.

M.: Of course, I don't. I'll bring.

S.: You know what I would like.

M.: And that is your coffee. I believe that the coffee-machine is one of the most important devices in any office or studio.

S.: [laughter] In our office it is for sure. We can't work without it.

M.: Do you know that there is some scientific study that shows companies that ban the coffee-breaks lose a part of their productivity. Scientists found that together with chatting during coffee-breaks, their employees discuss their tasks and that is what helps to find new ideas, exchange remarks and unite different activities of a group.

S.: That is... very interesting.

M.: Is it OK if I continue to reveal personal facts about you?
S.: Sure. Why you ask? Reveal as much as you want [laughter].
M.: Do you think you can be called a celebrity-addictive person?
S.: Well, no. I think I have this thing at a medium level.
M.: You mean you are as addictive about stardom, TV and glamorous magazines as our generation is on average? You like it all as everybody does, but you are not crazy?
S.: Yes, this way.
M.: I want to return to your days in the Agency. The way they prepared their so-called games, is not it too scientific? Why use so much of a method?
S.: I think it is a right thing. I think in sex, you can be free. And you can be absolutely free. I believe so. You may just do the things you like. But it is nice to use the experience of others and to listen to good advises. That means you can develop abilities and to be able to know how to please the other person. And it's very nice to know things like that.
M.: But doesn't it look too scientific? Doesn't it look really strange to you? All those terms?
S.: Well, no. It is not strange to me. It was too much fun to feel any strangeness.
M.: It's late. And I think there were all the questions

for tonight. Don't you mind to meet again when I have some more questions for you?

S.: Sure. Just call me. That is my own phone number because you always call me through my job.

M.: I know. It's just...

S.: You know, maybe you will interview me at my place?

M.: You mean at your apartment?

S.: Uh-huh, because it is more comfortable to me. I wouldn't need to go home. You can just ask your questions at my apartment.

M.: I don't know. It's possible if you want.

S.: I understand that it's more comfortable to you here, but at my place, it will be the same interview.

M.: OK, maybe. I will call you, and we will set it. OK?

S.: Fine.

Some Notes on Role of Multinationals in Sexually Repressive Society
from Dictaphone Record
by Martin

As I walk through the paths of the business center of our city that is also just the center of the city in general, I see corporate buildings towering over us. That should work as some sort of symbol. Architecture historically dealt with power and strength ruling over those who erect its pieces. From ancient times, a style of architecture was defined by the dominant political force in society. A few centuries ago the church played a dominating power in human culture. That was true that religion shaped the lives of most of the people. God was the thing the people feared most of all. And those who called themselves kings and emperors, and by this were entitled to hold the greatest power over the rest of the humans, were believed to be granted with their positions by Him. Two kinds of buildings played a most significant part in defining the architectural style. They were temples and palaces. That means houses of the gods and houses of those who were chosen by the gods. The national principle did not divide the styles of architecture. But religious one did. Entire Western European architecture shows a rather heavy influence of similar gothic style. Influence of European style might be found everywhere where European colonists set their foot. Eastern Orthodox tradition is different in its designs. It displays less of darkness, but more of white walls and more of gold leaf. All Muslim countries of Asia are connected by their architectural tradition. The spread of Muslim religion is historically linked to conquests of Muslim military leaders. Classical Asian architecture achieves its peak of development during the Middle Ages. This period's the most powerful conqueror was Tamerlane, the Iron Lamer. Tamerlane was one who collected not only lands and material treasures, but also the immaterial richness of Asian culture. He ordered to build several architectural complexes in the capital city of his empire - Samarqand. These buildings defined the designs for all lands that once belonged to his empire for centuries. As the lands were ruled by his descendants in that period of history. Tamerlane took the Persian culture as a model and adopted the Farsi as a primal legal language because Ancient Persia to Asia was something like Ancient Rome to Europe. One of the most noticeable elements of classical Persian architecture is a leaf-shaped arch. Under Tamerlane, the buildings with such arches were built in the Samarqand. And under his descendants, they were built in many countries all over Asia. These buildings had different textures of surfaces depending on materials available in a particular area, but their shapes were similar in many aspects. For example, Taj Mahal complex that was built by one of the descendants of Iron Lamer is similar in its shapes to many buildings not only in Samarqand but also in Chinese Uyghur province and many other parts of Asia. In India, you can easily define who built this or that historic building. There is a style typical to those who believe in reincarnation, a style typical to Muslims, and a style of those who were under the reign of Queen Victoria. Is it true that if a style of our most important buildings is shaped by multinational corporations, then it tells us who actually rule the world? And then, is it true that the multinationals had risen higher than governments? Many people in many places believe that the towers standing in downtown are the most important symbols of their cities. And more than that, such buildings are regarded as the symbols of progress and technology. They stand like the guardians in fortresses of the business centers protecting the essence of our contemporary corporate civilization. They symbolize the power of corporations. And that is why every multinational wants to build a skyscraper higher than that of any competitor. And it is especially true when corporations compete in the same city. Then happens what is called the skyscrapers race. It is a race not on earth, but a race to the sky. That was how according to the legend the Tower of Babel grew. Tower of Babel is a symbol of excessive pride and vanity. And it ruined itself when being not able to stand the weight of this pride. People became too different when they began to speak different languages, and thus they couldn't complete the Tower. That is what has a name of scale effect. It's when you need to do so many things altogether. But I actually have another point of view for the legend of the Tower. And through this point of view, it can be regarded as something having a serious connection to contemporary corporations. If people need to be similar to build the Tower, then the Tower will want them to be so. We are those who build towers and those who worship them. And look at our world - there is no difference today in architectural styles around the globe anymore. Everything becomes similar, like the bottles of Coca-Cola and McDonald's snack bars, no matter where it happens to be located. And similar towers are raised in all business centers anyplace where there is a business center. And that means anyplace where there is enough of money. And that also means all around the globe.

And that is what makes corporations repressive to sexual motivations of a human being. As we know thanks to Herr Freud, society is repressive to expressions of our libido. And corporations are major promoters of the modern social technologies today. They unite people better than military leaders did before. They fight to make people similar because this way it should be easy to sell them similar goods. Similarity like Ford's conveyor is what should provide more efficiency to producers. And sex as biological phenomenon implements the diversity at its very core. Sex as a biologic way of multiplication can be explained as a process when one unique genetic code mixes itself with another unique genetic code to create one more unique genetic code. That is what gave such advantage to creatures that performed sex as a way of reproduction in comparison to those who increased their numbers by mitosis. Sex gave to the animals an ability to create diversity within the same kind. That helped to accelerate evolution, and that helped to increase chances of survival. Diversity is a principal condition for sex because otherwise there is no point in it. And corporate culture favors the conveyor's standardization and similarity. Technological codes and technological way of multiplication with its regular linear math stand against biological codes and diversity. That is how it can be described – similarity versus diversity, corporations versus sex.

One may say that the corporate culture favors sex as

media for promoting the goods. There are a lot of advertisements featuring semi-naked girls and sexual elements. Such examples can be easily found everywhere from TV to giant shopping malls which, if to judge by their size, are replacing the temples as major spots for worshiping. But is it this natural kind of sexuality and sex appeal? In the nineties, top rank of fashion and advertising industry was blessed with the presence of such women as Claudia Schiffer and Cindy Crawford. Today, standards are different. Claudia was always a woman who kept smiling while walking by the catwalk of her super-successful career. Contemporary model is not a person who smiles too often. Does smile make a woman less attractive? I don't think so. Of course, a woman can be very sexy when being strict or angry. But not all the time! A contemporary model shouldn't smile too often, she should not be vivid, she shouldn't have breasts, and there are many other things she shouldn't. Maybe it's true that a model today shouldn't be too sexy. Maybe it's true that when a woman is too much interesting by herself, she is too much more interesting than the dress she should sell, and that means that she can't sell it so efficiently. The sexier seller is, the more you want her, or you envy her but not the dress she sells. And what is wrong with breasts? Why do contemporary models on catwalks should be so flat when we know that most of the people - including both women and men - consider it is sexier when there are some breasts? We know many famous women who manage to be very sexy while being almost flat. But still, that is the thing of natural attractiveness. There should be some reasons. Breasts deform the texture of the T-shirt or blouse that a model wears together with any print or pattern that is present on a tissue. And it isn't saying that the lovely breasts always attract some attention. A corporation wants attention to be paid not to sex, but to goods it sells. They want sex to be not a natural thing, but another media of the trade. And sex that sells is not necessarily the sex that excites. And that is why their version of sex can be so... unexciting.

Today, a woman with quite specific looks may really outcast many classically beautiful women. Beauty itself isn't always needed.

Probably, the nineties was a time when two different factors met in the middle. One was increasing and another - decreasing. But in that decade they met at their equilibrium levels. On one side, the nineties was a time when globalization made another jump, possibly it was a break-through almost as big as that happened in the post-war era. It was a time in the shade of events like the collapse of Berlin wall and the fall of the Soviet Empire. And on another side, western economies achieved that level of development when buyers would buy something not only because of product's physical qualities but also because of transcendent qualities of the brand more than ever. And brands together with companies owning them were big enough to give contracts that can make a model an international star. But they were not big enough and not sophisticated enough to have that firm control inside them.

Looking at the luxury industry, you may decide that there is a variety of sellers who offer their own goods. In every luxury store, there are so many brands to be found. But that is also true that almost every big brand is controlled by one of the two major luxury corporations. They are PPR/Kering and LVMH. Those names are hardly saying something to most of the people, but these companies have assets values approximately of 25 billion dollars and 45 billion dollars consequently. And they control the most of big luxury clothes, drinks, jewelry, and watches brands altogether with some other businesses. Carl Lagerfeld and Stella McCartney sold their names to them in the form of the brands. And it is not saying that Fendi, Prada, and D&G can't decide what will be on sale next season without their approval. There are only two companies, and it's like Pepsi versus Coca-Cola but in the fashion industry. Of course, there are some strong apparel brands independent of two giants like H&M, Zara, and Nike.

But they are few too. And they act in a very similar fashion. In general, apparel brands try to float in the same direction. Their primal aim is not your excitement, but their sales.

Another factor that counts is a decrease of personality's role in corporate decision-making. Previously, a certain person could have a significant impact on events of some little historical meaning. Heads of marketing departments and principal people of any corporation are mostly men. And men usually choose to be closer to sexy women. No matter in what circumstances they are if they have a choice they choose to be surrounded by handsome ladies, but not the opposite. And actually, women when not attracted this way also thought the pretty face on the poster might work. But today there are these smart computers with their smart software that rule the world. And those who are regarded as top rulers are only those who translate their will to others. There were times when shamans, priests, and druids had a big impact on human lives. They were telling the people the will of gods. And by this, they ruled them. And historians may think that they were lying to people in order to manipulate the crowd. Almost similarly, the data analysts read transcendent graphics and diagrams and explain them to others. And actions are designed this way. The only difference is that guys don't lie in most cases. Graphics are real, and they tell the facts, not the fairy-tales. Maybe if the economic analysis is one of our gods, then perhaps the corporate buildings are a kind of our temples.

A similar factor influences not only the world of finance and brands. But of course, it influences the media and entertainment industry. There are two major types of girls who appear nude, semi-nude or with lingerie or swimwear pieces on. First one is a famous woman. When a woman is famous, she can be sexy, and she also can be famous thanks to her looks to some extent. But famous woman actually doesn't need to be too hot with her face and body only, because celebrity status is what makes anybody as hot as necessary, no matter what. And there is a second type - an unknown but very sexy girl. Such type has no chance to appear on the cover of big magazine immediately, but she can be placed somewhere in the middle of contents. Mostly, this second type is used for photo shoots that feature these beauties in some sexy outfits like lingerie or swimsuit or just nude. Maybe it is only my private opinion again, but it looks like the difference in between average looks of those two types widened through a recent decade. That looks like that. A big celebrity doesn't need really great and outstanding looks to be declared a sex-symbol. She needs good lighting, a professional photographer, a makeup artist and other stuff like this, but not the looks as outstanding as those that the classic James Bond girls had. She may be somewhat average about her looks, but her money and status will add enough to make people think that she is a sex-symbol. Or maybe it is better to say that this would be enough for media to make people think this way.

And about Bond girls, did you watch recent Bond films? I think that the Skyfall was nearly as good as Casino Royale. But there is one problem. Bond girl line is not that strong as in classic films including Goldfinger and Diamonds are Forever. Berenice Marlohe is a good-looking woman, but I still think that they could introduce this line better. My opinion is that it is too much when Moneypenny gets sexier than the actual Bond girl. And when Marlohe was killed yet in a middle of the story, I didn't even feel pity. That is not right. Jeez, it's a Bond girl! That couldn't happen in the sixties. That time, Bond wasn't owned by a giant Japanese multimedia-electronics corporation. It was more like a family business.

In the sixties, stars had a special shine. Their shining wasn't like this of contemporary celebrities. Maybe it only seems to me, because classic and universally-approved things do always seem better than contemporary ones. But maybe it's not only the appearance when we talk about a comparison in between golden sixties of Hollywood and a modern industrial era of entertainment. Entertainment today seems to be more of conveyor than it was ever before. And as this conveyor works, people don't decide anything, but only stand near and press buttons they should press in order to keep the mechanisms going. In the sixties, there was such director as Alfred Hitchcock. He made a lot of successful films, and by this, he was an integral part of the Hollywood industry. But he also was a man who could make decisions. Examples are multiple. He could choose an actress for a leading part without too much of consultations or not thinking about what trends at that moment were. One of the principal trademarks of his movies was a permanent presence of beautiful shining blondes. There were Eva Marie Saint in North by Northwest, Tippi Hedren in Marnie and Birds, Janet Leigh in Psycho, Kim Novak in Vertigo, and of course, Grace Kelly in Rear Window and Dial M for Murder. He not only gave them parts. He also directed much of limelight towards their attractiveness. There is hardly a single director today who has such fame about his casting choices for the female lead. My guess is that today a director of the blockbuster-to-be movie is something like a principal person standing at central control board of conveyor called the movie production. His choices are limited within a range of a few buttons he can press. His actions are defined by what technical procedures conveyor can perform. Hollywood produces a lot of comics-based successes. But there are not a lot of movies that can be called both quality-made and oriented for a popular audience. When I say quality I mean the quality of plot and quality of emotions, the artistic merit. Hollywood today provides with all sorts of great professionals in a wide variety, except those who can create great stories themselves. There are a lot of masters of technology, but few of art. And the movie technology is what envelopes the art. But the art is the core of it. Without art, there is no sense, except money-making, of course. Billy Wilder was making movies for a broad audience gathering on Saturday night at cinemas from coast to coast in America and on another side of Atlantic. His movies were not some boring art-house. They were accepted by millions. And both audience numbers and box office were counted in the millions. Those movies are masterpieces, and the guy who directed them was a genius. Anyone who makes blockbusters in a row has no chance to be called a great master of cinema. Today. Wilder could choose to do things this or another way because he considered it to be a better choice. That could be only intuition, but intuition is an integral part of any genius. Today there is no place for intuition. It is too indefinite. And

corporations prefer to plan their budgets as correctly as possible. That is why personality defines nothing. This thing is too uncertain. But sexuality is a very personal thing. And that's much possible that the corporate politics, designed for more predictable business future, make real sexuality decrease. And some unnatural thing is placed instead of it.
And probably something similar has a place to be in the fashion industry. Yes, it is true that the celebrity designers like Carl Lagerfeld are still crucial for the industry. But they can't define what will be on markets and how to sell it. Claudia is a bit older than before. But she is still the owner of charming smile and impressive looks. She still looks great. And her looks are no worse than that of an average unit on Forbes Models Top Ten list. I doubt that the designers like Domenico, Stefano, and Carl himself wouldn't like to collaborate with her more often. But guys sitting in front of all-knowing and all-mighty computers tell that Claudia or someone like her wouldn't sell that well. And that is why such type of great looks may earn less than some models that are not that good-looking. There is more and more of standard for looks of a fashion model. One may say that there is a model like Kate Upton. She has pretty face and breasts that are heavy. And you don't know how she could become model our days at all. My opinion is that Kate Upton is a beauty who doesn't

define a general standard. She is not in the Fabulous Top Ten. She occupies some specific niche, and you hardly will find a model of her type having that success too often. Kate has excellent looks, and her breasts have it too, but that does not mean that she will sell better than some flatter girls. That is how the logic of fashion industry goes.

With the development of culture, civilization has a limited personal choice. And that may be somehow true about natural sexual intentions. A perfect example is a situation that occurred among European monarchies at the beginning of the twentieth century. As we know from history books, European monarchs were those who launched the world wars fighting against each other when indeed they all were close relatives. When limited in their personal choices, the highest European nobles were obliged to marry those who were equal in rank to them. That meant that their range was limited to a variety of a few European families that represented most powerful dynasties of that time. A result of that was that very soon they all had become close relatives continuing no matter to marry each other. And what happened to their genes was that an illness nested there. Hemophilia is a recessive sex-linked X-chromosome disorder. And that illness was common to royals of that time. Hemophilia means that a person has a specific problem with blood. Royals of that time indeed had the blue blood. Being obliged to act as society wanted them to act, but not in the way their libido moved them, not the way they wanted to do it, they developed an illness. For a person, it's normal to go far in the search for anything desirable. That is in our nature. That is how we are motivated to improve our lives and to widen the areal of our kind. That is actually a way the people went to space. That is why once Columbus set his foot in America, and that is why Armstrong set his foot on the surface of the moon. We always search for more and for new. And when we are limited, it is against our nature. We are searching for diversity and society would prefer to deal with the mass of similar items that are better for classification, systematization, and control. What I want to say is that repression towards individuality and sex can cause illness. And that can be not only physical illness but a social one too.

As society develops, it goes through a row of stages, and every next stage of history may show more repressive habits toward individuals. On one side, the society protects itself in general in vast extent, but at the same time, it may mean limiting person's individuality. Extension of unity in groups is growing the same way as the size of groups. It is a kind of social evolution from flock to clan, from clan to tribe, from tribe to nation. And what does it grow from the nation? It is easy to say that the people need to be united to achieve more together. And that proves that there is indeed some scale effect. It is true that a single human being won't be able to build a civilization. But it is a question of extent, a question of accurate scale. It isn't always true that the bigger, the better. If we regard it from this side, then we should admit that the Soviet Union was the best and the most efficient organization of people. Let's say - one of the best. It was a country where all people and all property was united into one strictly organized flock, into one corporation, if you want. That country was one of the most repressive societies of recent centuries. And it was one - if not the most - sexually repressive society of modern times. Everyone who differed from usual standard was under suspicion. Everyone who was unusual could be claimed to be an anti-Soviet element and by this be listed among things that should be taken out of the system in order not to bring any distortion in its synchronized processing. And that also meant the danger of elimination in this or another way.

Andrei Tarkovsky was probably the most genius filmmaker ever. Many apparatchiks responsible for the Soviet film industry considered his films to be anti-Soviet. But the truth is that in his films there is no single word of agitation against the soviet system. Tarkovsky just wasn't interested in politics. But his films were considered anti-Soviet no matter just because they didn't fit into a usual row of films about workers and villagers. It was enough to be individual in a way to make the system consider one dangerous. As we know, thanks to Freud, artistic movement into a person has sexual intention in its root. And it is not surprising that being strict toward everything unusual and toward the people of art, the soviet system was exceedingly repressive in sexual aspects. Homosexuality was prohibited by law in the country. And one of the most famous ideology taglines was - There is No Sex in the Soviet Union. Actually, it was about television of the Soviet Union, but no matter... I wonder where they took kids from. Of course, there was sex, but it was strictly repressed as a cultural element. The same way there were beautiful Russian girls. Contemporary models from Eastern Europe walking world's catwalks are descendants of those people who lived in socialistic countries of Europe. It is a matter of genes, and those genes were not imported to Eastern Europe together with Coca-Cola and American jeanswear.

In the Soviet Union, they couldn't display nudity of a woman. They could not, in general, because Tarkovsky allowed this in Andrei Rublev movie. They couldn't do it because their apparatchiks wouldn't let them. Today in Hollywood, the moviemakers can also be limited in such things too, because producers may want to get R or PG-13 to sell the movie to the family audience and to get more of the box office. Today in most cases, they will make a PG-17 rated film with the sex scenes due to specific reasons. The first case is a situation when a movie project represents a book adaptation, and it can't be even imagined without some evident sexual scenes, or it is a film which plot can't exist without such scenes. Another case is a movie where there is so much of violence supposed that it will get PG-17 mark no matter how many sex scenes it will have. These two cases are not usual for the biggest projects as they mostly represent some kind of family movie. And only in rare cases, a director will let sex and nudity appear outside these two cases. That may look to be an unusual comparison, but doesn't it make producers representing corporate giants and apparatchiks who represented a soviet regime similar, somehow? What if it does, at least partly? Soviets were a strict and centralized system, and that made them so sexually repressive.

Corporations today grow bigger and bigger. And it is no surprise that some of them become more powerful than so many governments around the world. And government nearly becomes something like another corporation with specific monopolies and specific rights serving the rest of corporations. Corporations would probably forget to deal with the government if they only could issue laws and declare wars and embargo themselves. Their size means more of efficiency for them. But what kind of efficiency is it? Is it efficiency on their side only or for all the people? There are a lot of questions indeed.

Their towers are growing higher and higher. And their influence grows too. And who knows what that means? And that is a question about how it will influence our everyday life.

Nov, 21-23
Private Audio Diary of Elise
by Elise

I spent those days in my hometown, in a place where I grew up. It wasn't mostly about meeting my family. Of course I met them, but in general, it was a nice opportunity to get away from my usual circle of life. I escaped my job place for three days, and that isn't bad. I continued to assist Martin's documentary projects. Mostly mentally. I read some few things from media and found some interesting thing about Susan's employer. But actually, I don't think it will help. And I don't think it has anything to do with Susan.

I went to meet my old friend. Maybe, a friend isn't a correct word. I would better say, my old acquaintance. It is one guy who knows me and who works for one of the papers in town. It was the only useful link in this place I could use for my professional aims. And that was the only way to justify my almost vacancy leave during the heat of documentary investigation. Subconsciously - and possibly even absolutely consciously, but trying to persuade myself it was subconsciously - I supposed that spending a couple of hours trying to get some information that theoretically might happen to be useful was what would allow me to spend the rest of time here at my leisure. It isn't that a lazing is my very favorite activity, but I just needed a little break. What I did was that I asked the paper guy to show me everything if there was anything mentioning a corporation Susan works for. Guy said that it's not their rule to show their archive to everyone who asks for it because it is mostly for internal use. I didn't know what he wanted from me. I just said that there was nothing so special about piles of old paper issues. And I didn't understand why I couldn't look for some couple of articles. He almost immediately said OK after that. And of course, I asked then whether he could let me access a digital version of the archive if they had any so that I could just type a couple of words into search to find articles I might be interested about. I didn't want to spend much time there. I promised of course, that if he wanted, he could watch me as I used their data and of course, I promised that I would not copy or do anything else about their files and papers except reading it. I said I would be in the eyes only mode.

To my surprise, they had a digital version of all their articles written in recent years. And a guy was even that nice. He allowed me to search it. But the problem was that the digital version - at least, that one I was granted access to - consisted only of names of articles with dates. That meant I no matter had to visit a storeroom where they keep piles of newspaper issues. As it appeared, activities of the Corporation that I chose as my interest for that day were more public than I could expect. There were at least three articles about them. One of the articles contained only an interview of one of their employees telling young people about advantages of working for the corporation. I considered this useless. But other two presented some interest. They had almost no additional connection between them, except the fact that those both articles featured one person as a principal figure in each story. But actually, their focus differed very much.

Articles appeared so intriguing that I probably spent a little bit more time in the archive room than I initially planned. And I even made short reviews on them and also copied their text contents with the help of my phone camera. All these operations should grant my consciousness with peace about my unplanned vacation. I knew what I promised to a paper guy, but I don't think someone will care. My promise was just a formality. It didn't matter whether I broke it or not.

First of the articles was about corporation's plans on their market future. They planned to present a new product that as they claimed will make a revolution in the industry. They didn't reveal what name it will have and told almost nothing about product's specs.

A reporter was telling how he did his best to get all possible information on this secret project and even proudly informed the newspaper readers that he got something on it what no other media source had in possession. And soon he was going to tell the world. His investigation gave some information about this new product. And I saw nothing sensational in it. I suppose he was exaggerating. And no other article by this reporter was released about the project to date. That means that he still didn't give the important facts he said he knew to the world. At least, I didn't find any other article about the Secret Project.

Another article was about scandal featuring one of the corporation's top managers. It was probably the biggest scandal their organization faced in a decade. At least among these cases that had publicity through media. It wasn't a great scandal to attract the attention of an entire nation, but there was something that might seem useful to Martin if to consider what theme he chose for his current investigation. The story indeed has some spice in it. One from the managing board of the corporation was fired after it was discovered that a person was using the call-girl services. At least, that was the version of a reporter. And of course she - and it was a woman - wasn't literally fired. A better phrase is that she saw her contract terminated. A connection between stories is the personality of this woman. She was one of the principal people responsible for the development of the Secret Project. I think that hardly will be useful for Martin's investigation, but at least, I believe he will find it interesting. I am almost absolutely positive about it. A story is indeed a bit unusual. There is a scandal. Actually, it is more correctly should be called a possibility for the scandal, because reporter himself isn't hundred percent sure about what was the reason for displacing that woman from her position. And there is a lot of speculation about ethics in the matter. The reporter wonders whether it's ethical or not to fire a person for something that is neither a crime in our country nor many other western countries. Martin should like this. Sometimes he seems to be crazy about ethics. Maybe he tries to find the perfect rules to act in any situation properly. He probably would like to have some code with some rules about how to do things with dignity everywhere and always. But I don't think it is possible to create such a code indeed. In our world – it's not. Thousands of philosophers were searching for something like this and found quite a little to become a legacy for descendants.

Soon I will go back to the city to which, as I understood being here in my hometown, now I belong more than to the place where I was born. All my miserable life happens there. And I will show

Martin what I found then.

I am not feeling sleepy, and so, I will spend some time reading and thinking, but no matter – end of a line.

Nov, 21
from Dictaphone Record
by Martin

My recent interview with Susan happened to be more unusual than previous ones. Maybe it was because Elise wasn't there and I felt myself a bit different. Usually, she doesn't make something special but looks like there is some specific reason why I employ her and why I should keep her near myself. She means something to my job.
This time it was somehow different about Susan and me. Actually, I can't say whether Susan felt it another way too or not. First of all, I started to notice how she dresses. I noticed it before, but I mean I didn't make some mental accent on it. I saw that she had jeans and green shirt with a zipper. But I noticed that her zipper was open down to some point in between her breasts only then. And I could see quite a nice piece of her flesh through a narrow triangle. I wonder whether she wore it this way before or I wasn't noticing. I just couldn't keep from thinking that she had lovely breasts. I even remember how lascivious thought flashed in my mind. It wasn't a thought about sex with her, but I wondered what her nipples were like right then. I wondered whether they were like on those photographs made on the

Caribbean seaside. Next thought was - it is good she can't read my thoughts. I am afraid I'm losing the ethics of my profession. It's not right to regard interviewee as a possible sexual object. I don't feel I do think about her exactly this way, but it looks like I almost do. At least I see her sexuality and entertain myself when regarding her this way against my weak will. At some moments I do feel I would like her zipper to be open even more down. And I feel I would like to know what kind of lingerie she prefers to wear. On those photographs where she enjoys the sun and sea waves with her entire body exposed to nature, there is no sign of any lingerie, of course. And maybe that is why I feel like I would like to know it. Is it simple briefs and laconic bra or something more delicious? Actually, it doesn't matter when a girl is almost perfect. And I can't do anything about it but admit that she is a sexy little girl.

Shame on me. On one side. And there is another one. And it is a healthy state of libido activity for a lonely man. I just need someone probably. There is one phrase from Jane Austin that comes to my mind now. Every single man in a possession of good fortune must be in want of a wife. It isn't a natural rule. Of course, it is a natural rule for most of the society, but not a rule of nature. Rule of nature may sound like - every single man in possession of

Mother Nature must be in want. We are designed to want as much as possible and never be satisfied because there is no limit which may stop Mother Nature expanding the areal of biological life. People are more specific than animals, and their wishes are more unlimited as their minds have more of imagination. And to wish you don't need to have an opportunity or ability to have what you wish for. All you need is imagination. We want the power, and money, sex, cars, and mansions. Maybe we want it all, especially power and money just to get more of sex. Sexual desire is root for all of our wishes as it always connects our complicated minds to the simple rules of nature no matter what.

Examination of Susan's Homework from Audio Record by Jess

Jess: Are you ready? Did you prepare your homework for today?
Susan: Yes, That's why I am here [giggle].
J.: You can begin. You just should remember those few recommendations I gave you. Do you?
S.: Uh-huh.
J.: And also I would like to add one little condition. That will be better if you tell a story featuring me and you, because this way that will be more practical. In here we always create stories where some of us should be present as characters. So you shouldn't be afraid to do so. Don't worry because all I would do is listening to you until you finish. And then I will make some corrections. Is it OK?
S.: It's OK.
J.: Then just begin, and you don't need to hurry. I have enough time for you.
S.: Well, it is kind of a school story. Location is a school room. There are two. They are teacher and student. And...
J.: That's a good beginning. Continue it.
S.: Well, and that is the beginning of a lesson. And you are the teacher, and I am the student. You wear

a classic teacher's costume. I would say. You have a tight skirt of medium length, and it perfectly shows the shape of your hips [laughter]. I wear schoolgirl's uniforms including a short skirt and white blouse. I wear white stockings also. And, also, then... I sit in front of you, and you are watching me seriously. Then you ask me. Did you prepare your homework? And I answer. Homework? I thought there was no homework for today. And then you say. No, Susan, there was homework. And I repeat my question. Did you prepare your homework, Susan? And after a pause, you add. There are only two possible answers, and I just need to hear one of them. If you keep being silent we will be obliged to spend the rest of the day here, and I don't know what your plans for the evening are, but I have things to do. You tell it all calmly in a low voice and without any hurry. You just state the facts. And then I say in a very unsure voice. No, ma'am. I didn't prepare a homework. And you say. Then you know what the rules are in our school. Don't you? And I say. But it isn't my fault I did not know there was homework. And you say then. Then, who did make this fault, Susan? And I say. It isn't my fault, and that's all. I won't blame anybody. And you say. I also don't want to blame anybody. I don't like to punish the schoolgirls, but sometimes there is no choice. Rules are rules. And in the school like this, we should respect them no matter what. Rules made our school one of the most efficient and high-rated institutions of a kind. People who graduate from our school are always a respected part of highest society. You are one of my favorite students. You always do well. But rules are rules, even for you. And it is... It doesn't matter why you disobey them. If you do, then you will be treated in a proper way. Even a good girl like you who usually scores the top marks has her life under the same rules as anybody else here. I do like you like a student, despite the fact I am not so sure that you will be able to graduate from our school. But of course, with my support, you will have the better chances. And no matter what my relation to you is, I just need to do it. Actually, it isn't time for a lecture, but it is time for punishment. And then I say. Yes, ma'am, I am ready for anything you give me. I become quiet, and passive, and obeying. And I stand on my knees in front of you, and my head is down. I am not looking at you but to the floor. You come closer and put your palm to my cheek. And you say. Not here, follow me. I rise. And you say. We should go to a detention room. And we go out from there and go through corridors. And then there is a staircase down. We go to the underground level of the school. It is designed in general like a dungeon. There are packs of different things for... well, for punishment, for punishing the naughty school girls [giggle]. And there, another girl appears. She wears black clothes. It isn't black leather, but instead, it is just a black uniform-like costume. And her clothes are not extremely fitting. Her hairs are black too. And she has a bob haircut. Let her name be Domino. It is Domino, because it sounds closer to domination and because it means something black-and-white. And she has black clothes and pale white skin. She is the one responsible for the detention exercises. And you say to her. It is her first punishment. Would not you mind if I treat her myself? I promise that if she gets naughty for one more time, it will be your work to do all the things in a proper way. She says. Sure, but if my help is required then just give me a sign. Or maybe it will be better if she just nods to you and doesn't say anything, but you both know what it means. Then you say. Stay here, and Domino will take care of you for a while. And then you go out of place to undress. And Domino looks at me and claps with her palm over her hip. And I understand what I should do without words. I move closer to her. And then I stand on my knees in front of her. And she roughly takes a shock of my hair into her palm. I look down at her shoes. Then you return. You are dressed differently now. You wear black clothes too. They are similar to those of Domino, but your size. You approach us, and Domino releases my hair from her tight grip. Then you and I, we go aside. And I stand on my fours then. I touch the floor with my hands and my shoes. The floor is cold, and I feel it. You bring a little pillow while I keep standing this way. You put a pillow down on the floor. And then you sit near me on your knees. Your legs rest on the pillow. You say. Are you ready? You say it almost softly, but almost without any emotion at all. And it is only a timbre of your voice that makes it sound so nice. I answer. Yes, ma'am. And at this moment there is no resistance in me at all. And then you move my little skirt up and reveal my buttocks. You tear my briefs into pieces with sure motions. And then you start to spank me. In the beginning, I show almost no emotion and then I don't hide that I like it. When you finish, Domino comes to where we are, and she bends a little. She then reaches with her finger to my pussy, and I give a loud breath out. She says. She looks excited. She is wet, ma'am. I suppose this punishment isn't enough for her. You agree with a nod. Then you move me making me roll on the floor and then I lie on my back. You start to undress me roughly. When I am completely nude, you stand up. I continue to lie on the floor. Pieces of my clothes or, at least, pieces that were my clothes before, are scattered around. You go to the chair. You sit in the chair. You start to take off a lower part of your black costume. You take off your shoes and then you slowly take off your pants in a single sure motion, sliding them smoothly over your skin. And then I see that there was no underwear underneath your pants. Your legs are nude, and your perfect rounded hips are nude too. You stand up and start to unbutton your black shirt, one button after another. You do it slowly like you have all the time in the world. You don't take off your shirt entirely, but instead, it only opens a stripe of your flesh from your neck down to your belly and down to... Then I stand up too and do an uncertain step towards you. And at this moment Domino slaps my hip roughly with her palm. And all she says at this instant is a single word. Down. I understand. And then I go down on my knees again. And then you say. There are some rules at this place, dear. You should learn the rules of our school better, or I don't know what may happen to you. And I say. Yes, ma'am. I got it. And you say. That's good, dear. In here you can't stand up until you are not ordered or permitted to. And it is better if you don't talk when you are not asked. After that, I only nod instead answer, and you keep being emotionless. And then... And then you go closer, and you touch a little pillow with your feet, and you move it to a spot in between your legs. Then you say. Come here. Domino slaps my hip again, and I crawl on my fours to you. Then you say. Stand here. And you point to a pillow. I place my knees on it, and I try to look at your face. At this moment you press my face against your pussy, and I start to leak it. I do it as long as you need to get satisfied with it. Then you order me to stand up. And I do. Then you walk me to a pole, and you put the palms of my hands behind it. And I lean with my back against it. And then you and Domino are tying my hands, and I am fixed this way. Then Domino entirely undresses, standing in front of me and watching me into the eye. And you take off your shirt, and now you are bare nude too. You come closer to Domino, and you touch her down there, between legs, I mean. And then... Well, and then it is some moment. I mean, it is such moment when I am afraid you will torture me with very special torture. I mean, you can caress each other and play with each other. And I can only watch it and feel excited to the limit, but I am not permitted to participate. And I can't get... no release. That's what I mean. You are keeping to touch her. But then you both come to me. One stands on the left side and another on my right side. And you start to kiss and to caress me simultaneously moving by my sides. And of course, I like it very much. And in the end part, you unfasten me, and we do more things if we have the strength for it after all we did. That's all [giggle]. It's an end of my fantasy.

J.: It isn't bad, indeed.

S.: Thanks.

J.: But I feel that I still need to make some

corrections. It is better to say that I will make a few recommendations. Don't you mind it?

S.: No.

J.: As I understood you had chosen the submissive-dominant type of plot for your story that can be used for a scenario then. Is it your favorite type of private sex-fantasies?

S.: Well, it is one of the things I would like. But I wouldn't say that I always fantasize about such things. I like different things.

J.: OK. But that is still what you do like. Is it, Susan?

S.: Uh-huh.

J.: Then I would note that it is an excellent idea to use something that excites you to excite others. But you always should remember that the other people may have preferences different from your own. That is why you should properly investigate other person's sexuality. And don't forget that there can be something what other people like and what can look not so sexy to you. The best if you are excited when you excite others. Do you understand what I am talking about?

S.: Uh-huh.

J.: Then, Susan, I would recommend you to try to feel what another person would like. That means that you should learn to know what is pleasing to a person before one tells you. One of the best methods is observation. You may observe how other person likes to do all things and just note it. Still, you can find something what may look not so fantastic to you but what is pleasing to another person. Another recommendation is to observe in both cases when you actively participate and when you don't. It has some complication in it. To overcome this kind of difficulty I would recommend you some simple but effective methods. For example, you can use what I call the extra-terrestrial method. That means you should imagine you are an alien creature put into a body of a woman with all of its senses and who has a mission to investigate a world of human sexuality. Do you understand, Susan?

S.: Uh-huh.

J.: You just may imagine yourself to be something like an alien inside female body who was sent to the Earth to learn people's sexual habits. Of course, you should remember that you were sent to learn the normal sexual habits, but not deviant. And at the same time, you should remember that there can be a wide variety of things within human sexuality that still means healthy human sexuality. You just learn about it to make a proper report. It is like being an actress who is a really great one. Do you understand? Do you think it is a suitable way to observe, Susan?

S.: Uh-huh. I think it should be a very good thing.

J.: And let's talk about the type of a story you have chosen. Submissive-dominant type is a widespread one as it gives a lot of advantages and represents something that doesn't look to be a regular part of human life. But there are also some nuances you should care about when doing things like this. I am not trying to give you a lesson, but I wish you to learn some stuff if you want. That means I would like to see you being more developed than you were before. And no matter how skillful a person is, there is always some room for improvement. And so, about S&M kind, I would like to say that the first and simplest rule is that you should ever care about your partner no matter whether you perform a submissive or dominant role. Mutual satisfaction through an experience of pleasure should be a primal aim of any sexual interaction. And you should also know what limits a person has when even this person is not sure about them. You may draw the boundaries together before the action begins and also you may implement a system of your secret language to communicate when something goes wrong. A good example is a use of a safeword. It is some word one may use when something goes wrong. In the process of the submissive-dominant game, submissive may be pleading to stop only to increase the pleasure. And so, you should be able to understand when it is a game and when it is true. It should be a word you don't often use in your ordinary speech. For example, I prefer to use a word basta. It is a foreign language word, and it fits well. I would use this word to stop the game when my partner comes across my limits. Also, you may use some gestures or other words that won't interfere with a process to notify your partner that you need some alterations and your partner may do the same with the use of same signs. Do you understand?

S.: Uh-huh. I do.

J.: It is crucial that you remember it isn't that real. It is a game. The pleasure of your partner in such delicate interactions should be not less than yours. You should remember that a word submissive doesn't mean a slave, despite the fact that this is how can be a submissive called during a game. No matter it's not the same. Submissive is just a role in the game, but nothing else. A slave is someone who does everything you ask about because he or she has no choice. Submissive is someone who has a choice and is a person who keeps all of her freedom and dignity with her. Submissive is someone who does choose to be this. If you play a dominant, then you should pick someone for a part of submissive who will like it. There is no way other. And now I want to continue with exact commentaries on your story. Do you want to hear it?

S.: Sh-sure.

J.: I recommend you to divide it into parts. For example, you may name it. Class, preparation, punishment, and final act. That may help you to analyze accurately. That will be good if you decide to make a scenario based on your story. Look into a folder I gave you. It will help you to understand basics and the general formula of the process. One of the most important things is that you should also understand what alterations may happen during the performance in reality. The scenario should never be a fixed item. You should have a possibility to alternate something in development or to do something this or another way at any current moment, except the element of a story that defines its development in general. Is it easy for you?

S.: Yep.

J.: And now I would like to note what was so good about your story. It is lovely that you used the element of a good girl going bad. Bad girls are attractive not because they are bad but because they go over limits, because they brake the usual rules. And people like to have something new. And sometimes to get something new you need to break the old rules. And thus it means it is very sharp to use an image of a good girl who breaks the rules. You made a right presentation. I mean the beginning of your story. Development of your story is perfect too. And the way you approached the final act is also lovely. Your usage of the submissive-dominant element is very satisfying. You used the advantages of this type correctly. And you made a lot of useful notes during the story. And so, I would give you nothing but top marks. For sure.

S.: Thanks.

J.: And one more thing. Who do you think could be Domino in your story? I mean who among girls?

S.: I don't know. I think it is not that important. They all are great. Maybe, well, that could be Barbara or Jane or someone else.

J.: I suppose you are right. They all are great. Before we finish our meeting, I just would like to tell you that you should not treat me like your teacher. I am not a teacher. I am only a simple woman who knows something well and who shares her experience. And we are equals here. I believe that it is you who is a teacher for yourself and the whole world around you is your school. No one can teach you better than yourself, dear.

Nov, 26

Private Audio Diary of Elise

by Elise

I am back in town, and it looks like town didn't change at all. There are same streets and buildings and same people hurrying to their jobs when morning comes. I prepared my papers on the corporation for which our little Susan works laboriously placing some documents from one spot in the office to another. To my surprise, Martin liked them more than I could expect. He said that this most probably wouldn't be useful, but at least this was very interesting for a general view of corporate culture. And that was all I could hope for. My vacation was justified.

Martin today was moody to make the philosophic notions. He happens to be in such state time after time. That is one of his most usual habits. He made a speech devoted mostly to an influence of media and entertainment giants on our world. I would not say I understood all of it. Actually, I wouldn't say I was listening carefully. But what I got from it was that Martin believes that the corporations today are something instead of Catholic Church with its inquisition. He stated that the corporate machinery, which we now meet both as employees and customers, is suppressing individuality and that leads to degradation of personal quality in the society. And that's also true about our culture and celebrities. He was saying that our stars are not that cool as they were before. Martin sometimes sounds like a person who would feel himself better in the sixties than in reality of our days. He would enjoy the time when there were still living Beatles and Pink Floyd, Fellini and Antonioni. And there were Steve McQueen and cars like Ferraris of 250 series. Steve McQueen was what a final paragraph of his speech was devoted to.

I suppose I wouldn't agree with everything he was saying, but at least there is possibly some point in it. In the sixties, it was Steve McQueen who was the King of the Cool. And who we have today on the top instead? Justin Bieber. That is what we have. It is too early to think about making any bucket list of my life, but I wouldn't like to be considered a part of the generation who worshiped Justin Bieber. Imagine that this kid earned in a year more dough than Steve McQueen ever did in a similar period. I am sure Steve McQueen never had that money in one year. And the comparison is a bizarre one. I wouldn't say that I would prefer to live in the sixties, and it isn't because the internet didn't exist then. But maybe in general, I just don't want. But at least I prefer Steve McQueen among these two. Do stars become

smaller? Do they become, well... more ordinary? Martin could make a speech about it, but not me.
At the end of a day, we decided what we would do then. We shared the tasks. Martin asked me whether I would like to talk to Susan for one more time or would I prefer to work with information instead of it and I chose latter. Information, not Susan.
Going to bed and end of a line.

Nov, 26
from Dictaphone Record
by Martin

Nothing extraordinary happened this day. And I wouldn't say I found some new information able to shed light on the investigated matter. The only new thing I got is that story that Elise told me. A story is about one top-manager of some corporation involved in what possibly can turn to be a sex scandal. A story is exciting, and again there is sex. I am still feeling myself moving like a ship through the smog of sexual fantasies of others, not knowing what land I will find after crossing this Sea of Carnality. I am also afraid that I can meet storm in my way. And I still don't know what ship I have. Is it a large brigantine or just a simple vessel boat? We will see. After smog goes away. I hope this kind of smog won't completely poison my mind. Indeed I feel I was already influenced by sexual sensations brought to me by this story and by Susan. No one can stand such thing, I suppose. That should be quite a normal state of a normal man in such situation. But there is still a question of ethics.

I remember when we met with Susan recently, she was talking that it probably would be better if we met at her place. I understand that it is more comfortable for her and all of this. But no matter as a journalist I cannot meet her one to one to talk about sex at her apartment. Oh, can I?.. It is a bit more private. And more than that, I am almost sure I would like to do so not as a journalist but as a man. And I am almost sure I would like to see her in bathrobe or no matter with fewer clothes on and being closer to her private bedroom. Yes, I would like it. And that is a problem. The thing is that when she just mentioned about such an opportunity, I didn't tell her that we should better keep things going as we did it before. Of course, she is an interviewee, and I am the interviewer, and that means I should make her feel as comfortable as possible and make some changes for that if she likes. She has a right to ask for some little perks. But, no matter, being in the studio is what still keeps an invisible obstacle against deeper privacy. And instead of firmly refusing her, I said that I didn't know and that I would call and tell her!

And today when I was deciding whether Elise should come to assist me in a next interview I wasn't sure, and I told Elise she might not come if she didn't want to. Maybe subconsciously in both cases, I was leaving an opportunity to myself to meet Susan in the more intimate surrounding. And Elise chose to work on something else. That means I will meet Susan, who attracts me more and more as a certain sexual object, tet-a-tet for one more time. Do I go against own ethics? Actually, the entire story is filled with sex to an extent when you can't avoid it. Of course, if you are not a robot. At least, I have a pretty nice excuse. The situation is not a usual one. I also would note to encourage myself that someone other would do definitely more to Susan than I did. And now it is all more complicated as I know something about Susan's private sexual fantasies from a record of her talk with Jess. The existence of such record makes them not that private, but still, this record wasn't made to be public. I never wanted to be any teacher, but I feel for sure that I would like to have one of parts in some story by Susan.

Maybe the real problem is that it seems to me that Susan somehow - knowingly or only subconsciously - wants to do things with me. And right now I am not sure that it only seems to me so. The way she talks and sometimes the way she looks at me that is what made me think so. Maybe she just entertains herself with a little of dirty talk. Or is it something more? And probably all of this is somehow true. I hope I wouldn't get trouble with some sex-harassment issue. But what can I do? I can't stop. The only thing I can do is to continue in the same direction.

Description of Video Three
from Dictaphone Record
by Martin

On this record, I will explain contents of another video to be sure that I will have some kind of verbal copy of it, in case the original that was provided to me on pretty specific terms won't be available. I would note that this video similarly to previous one is also made of two parts. There is also one crucial difference I would like to note. The video bears doubtless signs of editing. There are cuts in its current. I would also note that there are other files. And they don't bear any signs of editing and represent what looks to be the original videos that were edited to compose a single file. Footage that I would call original represents video made from a single camera and is not interrupted by any editing cuts. And a final file I would call a composition. Now to what we have. First part has an event that happens at the shooting site. It seems a little strange as you realize that it is a film about how someone else films. There is a couple of professional digital cameras in view together with some furniture like sofa and armchair. There is also some other equipment including lights. In the beginning, a tall dark-haired woman appears on the stage. I suppose I know who she is. My guess is that this is Jess. The Mistress. She enters a frame together with a couple of men. One sits in a chair in front of shooting site, and another stands behind one of the cameras. Jess wears... Well, at least, I would say that she is fully clothed. I mean she has clothes enough to go outside and not to be regarded as someone crazy. She has some shirt and some trousers. It seems like she poses in front of a camera. Man in a chair tells her something time after time and makes passionate gestures. After some time, Jess goes out of view and returns now wearing fewer pieces of clothing. And together with her, there is one new person. It is a girl who isn't that tall like Jess. And it seems like she corrects her makeup. I would suggest that all this represents shooting some scene of some film or something else. I am not sure because Jess is only one in front of a camera and it looks like her role has no words or there are not a lot of words to tell. And thus she is an actress. A little girl is a kind of makeup artist. A man in the chair is the director and... another one is his cameraman and assistant. Looks like this.

Then even more figures appear on the scene. They are two girls. And it seems that they occupy a position of passive watchers. They keep talking. At least, it is one of them. She keeps cocking her head telling something to her friend. And it takes some time for me to suggest that it is most probably Jane. I can't see her friend's face as she keeps herself with a back of her neck toward the camera. Sometimes there is a feeling that she will turn her head right now and I will be able to see her face at least vaguely. Quality of tape would permit to see it only vaguely from this distance. All I know is that her hair is dark and she has a tail. They watch Jess and her doings as lady keeps changing dresses and posing on the sofa. And things go this way until a certain point when activity on the shooting site decreases and it looks like that they have a break. A man, who I suppose performs director, seems to smoke. That seems a little grotesque to me. After he begins to fume, Jess approaches him and tells him something, and he throws a cigarette into a litter box. Then Jane and her friend stand up slowly and approach Jess. They have some short talk, and then Jess moves away from them. She seems to have no emotion. Jane seems to be unsatisfied somehow. Maybe that is what her indecisive pose tells me. She seems to get frozen in a strange pose for a while. And at this moment Jess goes away, and Jane keeps watching her back until she probably disappears from view. Jane's friend stands motionless near her. And that is all that can be considered remarkable from the first part of a video. Two girls, I mean Jane and her companion, do nothing special, but talk a little and then go away from the view of a camera.

Next part happens at what seems to be some luxury hotel room. Or it can be some room in a mansion. There are two girls from previous part. I mean Jane and her friend. And still, a face of latter one is unseen. They sit and talk. They don't seem to be too active or something. They moderately express their emotions. They spend some time doing nothing special. In addition to their conversation, they drink a little and enjoy strawberries. I am not sure there are strawberries exactly, but I think it is most probably them. There is a bowl on the table full of these strawberries in a reach of hand. After that, they watch TV. Jane goes to a TV panel and switches it on. They change their positions sitting in front of it. They talk with some animation. I don't know whether it is connected to what they saw on a screen or not. They don't devote a lot of time to this kind of activity. They go to another room. Another room is similarly decorated, but I can see a difference in furniture there. That is why I see it is another room. They talk sitting on a large sofa. Jane stands up and goes away for a while. Her companion sits on the sofa alone, and I still can't see her face, but only her tail and her neck. Jane returns carrying a bowl of strawberries with her.

They talk and eat strawberries again. And then there is a new event that can be called a turning point. The third person appears. It is a tall and dark-haired woman. It is Jess. She talks to them, and it seems like she smiles. She shows some signs of friendly behavior. She makes a handshake with Jane's companion. I think it will be right if I call her Miss Incognito from now on. That is to make things easier. Jess makes some emotional gesture with her hand and smiles as it seems. She even bends her body a little like some schoolgirl who can't keep from laughing. Right now I think about where I could see such motion before. Oh yes, of course. I know where I saw it. After this, Jess goes away to some other room. I suggest she went to redress or something because she probably had just arrived.

Ten minutes later she returns to a room where Jane, Miss Incognito, and strawberries are having fun together. Now she has a big white bath towel wrapped around her body. She probably has nothing else on as her feet seem to be bare. She approaches girls on the sofa, and it looks like she is ready to take a seat near Jane, but then changes her mind. She stays close to them. Jane tells her something. She tells her a couple of words too. And then Jess goes down on her knees in front of Jane. They keep exchanging phrases. Miss Incognito seems to be uninvolved in their interaction. Jane slightly slaps a cheek of Jess and tells her something at the same time removing her towel from her shoulders in few slow and sure motions. Instinctively, Jess puts her hands across her breasts. After a couple of seconds, Jess stands up now being bare nude and goes away again. I would say that now I really don't understand what the hell is going on. That is a pretty strange game they play, I suppose. What is it all about?

In few minutes Jess returns. She didn't wear anything. She is still completely nude. She has something in her right hand. It is some small circle and something that seems to be a stick. She comes closer to the girls on the sofa and then goes down on her knees in front of them. She bends her head down and holds out her hands offering the stick and a little circle. It seems like Jane keeps talking with Miss Incognito almost like not noticing what's going on. Then, a few seconds later, Jane moves. She stands up and approaches Jess. Jane takes what Jess holds from her hands. This circle, it is actually a collar as I got it. And a stick is not a stick, but it's something like a whip. It looks like something that is used to whip the horses. Jane tells something to Jess and touches her cheek with tips of her fingers as it seems. Jess stands on her fours. Jane says something to Miss Incognito, and she rises from the sofa and comes closer to a spot where Jane stands over nude Jess who still stands on her fours without a single motion or any intention to move. Now Miss Incognito stands in a single step from Jess. While

Jane stands with her knee close to Jess's face. She can touch girl's cheek with her knee making a little movement of her leg. Jane moves her palm over a body of Jess. She moves it over her back. And then she touches her breasts. And then she moves it over her belly and down to a spot in between legs... Doing this, Jane bends and then goes down on her knees for a more comfortable position. She spends no more than a minute for such caresses. Then she tells Jess something, and Jess answers with some short phrase. Jane then softly touches buttocks of her submissive. She caresses them and then even kisses them. She says something and then she begins to use a whip. She only touches every side of Jess's bum once. She does it very softly like being afraid to hurt her. Then she puts a whip into the mouth of Jess. And then she spanks her with the palm of her hand. She stands up and says something to Miss Incognito. And after this, Miss Incognito takes her place sitting near Jess. And while she does so, there is a moment when it seems I will be able to see her face. But it doesn't happen. She almost turns her face to a profile view. Then she starts spanking Jess in a similar fashion as Jane did it. She slowly begins like being not sure and then intensifies the motions of hand from up to down. Jess starts to respond with what seems to be motions of pleasure like she was doing to Jane's touches, but more vigorously. After finishing spanking, Incognito removes the whip from the mouth of Jess and places her hand close to her lips. Jess seems to caress Incognito's fingers with her mouth. She kisses and leaks them.

Then Jane makes Jess stand on her knees instead of standing on fours. Jane goes to a drawer. She opens it and produces something like a rope from it. She fixes hands of Jess behind back with it. She kisses her. And both active girls – Jane and Incognito start to caress Jess who pretends to be their victim. And then they unfasten her and start to undress. As they keep undressing and caressing Jess, video interrupts. And in the videos I would call the original files, I also didn't find the continuation of this sexy story. Actually, I suppose I know what was then. I am quite excited, but I am not that crazy about watching these videos. Anyone would be a bit aroused if being forced to watch this, but there is another thing. I believe that then it was something the same what happened before in previous videos. That should be what the Agency girls would call the final act. But I would like to know why someone would hide something from me when this someone was going to reveal everything to a broad audience. Was it on purpose or accidental? It is for the first time that I have some particular questions after watching the video file like this. Especially, I am concerned about Miss Incognito. Why protect her?

Maybe it is accidental, but her face wasn't revealed even vaguely. Maybe it is a normal delicacy. Someone just doesn't want to involve a person who has nothing to do with this. It is very fair in case. Another thing is a question about the edition of this video. Why was it this way when others were the plain single camera non-interrupting records? Is it accidental or not? Should be there some clue about it? Maybe there is nothing like this, and I just grow paranoid inside my brains. I have the originals it is made of, and that proves... Or it doesn't. I still feel I know too little to understand what it all really means. Also, I don't know why I can't hear what they talk about. If you can implement the surveillance cameras anywhere why can't you do the same about little secret microphones? Is not it natural to give a picture in one single file in full view? Of course, I have the enormity of different documents. And it isn't a big problem that I should work a little to put all them like a puzzle into something one, but still, there can be something that is hidden from me. On purpose? I just smell that someone plays with me. What I smell actually is a scent of danger. I can't stay out of it. It is everywhere I go to, mixed with the scent of sexual desire.

Nov, 28
Susan's Interview Six
from Dictaphone Record
by Martin

Martin: About your first homework, did you do it, finally?
Susan: Yes, of course.
M.: You saw what was in the folder?
S.: Yes. For me, it was pretty exciting and educating. Indeed.
M.: Did you find something unusual?
S.: I think you may say so.
M.: You said it was educating. What was that you learned from it?
S.: I suppose... general things. It was some interesting stuff.
M.: Can you describe it somehow in more detail? What was the thing that was new to you and that was of the biggest interest for you in it?
S.: It was the sharp reversing element.
M.: What do you mean, sharp reversing?
S.: In this folder, I found a particular demonstration of what is called a sharp reversing element. That is when things dramatically change to increase the excitement. That is a psycho stuff.
M.: Psycho? You mean it is connected with

madness?

S.: Ah... Well, it is crazy, of course [giggle]. But I actually mean it is about psychology. It is a psychology thing.

M.: And what does make it so different? This psychology element, why does it have to be so different from other things involved?

S.: That means... that it isn't only a situation that physically shifts, you know, but it is also an influence on human sexuality through person's feelings. And it is a very sharp thing when you put them to one side, and then you move them to another, opposite one. That creates the greatest sexual transformation. Yep, it's a transformation. And it is like pulling the string. Or it is like using a slingshot or sort of catapult. The more you pull, the more energy is produced when you release it. And that means it moves from one psychological point that is not desirable but is very emotional to another, a very desirable one. It isn't just changing those things. It is changing the personal attitude to them. It's playing about feelings. I suppose that it is pretty dangerous and that is why it made me so excited to see how it can be done properly. It is a great idea indeed, but in fact, I suppose it is complicated to perform such things without necessary experience.

M.: I am not sure I do understand everything you talk about. It isn't that you explain incomprehensibly. I just need more facts about it to get the picture. Did I get it right - you talk about something when you put a person down, and then you give this person something desirable, some pleasure?

S.: Yep, I am about that.

M.: Can you tell me more about that?

S.: More?

M.: Yes. What exactly can it be used to put a person down to elevate him then? Do I ask a right question?

S.: Question is right. It's not easy to explain.

M.: I understand. But I would like it if you tried to, Sue.

S.: Well [giggle], OK. It is most probably something aggressive. Aggression, you know, works well.

M.: You mean you need to do something causing a pain. You say you need to hurt a person. Is it not against the rules then?

S.: No... Well, Yes, but... It's not about pain, but you may say it is to hurt. You should hurt somehow, but you should mentally injure, you know. And it is pretty risky if a person isn't well-known to you. I mean, you should be sure. And then this aggression that burns into the heart of a person. It should be soft, but it should be enough to make a person feel emotional. And then you may use it to transform it into sexual impulse. I think you can't transform it into something sexual, but when it is soft, but

already burning, I would say, you can use it to reinforce the sexual sensations with it.
M.: I want to fix it. You may provoke some negative, or better say aggressive, emotion in a person to use it for increasing the power of his sexual feelings. Is it this way?
S.: Yep. You understood now [giggle].
M.: Is it some method?
S.: Yes. That is what employs a sharp reversing. Or you may call it a U-turn, or shift method.
M.: Don't you think it is strange to use any aggression or even just a possibility for it in sex? I mean sex is something about pleasure, and aggression is something different. It is more often about stress and conflict. And sex means satisfaction and mutual consent.
S.: Well, sex and aggression do have many things connected.
M.: You mean it is a psycho thing?
S.: Um?
M.: I mean it is in human psychology to connect these two things.
S.: Yes it is. And you know, in this case, it is more about the possibility of aggression than about real one. That means that finally, it is not an aggression, but it keeps its impulse. A pretty way to understand it is to talk about energy plant.
M.: The energy plant. I am intrigued. We're going to

talk about the energy system of our country. That is a novel thing for us indeed.

S.: Oh well [giggle]. You know you are really funny.

M.: And you are lovely companion tonight. With you, it is better than alone. For sure.

S.: O-oh thanks. That is so nice of you. And you're a really cool companion for a night too. Would you bring some coffee?

M.: Sure, and you keep telling me about the energy plants.

S.: Oh, yes. Energy plant. That means... Well, you can imagine there is energy plant, and there is the thing that works using the energy it gives. It can be something like your computer, for instance, or TV, or any powerful machine. And the more energy a plant gives, the higher performance a machine gives. And this way... are you listening?

M.: Yes, of course. It is pretty smart. Keep going.

S.: Yes, it's exciting. It's interesting. Well, and you need to generate as much of power as possible. But what if there are some specifics about your plant? What if it can only give a lot of potential only when working not for your machine, but for something else? It can be such plant that works well when you launch your computer or iron, or TV. I mean it starts well with something, but not with the machine you need to work vigorously. But you need to know how to make your machine work vigorously, and you need this plant for it, but it is designed for a different purpose. Then you start your computer, and it starts the power plant. And then suddenly when power plant generates enough of energy you plug your computer out and connect your machine to it. And this way you use the heat generated for another purpose for something you want.

M.: Do you mean aggression works like something like a plant to generate the energy, and then you redirect it in the direction of sexual desire?

S.: That is it. Correctly.

M.: That's an interesting point of view.

S.: What are you thinking about?

M.: It is an interesting connection to natural basics of human psychology. A human being is naturally a hunter and gatherer. He is designed to fight and to explore. And mostly there are two basic things of nature we do to other people. They are searching for a sexual partner and competing. That means we challenge other people and try to attract them simultaneously. And when you hurt someone, you make him defy you. And that can be effective if you can put this two into one. Somehow.

S.: Oh, I suppose that is what it should be. I think you understand it too. It's about human nature.

M.: Now I see it was very evident. But I just needed some comments. Do you think that is why dominance and submission are that popular? I mean that there can be some natural links to the psychology of humans.

S.: I think... I think you are right. But there are some more reasons for it too.

M.: And what are they?

S.: Well, it's about surrender too.

M.: What does it mean, surrender, in this case?

S.: Surrender. It means that during sexual intercourse you should somehow surrender to another person. You have to open yourself to a person who pleases you, just to receive more of it. That is very important for having a really satisfying experience. It is pretty important for having a sexual gratification and for having an efficient orgasm.

M.: But when you have an orgasm, is it not enough? When you have an orgasm, does it not mean that you achieved your primal aim in sexual intercourse? And then, does it not mean that it was efficient?

S.: Yes, but... No. Orgasm can be different. It can be more or less efficient. It can be longer. And to have it you should surrender your sensitivity to another person. And for many people, it is a complicated thing. They just can't avoid using their defensive mechanisms, or it's something like this. And when you are submissive, you are playing your part. And according to rules of this game, you can't defend yourself from anything coming from your dominant. And actually, a good dominant is someone who pretends to be so careless about you. It is a sort of game. True is that when you are submissive, your dominant can do things to you and you receive it more efficiently as your entire defense is that down. And that means you get more of it.

M.: You mean that is what helps to break the limits between sensuality of partners?

S.: Yep, It's kinda that. And there is also the fact that the dominant may represent some parent figure to submissive. Dominant takes the entire control, but the whole responsibility too.

M.: Partner figure?

S.: Parent figure, actually.

M.: A parent figure? Yeah. I see. Do you mean it is something like Oedipus complex or Electra complex?

S.: What?

M.: I mean it is a psychological theory about how human sexual preferences are influenced by relations with parents.

S.: That should be that. Yes, I think it is. I believe that our sexuality, you know, starts to form before puberty. That is what the psychologists proved. And then it is influenced by what experience we have. And it is also influenced by a biological program according to which every one of us should be both a child and parent. And that also forms our sexuality in some way.

M.: You mean... roles of the son and father, and roles

of daughter and mother that are programmed inside human being by nature are influencing sexuality?

S.: That's what I really mean. I mean that you should partially perform these roles to get more of it because it is such a game of nature. Because, you know, sex was designed to make kids indeed. But we usually use it differently. We can make love for pleasure. And so, to have this pleasure, we should move by this way at the end of which we could have kids. But if we don't want kids, but we really want a great pleasure, then we should go through a big part of this way. The same thing is about being a mother and daughter.

M.: That is what corresponds to your metaphor about the power plant?

S.: Metaphor?

M.: I mean your idea about the energy and the power plant. That is where it applies again.

S.: Oh, yes. Sure, I think it can be.

M.: Do you mean that a dominant woman is someone who takes a role of mother somehow during games like these?

S.: Yes. She takes all the control. And submissive is only doing what she says to do. And this is how this person has no responsibility and no need to decide about anything...

M.: That is what we can do only during early childhood when entire responsibility rests on

parents. And you are free, but you can't understand it. And when you are older, you can understand what it is like to be free, but you can't be it anymore because you can understand. I mean you are too conscious to let yourself be it. And society won't let you be that free when you are conscious enough. I know a lot of people who claim that they would like to be kids again because it was a time when they had no responsibilities they have now. That's... You are telling some novel things today, Susan.
S.: Oh, I am in a great shape today [soft laughter].
M.: And so, there are those two connected factors – ability to surrender and some sort of the parents-kids complex.
S.: Yes. I suppose it is. I just think all those things work well and that is why people use them so often. You know, Jane once told me that she had known a woman who was on top. I mean, she was a top business person, big boss. And thus she had the heavy responsibilities and many difficult problems to solve on her job. And, you know, she liked to play such games. And she also liked to be submissive, because that helped her to relax. And she even understood it herself that it worked this way about her. She knew what she liked and why she liked it. You know, when you have all those responsibilities with thousand people under you... under your command and a little time for private life, it is more

difficult to get really relaxed. And she used such things to achieve it sometimes. She just got submissive, and by this, she took it all off like she took off her clothes. She just floated through it. She floated through her sexual sensation, I would say. Sometimes she liked to close her eyes and to have something cylindrical put into her mouth by her partner. And she imagined that she played some sort of bitch or a bad girl or someone who was taken under control, maybe even against will. She imagined that it was some low-placed employee like a guy from the very bottom of the office hierarchy or a guy from a parking lot who did it to her. And she also liked to imagine it happened at some place at night where accidentally one could see her doing this, being totally abused by her desire. It could be a place like a parking lot or corridor in an office building where she worked late at night. Another her trick was that she would ask her girlfriend to play some sort of soft dominant. I don't know maybe she also did such things with a boyfriend if she had one. Someone whom she really trusted, because Jane thought she was bi. You know, then she would tell that she was a bad girl and she made a fault. And then she would just tell her real problem from her job. And she would ask to punish her because that is the only thing that would make her consciousness relaxed. She would say she really needed it. And that you do need to do it to her.

M.: You mean she used it to relax about her real professional problems? She used it to overcome stress?

S.: Uh-huh. She did. She was a pretty smart woman. And she was a real boss with lots of personnel under control. She had so much of control at work. So, then she would like to be controlled somehow to get relaxed, you know. I think it is not a bad idea. That is what so good about being submissive. And of course, it is a bliss to be dominant when you give someone pleasure and relaxation. It is better than being able to give a massage [giggle]. It is always good to please and to make someone relaxed.

M.: That is what we need. All of us.

S.: Sure.

M.: You tell the things today, Susan.

S.: Thanks. But please don't call me Susan. Call me Sue. Just call me this.

M.: But Susan is the name on your ID. Why not?

S.: I don't know, but Susan isn't me. I am Sue. And Susan is someone other. It is someone with... It is someone who is more... serious maybe. Someone not like me.

M.: You just like how it sounds?

S.: Yes.

M.: Then, just Sue. I will call you Sue, but not something else.

S.: Deal [laughter].

M.: I would like to ask a couple of questions of a delicate kind if you don't mind.

S.: Sure. You're welcome

M.: Is it true that you can be considered a person with some... sufficient experience in sex?

S.: Yeah, I think I can be called this. I wouldn't say I know more than others, but my experience is sufficient. I guess.

M.: I mean that you may have a little more of such knowledge than an average person.

S.: I think it is so.

M.: I read once that there is some quality of complimentary dualism in people's preferences. That is what usually is called a road with two-way traffic. I mean, there is a suggestion that if a person likes to dominate, this person will also like to be submissive. Do you think it is right?

S.: I suppose it is. Many people are so. If they like one side, they like the other one too. But many prefer submission or dominance only.

M.: So, it should be right.

S.: I suppose, yes.

M.: And don't you think it is difficult for some people to be submissive? For some people, it is probably impossible to take part in such games.

S.: Maybe. It is a personal choice. But there is nothing complicated about having fun.

M.: I think sometimes it is the most difficult. In

some consequences, it can be difficult to relax and to have fun.

S.: Do you think so?

M.: Yes, in consequences. How do you think - what makes people want to be submissive? Is it just being kinky?

S.: I don't know, but maybe it is just about enjoying the new things. And there is nothing wrong with being a little kinky. Just someone can be submissive and someone can't.

M.: You mean it requires something like a skill?

S.: Maybe, if you call enjoying sex and pleasing others a skill. It's like a strip-tease.

M.: Strip-tease?

S.: Uh-huh. Someone is a great strip dancer, and someone is not. But it doesn't mean a person is not a good lover. And all this submission. And surrender. It's quite personal. You can undress immediately, or you can do it slowly. Also, you can do it in some delicate or intriguing way. It's like a strip dance. It's kind of game. But you don't just pretend because you use your sexuality. And sexuality never pretends. It is the most real thing. You may just take your defense down immediately, or you may surrender little by little like some strip dancer who teases person and intrigues by taking off one piece after another. That is why it is so good to play a good girl who goes bad.

M.: What do you mean?

S.: I mean, in the beginning, it is a good girl who has her defense active. But inside she wants to be pleased, and she wants to surrender. And when you surrender in this way you do it slowly. You don't show it immediately that you like it, but you do it after some time. There is a... transgression of a kind. Yes, that is what it is called – transgression. That is like a strip dance of a psychological kind.

M.: There is something sexual in dances. It is most primitive, but also most natural and probably historically the first way to manifest personal sexuality indirectly. I mean it goes well with culture.

S.: When you see a person dancing well it makes this person look sexier. Everyone knows.

M.: I would like to ask you a question that may look strange to you, but please don't think it is strange. Just answer it.

S.: OK.

M.: Don't you think... Don't you feel that there can be something strange about all these things?

S.: You mean the submission and dominance?

M.: No. I mean the whole thing. I mean the Agency. Don't you think there can be something strange about them?

S.: Well, no. I think it is better to call it unusual.

M.: And then, what do you think is a difference between strange and unusual?

S.: I think... I suppose strange can be something you

can't comprehend and maybe something wrong about some person or thing. And unusual is about learning something new, but it isn't bad.

M.: Got it. Well, do you need to go home?

S.: Well I have nothing urgent, but it's time.

M.: OK. I would like to see you next time.

S.: Can you see me home, please? That would be very nice of you.

M.: Sure if you need it.

S.: Please.

M.: And Susan... Sue. One more thing.

S.: Um?

M.: Do you think there were strawberries?

S.: Strawberries? What strawberries?

M.: Forget.

S.: Oh, yes. It was strawberries. Sure.

M.: Ah... you like them? I mean strawberries?

S.: Yes, I adore strawberries. Recently, I always have some strawberries at my place. And do you like such things?

M.: Almost everyone likes sweet strawberries. That is a great thing.

S.: Sure. Everyone likes. You know I eat them often. I mean at some moments in my life. They make me feel better when I eat them. You know, I don't bite hard. I think you should feel it. That is why. I just suck and then touch a berry with my tongue to taste it better and then I just swallow it.

Some Notes on Celebrity Sexuality from Dictaphone Record by Martin

There is something specific about additional sexual attractiveness possessed by a person who bears the status of celebrity. The thing is that natural sexuality comes from biological process and celebrity is an invention of society. And thus sexuality is a manifestation of Id through convenient ways. And celebrity belongs to Superego if I would use the terminology of Freud. Celebrity has all the conventionality of human society. It is not a real person, but something like an image of a person. And this way it may represent some artificial Superego. Individuality is what plays a vital role in sexuality. One who has no individuality can't be sexually attractive as a process requires the possibility of unique biological materials exchange. But celebrity is something that becomes more and more connected not to the human ability to express a unique individuality, but to the commercial ability to sell standardized goods. Many years ago one could hardly imagine Elizabeth Taylor featured in a commercial of Coca-Cola. Cleopatra couldn't just sell some beverages. Today no person can't be imagined to be a promoter of Pepsi drinks, Gap clothes or Sony gadgets together with so many other things on a list. And even more, those who sell goods today are considered to be bigger stars than those who don't, in most cases. There are only a few stars who completely avoid the path of becoming a professional promoter of internationally-sold goods. Forbes lists evidently gave their praise to those who grossed bigger endorsements from their interactions with multinationals.

Again remembering about the Tower of Babel, I would note that it may mean some sort of sexual repression from society. To sell goods, the companies may tend to create the star characters that would be as primitive in their core as McDonald's menu. That is to be able to fit into any part of the world, into any type of people. Famous fast-food seller tries to replace complexes of unique national cuisines. Similarly, the corporations may like us all to be as similar as possible. They would like us to have similar preferences. And that is against sexuality as it bases on person's individuality. We are taught to love something that the lots of other people love. And Olympus of Stardom is not a place where a wide variety of divine creatures can live. This place is too narrow indeed. And as people are different, they should search for different opposites. But corporations may like to implement some standard kind of sexuality or beauty into our lives just to sell more goods to wider audiences with the help of it. That is what can be regarded as sexual repressiveness of society. It tries to create artificial superego suppressing person's Id. And thus, it suppresses person's natural sexuality.

Of course, there are some things about the general attractiveness of stardom that gives it a reason for being. Maybe it is just a question of the extent. A matter of the possibility for variety. We have a desire for money and higher social status, and the chance of getting it makes us work harder. That is the basics of the capitalist system. The problem is that some talented people may be put outside the industry just because they don't fit in. I believe that the talent is sexy. But stardom is not always about talent. It is more about fame and position. It is also for sure that when someone other's higher status outlines in front of us, it may give us different feelings from adoration to a hatred that make us try to challenge and to win the race to stardom.

The sexuality of big stars may indeed seem to be very unnatural as it is the thing unreachable for us. No one can live and sleep with the star. It is almost the same thing as trying to sleep with Minnie Mouse or something. You always live with a real person. A human with a body, but not a media image made of abstractions. Yes, it is logical to have some comfort as it provides a better starting point for sex. Star is one who has money and comfort in life. But actually, you don't need to be a big star for that. You need to be prosperous and maybe to belong to an affluent society. Maybe to be a local star. Someone can be very sexy just this way. It can be a most beautiful girl from fitness center or prettiest lady from your job. But then why big stars?

In a society that is so fixed on money and fame, shouldn't most of the people feel some envy? Maybe sex is regarded as the best way to replace the envious feeling with some another carnal sensation. What is the first association after the words star and sex? I am sure that it would be a scandal. People would like to make love with someone sexy, no matter whether it is a star or not. But for a good scandal, they need a star. A considerable portion of our entertainment industry stands on a set of celebrity scandals.

That is the hottest topic now. Celebrity sex scandals. Didn't you think that the people like to know about it not because they feel shame for society, but because they like that such things happen to stars too? Sounds crazy? Maybe not. For a person of contemporary to make love to a star would mean to be equal to the star in some way. It is not true that the people want stars. The truth is that they want to be stars. Sex is associated with possession. So it may mean to diminish someone's divine status to a status of a regular sexy woman or becoming something like a star.

Game Scenario
Provided to Susan
Paper Document
from Archive of Martin

Title: Star Track to Submission.
Supposed parts: Star, Starlighter, Friend.
Object's role: Voyeur, Assistant, Active Participant.
Elements: Celebrity Fantasy, Dominance and Submission, impulsive redirection and guilt-into-desire transgression.
Part specifics: Star is someone easily showing her neglect of others and pride about herself. She is a person of a prominent status, and that kind of behavior seems regular as a part of the popular archetypal image of the celebrity. Starlighter is someone who has a sure acquaintance with Star and possesses some different features of character. That is a well-humored, open and communicative person ready for friendly assistance. There is no gender preference recommended for part of Starlighter. Possible performers are a heterosexual man, a lesbian or bisexual person. The central line of Star's part is transgression from an image of dominance in the world of fame to submission in reality. The central line of Starlighter's part is opening new sexual horizons. The Friend has the central line to be

repurposing a possible sharp hatred into soft sexual desire in reality.
Notes from Object's preferences analysis: Despite the fact that there is no proof that the Object is deeply interested in celebrity sex, it can be stated that the Object has interest in stars' lives not less than usual. And also that the Object is evidently interested in exploring new horizons in sexual life. That also should be noted that the Object is more interested in an ambiance of the sexual act than in the irregular performance. That means the Object is interested in new interesting sexual partners and their stories. Analysis proves that the Object is equally interested in sex with both men and women. Its status is bisexual. Object's preferences were available for proper investigation, and that gave a basis enough to define them. Object's basic preferences include regular interaction and oral sex. Object's basic preferences do not include anal sex and double penetration. Object's playground preferences are varied. Playground preferences include finding new items to add to a list of games.

Setting
Required: Shooting equipment, star commercial video, additional actors' assistance.
Stage sites: Shooting site, home location.

Story and remarks

Part one: Starlighter meets the Friend (Object) and tells that she would like to meet one of her acquaintances. They both go to a shooting site where the shooting of commercial promo happens and where they meet Star who happens to be that acquaintance mentioned above. It is crucial that at this stage of story Starlighter should create positive ambiance for Friend. And thus latter one should feel relaxed and confident. Nothing should give to Friend an idea that the Star wouldn't like to make acquaintance with her. Starlighter and Friend spend some time watching Star at work. That should create an image of the celebrity status of Star. To improve this with additional features Star may choose to show the signs of neglect or any signs evidently indicating her higher social status toward assisting actors who perform cameraman and director responsible for shooting the promo. When Friend perceives celebrity image of Star sufficiently, next stage opens. At this instant, the Friend should be ready for friendly or at least for the better-than-neutral behavior of Star. The Object should expect to have a beneficial status of friend's friend. But at the same moment, the Friend (Object) should feel a growing excitement of this anticipation. It is strictly recommended to be very careful while performing an interaction that implements manipulations with an emotional sphere of the Object as it represents vulnerable and sensitive part of human personality. The Friend escorted by Starlighter approaches Star. It should be noted that in this story, Starlighter is also representing the role of a so-called Starlinker. The Starlighter may suggest that three of them may have a nice dinner together or Starlighter may suggest any other kind of social activity. The Starlighter may note in this or other way or just may give an indication that it will be enough if Star has a little time for this and thus show understanding of Star's inability to spend a lot of time out of her celebrity duties. When being presented to Friend, Star refuses to give any friendly behavior to the Object. She keeps showing a neglecting behavior, keeping her line of a person who regards others like inferiors to herself due to own status of superwoman. Star may use phrases like: I am too bored for that today; What do you all want from me?; Leave me alone; similar phrases. It is also possible that the Star may use phrases expressing the ruder characteristics: Get off; Don't get in my way; You better keep away from me; phrases employing foul language and similar phrases. Also, Star should support an image with some manner of behavior. Her motions and expressions of a face should supplement her image of a person neglecting others. In Object's mind that should create the image of an archetypal celebrity who thinks that the other people are not for the count. After a short exchange of phrases of different meanings, Star goes away paying no attention to the rest of group. The aim of this stage is a creation of a specific image of Star into the consciousness of Friend and thus creating an impulse of emotional heat connected to the possible aggression of the Object. Star should softly hurt the feelings of Object in order to produce psychic impulse in the latter. Also, Friend may start to grow suspicion that the relations of Starlighter to the Star are not that close as it was initially supposed.

Part two: Friend and Starlighter are spending time at home location. Location is supposed to seem a home place of Starlighter. The two of them do usual things that are common for friends. A good portion of chatting is recommended. At this stage, it is the responsibility of the performer of Starlighter's part to create a relaxing environment for the sake of Friend's comfort. This stage also can be marked as unrecognized anticipation. During this stage, participants should watch the fake promo video featuring an image of Star character. A video should be prepared and shot previously. Preparation of the video includes the creation of a fake brand product that should look essential to the Object. A video should not be too original in order to represent a believable typical glamorous brand promo. That should be a short video featuring an image of Star presenting fragrance, lingerie or another type of product which presentation is typically connected to model's sexuality and attractiveness. Most probably that should be another video than that which as supposed should be filmed at shooting site that the two visited previously as an intermission between two parts will be not long enough. Supposed promo may be presented at this moment only in the case when such intermission is long enough. That may happen due to unforeseen obstacles, but in general, the option is not recommended as long waiting may diminish emotions generated by the Object during the first act and thus diminish their possible effect. It is recommended to reveal this video commercial as part of usual TV broadcast to increase the impact. When the Starlighter turns TV set on it should look like Starlighter tries to find something interesting on one of the satellite channels by chance. But instead of launching one of the channels, Starlighter should launch a prepared piece of video including a supposed fake commercial put in between records of real TV shows.

Watching the fake commercial should reawaken feelings of day one into the heart of Friend. After watching TV, a next stage opens. At this moment Starlighter may provide the Object with soft innuendo on the possibility of something funny happening then. What happens is that the Star arrives at the spot. She comes to the place and goes to two showing good mood and most friendly behavior. When appearing in front of Starlighter and Friend, it is recommended for a performer of Star part to smile. Greeting Starlighter, Star should give all possible indications of a close friendship between them. Star may use phrases like: I'm so glad you came; That is so nice to see you; You look fantastic today; It is nothing like having a best friend home when I need a friend so much; We are going to have a great time; similar phrases. In return, Starlighter should note that they need to talk about one thing about her (Star). And then Star leaves the room to have a shower. She informs two on this, also telling that she will be back soon to enjoy their company. At this moment it is supposed that the Object most probably starts to believe in close relations between Star and Starlighter. During the time that will be required for Star to take a shower, Starlighter should do nothing to ruin doubts of the Object about the behavior of Star toward her. Instead, Starlighter should leave an entire difficulty of emotions (if such problem exists) to be experienced by the Object. Starlighter keeps chatting and entertaining Friend with no indication of notice for a change in the mood of Friend if such change happens.

Approximately in ten minutes, Star returns being

wrapped in bathrobe or bath towel only. She tries to join a conversation becoming a third equal element of the group, but Starlighter prevents it. Starlighter explains her softly but firmly that they need to talk she *knows what about*. She may increase seriousness in her tone after some time. Star should keep trying to turn Starlighter's words into a joke, but not try to resist, answering softly. That should not take a lot of time as this should become a short bridge into next part of events. At this moment Starlighter may use phrases like: You know you were really naughty this time; I know you didn't want it, but it is still your fault, dear; Don't spend my time honey, because we just should do it; You know how much I love you, but I should punish you; I know it's your childish jokes, but when you do like the bad girls do, you get punished; We both agreed that I do it to you in such cases; similar phrases. The manner of Starlighter at this instant should display no aggression, but only a firm softness with a possible light shade of tenderness. The Starlighter should employ a manner in which a good caring teacher educates and in which a deeply loving mother treats an adorable child who at this moment needs to learn some essential rules of life. The Starlighter should make it clear that what will happen next is a previously agreed punishment that the Star will face for hurting Friend during the day one. It is crucial

that the Star shows a behavior opposite to that she displayed on day one. Star shows no real confrontation and disagreement. She may indicate that she doesn't want to get punished in the presence of a third person, but softly and not insisting. She may softly plead and then she may show her full readiness and show that she is under control. During pleading she may stand on knees letting her bathrobe fell, revealing her body.
The Starlighter at this moment may use the phrase: You know what you should do; or a similar phrase. Then Star silently agrees and goes out of the room. When she soon returns, she brings horsewhip and collar. She goes down on her knees, lowers her head and gives these items to Starlighter as a sign of obedience. After this moment Starlighter should make it clear who holds the control over the situation. From this moment on, Starlighter should decide on the intensity of Object's participation that may vary from voyeurism to active participation. Starlighter then should make Star standing in a position comfortable for spanking, most probably on fours. Then Starlighter should start spanking and then ask Friend to continue if being sure in Object's readiness for active participation. The Starlighter may use phrases like: I think I need help with this naughty girl; Would you help me, please; That will be most correct if you punish her well; similar

phrases. During spanking, an actual using of horsewhip is not recommended. This item might be used as a symbolic element. The Starlighter may put a horsewhip into the mouth of the Star, like pretending that the process will be painful and that is to prevent loud shouts. The episode should not present a real punishment of the Star by the Object with the help of Starlighter. It should represent a sexually attractive interaction. It is the responsibility of Starlighter to help Friend to transform the generated emotions that may be close to hatred into sexual desire and excitement. At the moment when the performer of Star character feels willingness of participation expressed in actions of the Object, she should openly display signs of receiving a pleasure marked with increasing intensity. When spanking is finished, Starlighter should instruct or give a clear notion that the Friend may give her hand with which she spanked the Star for kissing by Star. That should serve as a sign of full obedience and gratitude during this part of the game. Next recommended part of *punishment* episode is the performance of cunnilingus received by the Object. At this moment Star should not display any protest against sexual interaction with the Object. She should do it delicately and with the best quality possible. As it is seen from insight analysis of Object's preferences, Object prefers to grow an excitement as slow as possible, performing fast sex only like a possible way for additional variety in sex life. That is why a slow beginning and gradual development are recommended. Also, it is possible to give no orgasm during cunnilingus to the Object, but only to heat the Object's senses up and to postpone the culmination to the final act. If Object won't be ready to receive such kind of interaction, then it is recommended that the Starlighter takes its place, but this development is less probable than the opposite version. At the end of *punishment* episode, the entire trio should become equals losing the statuses of submissive and dominants as these statuses are needed in previous parts of the game to open sexual emotion in participants. It is true that a submissive has the comfort to reveal his or her sexuality to others while being not limited to anything. But for dominant, it is possible to get excited and by this to be moved to sensitive openness when watching the excitement of submissive. The whole episode of *punishment* should bear a light domination-submission character as rough sex is not among evident preferences of the Object, but that kind of interaction may prove to be very interesting to her. Little by little *punishment* episode should transform into the final act. During the final act, a variety of caresses is recommended. Performers should show their best skills and creativity together with

openness for pleasure to please the Object.
Additional remarks on impulse redirection: This sort of instrument should be used as carefully as possible due to evident obstacles. In this story, there is a supposed use of mechanism redirecting possible emotional energy generated by feelings close to hatred and aggression into energy fulfilling the erotic desires of the Object. Such use if performed carefully and in a proper manner may create additional psychological depth for experience during the sexual interaction. It should be noted that an actual interaction should bear no signs of hatred and aggression, but instead support a full transformation of energy from one kind to another.
Participation of the Object: It was revealed that the Object is the person with high social status who prefers to keep details of her intimate life in secret. That means the performers should create a particular environment to make the Object feel free and comfortable. The Object should be sure about the safety of events happening during the story. It is also revealed that the Object previously experienced a sexual interaction in a group involving elements of a game. That proves that the Object may have a strong inclination to active participation after some point of story's development. It is recommended to stimulate active participation of Object by friendly encouragement. Providing this encouragement is the

responsibility of Starlighter. The same way it is the responsibility of the same performer to hold the general decisions depending on circumstances.
The rest is improvisation.

Some Notes on Common Fantasies
from Dictaphone Record
by Martin

Why are some sexual fantasies considered to be more common than others? It looks like that the people are very individual about many of their intimate preferences. Is it only the influence of media sphere that shapes the dreams we dream? I suppose that in this case when even it is some influence of media, it still can be only partial because media would no matter choose something most common to sell it in the form of a mass product. That means that the people still reveal their sexual fantasies themselves. Maybe this sphere is so intimate that even a corporate might can't break it. But then if there are common things for a vast quantity or even most of the people around the globe representing different nations and social groups, it means that it should have some biological reason. Everything that the people have in common in their behavior and psychology most probably can be explained by basic biological intentions of the human creature. It is almost like stating the fact that most of us have two eyes, two hands, two legs, and one head. Or it is almost that. For example, the most common fantasies that work well in the sphere of sci-fi production have a certain basis for their existence. That makes people dream those dreams. Awake. Generation after generation. Founding father of contemporary fantastic fiction Herbert Wells presented the major kinds of sci-fi fantasies including the hostile alien intervention, the mutants, and the time machine. There is something in these fantasies that provokes the strong emotions in many people not depending on their status in society. Time machine is a popular idea through ages because we are used to reflection. We keep thinking about what I would do then in my past if having the opportunity to rewrite it. That makes us obsessed with an idea of traveling in time no matter how impossible it is in reality. Other two basic kinds of sci-fi fiction are easily explained by biological reasons. And note that there is definitely more films about mutants and hostile aliens than about time machine. Actually, the idea of time traveling is more popular in Japan than in western societies as the eastern nation shows more of introverted reflection. Westerners tend more to express their biology. We experience an intense emotion facing an alien invasion on the silver screen not because we have a biologically predetermined fear for aliens, but because we are much afraid not only of our own extermination, but also we subconsciously fear our kind's extinction. Group of scientists claimed that they registered a minor baby boom in the US after September 11 events. Those scientists connected this happening to the fact that during this period the American nation subconsciously felt some possibility of their group extinction due to extensive negative information in media. And mutants' fantasies are about massive changes into human genetic code. And we are, of course, subconsciously afraid of this too. Mutants are something like a wrong result of genetic development. That means failure to all the process of genetic recombination. And if sci-fi fantasies can be understood to exist on the basis of what I probably would call an adrenaline drive, then probably sexual fantasies are fed by its opposite – the endorphin drive. And of course, nature won't supply as with pure endorphin similarly to a drug dealer who won't sell for free. That is why we receive it mixed with oxytocin, and this fact is what can help to understand psychological side of most common sexual fantasies. Psychology tends to be a science. And science is what takes mostly the mass cases into account, not caring too much for particular individual cases. So, that is what establishes a strong bridge in between psychology and biology. It is considered that Freud experienced a significant influence by Darwin during his time at Vienna University. But then what it should be?

Simplest and most commonly efficient way of analysis represents a process of comparing lots. That is why to move on, I need to answer the question about what the most common fantasies actually are. Today we see things including BDSM elements in too many media sources what proves that this sort of fantasy is a quite common one. But it is also a question about how much of that and what exactly of that the people like. I am seriously doubtful that most people would enjoy sadomasochism because most people don't enjoy beating each other. Maybe we are becoming softer than our ancestors were. But what seems to me rather evident - despite the fact that I can't find proper statistics for it, but only some opinions of some sexology authors - is that we are becoming kinkier.

Today people have submission-dominance fantasies probably because that is a kind of story that means some unusual steps of interaction. Before, simpler things were enough. Fantasies, as I suppose, were differentiated by style of outfits. Today, people watch the videos where partners do a lot of unusual things to each other. But just before the sixties for Nabokov it was absolutely enough to use only some innuendos to make Lolita the most scandalous book ever. And it became a commercial success. In the second decade of sexual revolution when erotic film industry saw its greatest rise there were films like Emmanuelle and Fruit is the Ripe devoted mostly to discoveries of sexual life by some girl who served as a protagonist in the plot of such feature. Emmanuelle was just about a girl who was making revelations that would seem today too simple to surprise anybody. But that time the movie became a hit. Softcore scenes featuring a sex-exploring lady were enough to give this movie the more than eight-million audience in France only. Nothing like this is possible today. It looks like authors themselves will consider their video insufficient if there is no juicy cum shot covering a face of an actress with a biological material of her partner. Now people fantasize their stories being educated by a porn industry since sweetest teen years.

Previously it was enough to have some beautiful girl who wears and then takes off her lovely outfit. We all know what those outfits are. I mean those most popular ones. The list will include nurse, teacher, schoolgirl, stewardess, and maid. It may also include cop woman additionally. For years I tried to understand what unites those characters. Frankly, I tried to do so for a couple of recent years. And it looks like that I finally found the biologically based reason that explains the frequency of these fantasies. And even more, it gives a link to submissive-dominant kind too. When I suddenly got it, I felt like having a revelation. That seems to explain so much. And that seems to be able of being a guideline in the sexual life of a person. At least that is what it is for me. Of course, it didn't happen in my mind in a single second. These two years, or at least in recent months it was forming in my mind, but when finding a proper shape, it came to me with a feeling of revelation. That probably can be partly explained by the fact that such reason helps to unite knowledge I gained from biology, psychology and sexology sources into one point.

My guess is that we should look back to human childhood. Society approaches a single individual by descending from its aggregated mass down. That is why society is based on rules of scale effect. It cannot treat a person individually but instead it created a variety of groups in which a person can find a place. But if the actual scale effect is considered to be wide enough, then there is no real variety of such possible aggregation. That is why in general when we talk about the sexual development of human being, we divide entire population into two parts. There are kids, and there are those who are not kids anymore. That means having or having not the right to any sexual activity according to norms of society. That is what I would call the condition of discrete gradualism that exists due to a massive scale effect. But the truth is that the developments of a human being including such of sexual character are not discrete, but continuous. Society treats us like a part of some group. And thus for society, our life represents transforming from a school pupil to a college student and then to a working person and so on. And the same way it is judged that we exist as kids and then suddenly we become the adults. According to this logic, we should become fully sexually developed in one day. But that is not so. Human sexuality develops not in sharp jerks or suddenly overcoming the stages, but as slowly as the whole human body and mentality do.

That is what created a conflict in between society based on a discrete logic of aggregation and our continuous nature. When we face a society in a massive form for the first time going to the school, we start to ask ourselves whether it is right or not to visit this place where you are treated like one from a mass. When strong enough, our subconscious struggles against any attempt of society to make us conform because that means losing individuality and future sexual attractiveness. That means that our sexuality starts shaping itself in early years.

And in early years, the humans are not oriented to an opposite sex same way as adults. Different elements that are programmed shape it. From evolution theorists and researchers of nature, we know that the mammals are able of experiencing a biological kind of love to their kids on earlier stages of evolution than primates. When I say a biological kind of love, I mean that an animal, for example, lioness, experiences a flow of endorphin into her brain when watching and caring for her kids. There should be two circumstances. First is that the mother should know that these kids are her kids. And animal mothers are rarely mistaken about that. And second is that they should look infantile enough to make her care about them. That probably means that a next stage - development of inter-gender emotional relations, that were initially shaped like a process of reproduction and thus like a process of giving birth and care to kids - was nothing but a double use of this function. It is like an evolution of mobile devices. Do you remember what the old phones were like? Today we use many useful apps installed on the same device. That means that we can use same OS, same processor, and battery when launching a different function. And that gives to our phone a multi-functionality.

That may explain the Oedipus and Electra complexes. There is a biological basis. Our sexuality forms depending on our realization of roles like the son-father for boys and daughter-mother for girls. That means that when searching for a woman, a man searches for mother and daughter into her. That means he seeks for her sexuality that will fit his own. And it is similar to a woman. That also means that a connection is not between father role and mother role as society teaches us, but it is a diagonal connection in between role of a mother in woman and role of the son in man, and in between role of a father in man and role of the daughter in a woman. That also probably gives an additional explanation why Humbert's relation to the miss Haze is so unnatural. He was searching only for a child, but not for a mature woman who possibly can be a mother herself. Thus he wanted to control a person and didn't intend to stimulate her development in general. He didn't care about her real freedom. So, he perceived her as a stable element stuck into a stage of human being not because it was true, but because his perception didn't allow it another way. That's probably the additional explanation why healthy human sexuality always searches for an adult person. The thing is that a process requires not a single link, but somehow a set of links. The system is a bit more complicated.

Society teaches us that there is a father-to-mother direct link as it is supposed to be in a marriage. But that's not exactly so. But as the evolution shows, nature initially supports - with endorphin first of all – the link in between parents and kids. Gender relations represent a partial borrowing from this complex of relations. And that is what makes much of the difference. Society created marriage and its rules. And it keeps promoting this institution. I wouldn't say that it is a bad idea to marry someone, but I would say that according to nature, marriage is an entirely conventional creation. And thus there is no this kind of link in between a man and a woman as something absolutely independent. We are taught that it is so. And we are also taught to perceive the childhood and sexual maturity as two absolutely non-corresponding things. Another thing is that nature wouldn't give to a human being only a parent role not providing with a child role as it would create inequality in a pair. Such inequality may mean the inability to represent a sufficient element inside a chain of evolution. Nature in many cases supplies us with two opposite sides that work simultaneously, but not gradually one after another. Only this way we can integrate into a possibly infinite biological process of the reproduction.

And that is what explains nature of the most common sexual fantasies. In most of them, we see a possibility for something like the active-passive relations that are common for relations of a parent to child. A nurse is someone who knows better about how to deal with the illness of her patient. A patient is sure eligible to be passive because he is not able to deal with his illness due to lack of the medical experience. In this sort of a game, an illness metaphorically represents a yet unsatisfied sexual desire when the medical experience represents the sex experience and sex skills. Men may prefer this kind of fantasy because nothing is humiliating in the situation. There is the logic that says that it is normal to be a patient when you are ill. Many men would consider it to be not a proper men's style to allow a woman's lead. According to the traditional stereotype, a woman should be passive, and man should be active. But true is that to receive a good orgasm you actually need to lose control. And that is what so good about such fantasies. Other outfit-equipped characters like the stewardess, teacher, and maid are similarly representing the personage who will take care. That is someone who will take control over your pleasure. That is what a parent does to kids. If to come back to the Freud theories, he divided a human mentality when regarded in the sense of relations of human nature to human society into three parts. There is Id responsible for our nature, there is Superego responsible for our image in society, and there is Ego that struggles in between Id and Superego searching for a balance. The position of Ego is what defines our problems if regarded from this standpoint. We need to have the Superego to be able to integrate into society, to be a successful part of the whole flock. That means we should earn money and make a career. But our actual chemical happiness depends not on Superego, but more on Id. I say chemical because I mean that to feel happy or really satisfied the same way as to receive fantastic orgasm, we need our organism to produce specific chemical combinations. The endorphins, for instance. That means we should make our Id work. And when we block our Id, we cannot receive the happiness or orgasm. We need to let it go. That is what explains the most common fantasies.

And if to talk about schoolgirl then, it is evident that a schoolgirl is a reverse of a teacher. We are programmed to stand on both sides. If you like to be a school student you may also like to be a school teacher. That is quite evident. You hardly will find lots of young women who decide to teach kids in schools and had chosen this profession, but who were the bad pupils during their teen years. That also partly explains the tennis girl fantasies. Sexy tennis girl from such lusty dream has more of a schoolgirl and less of a sports pro who cries during serving the ball like she is a big cannon releasing it into the target. Such girl is probably some nineteen-year-old student of a sports academy. And remember that there is also a university factor of tennis.

And parents-children relation complex is partly redirected to create the bound in gender relations of similar closeness. That is what also explains the popularity of submissive-dominant games too. It does not explain sadomasochism, but that explains SD of BDSM as it represents another image of active-passive sexual behavior. Despite the fact that many internet sources claim that the scientists find a proof of the usefulness of sadomasochism, I would not support this opinion in general. My opinion is that those web-pages and other media like the TV shows devoted to the theme of sexuality don't represent the research groups. And their chiefs are not the real sexologists but the media people. Those studies usually somehow find that the sadomasochism improves some aspects of organism's activity what can be considered to be a proof that the sadomasochism probably increases health as people practicing it are healthier on account of these organism's activities. First of all, the health of a person is more complicated than this. And second is that in general there is only one primal organism's activity that says that the sex was pretty good and beneficial for an organism. And this sort of activity is usually called an orgasm. There is no scientific proof that the sadomasochists averagely receive the better orgasms than most of the people. Actually, the more complicated your way to orgasm is, the less chance for it you have. That is what at least seems to be logical. My opinion is that the sadomasochism is quite a specific kind of activity that can be normal only for a small part of people. Freud saw such behavior as result of a childhood trauma that led to a person's association of sexual activity with the sadist activity. And extensive use of BDSM both in real life and in media doesn't prove the opposite. BDSM is a term that embraces a wide variety of sexual practices. It is one thing to use a little of bondage and soft spanking, and it is another thing to hurt a person physically. Light spanking may appear to be pretty pleasurable to a variety of people - if not to most of the people - as it creates pressure on the part of a body that has a thicker sort of skin and then is less sensitive to the pressures. Pressing woman's breasts too roughly may really hurt as this part of a body is very sensitive and has thin, delicate skin. That is why sexologists recommend mostly subtle touches in this area. But hips are different, of course. And so, some spanking can prove to be nice. But then it is not sadism of course. I even would risk making the notion that the sadomasochism is not natural for most of the people, but can be useful for a minority of people.

Improvement of some physical activities may be connected to a release of adrenaline that improves animal's ability for survival. That is when having some stress. But sexual interaction is mostly connected to the relaxation. There are two major groups of instincts. One is about survival, and another one is about reproduction. They complement each other and thus, they occupy the opposite sides. Sexual interaction is connected to release of the oxytocin. This hormone makes us social. Its general effect is a creating trust and relaxation toward another person. Normally it creates a feeling of trust and relaxation during sexual interaction and thus prepares the ground for a good orgasm. To receive an orgasm, you need to be relaxed. Oxytocin appears on the stage of evolution earlier than a human sort of gender interactions. Oxytocin is able of creating a strong feeling of a bound to the child into the mind of any mammal mother. During lactation, the mother receives three major hormones. They are oxytocin, prolactin, and endorphin. That creates a feeling of bound, relaxation and pleasure. What are three major hormones a person receives during the orgasms? They are same three actually - prolactin, oxytocin, and endorphin. That theoretically explains some rare cases when women are reporting to have a feeling close to orgasm during lactation. That also probably proves that there is a particular link in between love of parents to kids and love of sex partners.

It may mean that a normal relation of sex partners should represent aspects of such relation. That also supposes altruism toward a partner stimulated by oxytocin as kind of natural behavior. Some researchers report that the most of the women are fantasizing about being submissive. But true is that being submissive in the sex game is not being abused. That may only mean that a woman wants to be treated like a passive side what means to receive pleasure and being pleased by another partner. And it's nothing else. I mean nothing like being hurt or really abused. I would like to say that the people are not predestined to hurt each other during sex, but only to take a passive or active position. Sexologists claim that a person should take a passive position to receive a full orgasm. That is probably due to a role of Id in receiving pleasure. To get more of pleasure you need to make your Id free from your Superego that chains it. That is why so many people say they would like to be kids again. Kids are those who don't recognize any their status in society and this also means they have no responsibility. The problem is that they can't embrace this quality like the adults do, not being able of social recognition.

That easily can be connected to one ancient myth with which help the hundreds of generations were educated. I mean the Adam and Eve's exile from Eden. Being in Eden they were not able to recognize its quality as the blessed place, but when they lost it, they started to regret this loss. They actually lost it because they were able to understand losses. They recognized the evil from good, and that made them responsible for the evil they may do to the others. And those who are able of self-recognizable evil have no right to stay in the Eden. And since the ancient time, we regret our disability to find the keys from Eden's gates. And the Eden is less something like a place but more sort of condition. It is considered that a human being shows some rudimentary signs of previous stages of the evolution during the in-utero period. That is, for instance, the gills similar to those of fish, what shows that the mammals originated from the sea species. Maybe that can be said to be true that a person also repeats some stages of psychological evolution during early childhood period. During childhood, a person easily manifests one's Id and doesn't manifest a strong Superego as it is not yet developed. Many religions claim that the kids are blessed creatures as they don't mean any evil. They don't mean it because like the animals they don't recognize it. Adam and Eve as we know were exiled, but not the animals - except serpents, of course, that were damned to crawl on the surface of the earth - because they still were not recognizing the evil. In a time of childhood, people are easily enjoying simple things connected to their biological intentions like being with mother or eating tasty food, but don't recognize how good it is on that level of recognition. And then the Exile happens. We are given the status and responsibilities. And society does its best to make us want a bigger status and more of responsibility.

During sex, we are given the extraordinary

possibility to enter the Eden for a short time. A person may become similar to a child in one's revealing intentions of Id and losing the limits of Superego, but still being an adult able to recognize the good and evil, grief and happiness, pain and pleasure. That is why it is so important for the sex partners to be like the kids and like the parents simultaneously in some aspect. And that completely explains nature of the most common sexual fantasies that are mostly about taking part of a passive or an active element. Nature stimulates us for some sort of altruistic behavior the same way as about receiving it through the release of oxytocin and our want for endorphins. And these fantasies are not about humiliating or abusing each other, but about the mutual comfort and pleasure.

Nov, 28

Day

Private Audio Diary of Elise

by Elise

Today we devoted most of our time to discussing our documentary projects. We were talking about what concepts we can use. And Martin started to develop his theories about society. And so, we were talking about many things like prostitution, fame, scandals, money, and many other things.

Martin proposed to regard stardom as some social merit. And it is something you need to deserve it if you want it. And if you kinda want it, then you need to do something what you maybe don't want, but what the society wants. And thus stardom is quite an instrument for the society. Society doesn't need us all to be stars, but it wants us to want to be stars. Kinda. It tells the people that everyone can be a star. And that's what reminds, as Martin said, about the porn industry. In this industry every performer no matter what is called a star. A porn star. In a more natural situation, at least in theory, we could be more satisfied with just some level of prosperity. But instead, we have no limits on our want. And in our society, we accept some very high level of prosperity as a necessary one. It's not even a luxury to us. We feel it should be almost like a basic level. And then we are ready to do anything to achieve the level. And that's what makes us more similar to the prostitutes or porn stars. And of course, it's some saying. It's not that all is complete shit. It's just in this way. And it all works no matter whether you have a low start or you are high-positioned. We keep our lives being full of pretense. You know, porn stars are those who pretend their reaction to things they make too much. And prostitutes often do things they didn't want to do. And in a situation like this, you always need to pretend to be accepted by society, or you need to be pretty infantile, an unconscious person who doesn't feel about it this way. That's why, maybe, we now have so many childlike stars. Previously, famous people were more like adult men and women, and now they are like kids in many things. And at least in this, I agreed with him. And also maybe people don't want prostitution to get extinct. They want the dirty women to exist so that most of the people would look better in comparison. And people especially like to find out that someone from a high position faced some big troubles. So, we all kinda prostitute ourselves little by little and blah-blah-blah...

At home, I watched some documentary about prostitution to know more about the matter. I also had some other entertainments, and maybe it wasn't such a bad day after all. Now I am going to sleep. End of line.

HELEN

PART THREE

Description of Video Four from Dictaphone Record by Martin

Next video represents a record of another sex game performance by the Agency. I should note that there is no need to spend much time on its actual description as girls used a scenario similar to that which performance was explained in the description of video one. So, this was a similar story about watching the others having fun across the street. But I still would like to note about differences.

In general, many things were the same. It seems like performers were same girls including Susan and Jane. Differences were mostly about the Lead Hero. And there were some minor differences about other things. For example, girls used a telescope on a tripod to watch those who played across the street. Also, that seems like Susan didn't watch through its lens but was more occupied with communicating to the Lead Hero. This person was one element that made a real difference about the events. First of all, I would note that I definitely can say that this was a woman. She behaved rather openly, not trying to hide. She talked with girls and was readily receiving what they were giving to her. It looked like that all three of them were relaxed about each other. She and Jane were looking through a tube time after time, but it looked like that they were more interested in each other than in things that were happening across the street. It seems like they used their voyeuristic option like some spicy addition. And Susan was supporting their pure erotic entertainments pretending to be an interested voyeur. I would also note that a location seemed to be a similar apartment in some rather tall building and as camera position was similar too, many things seemed identical. And another thing that seems important to me is that there was no any supporting footage about what exactly those who were on the other side of the street were doing. I suppose that there should be something similar. Probably there was another lesbian play or something that should be exciting for a so-called object.

I don't know whether I should consider it to be suspicious because previously I did not feel that the source tried to hide something from me. Mr. Shadow should be a very mysterious character and what is on his mind should be covered with some sort of mystery. Returning to the role of an object, I would say that her behavior really gave me what to think about. The most unexpected thing happened because I think I saw her face. I mean I suppose I will be able to identify her if seeing in real life. Right now I am trying to extract a still from a video. The one where her face can be seen. I hope my sources, including

Mr. Shadow and whoever may stay with him or behind him, don't think it is improper behavior. I just really may need this photo for the purposes of investigation. Yes, of course, it all seems like they give me everything I should know, and I tell others. But then why did they hire a professional? They could just publish it all via the internet. And I am a journalist. I should search for the facts to prove or to disprove the story. Why did they instruct me to interview Susan? Is it to have fun or to have another proof? Little by little I start to feel that I like Susan somehow. And I am afraid that is also somehow connected to my sexual affection. She is indeed a nice kind of talkative girl. But a girl like her hardly can be a skillful liar. I suppose that it is quite evident that she didn't see these videos and thus her stories where she correctly describes events prove that these videos are not fake. She gives the facts of proof. Doesn't she?

And now as I just got the still I need, and I am watching a face that I think I will be able to recognize, I would like to tell how it happened. In the process of a game, this woman, who served as an object for Jane and Susan, was developing her sexual openness slowly. She came to the point where she openly started to caress Jane and Susan. But more it was Jane. It is interesting that both of them didn't undress in process. They only unbuttoned themselves a little. And woman touched them mostly through the tissue, pressing parts of their bodies as it seemed tighter and tighter every next time. She also touched them in a few available open parts like the neck and face. She touched them there softly with the tips of her fingers only. And then reaching the top of her delicate excitement, she started to undress. Her excitement was actually so delicate that it wasn't that evident she had that sort of experience. It was definitely less evident than with the previous objects in the previous video pieces. She slowly undressed, moving softly. She indeed was very delicate about herself. And it seemed like that took some time to finish an entire process. At least, that is what it seemed to me. I measured it then, and it appeared to take some minutes, not hours. But she really was taking her clothes off in no hurry. And she, of course, took off her stockings perfectly like it only can be in some classic sexy movie. And then she stood barely nude in front of a window in this apartment that is probably her apartment. And she wasn't doing anything really dirty. I mean she didn't look like any kind of porn star at any given moment. She was elegant with any move she made. She only caressed herself similarly as she did it to girls previously. She was softly touching herself with just the tips of her fingers making some soft round motions over her body. Three of them seemed to enjoy her nudity and her beauty. Suddenly her fine body seemed to be a center of their little private universe. And it wasn't that important what was going across the street. She has a nice body, that woman. She is a little taller than average, her hips are rounded, and breasts are not the big ones. And then she moved from her spot that a second ago was the center of attention for all the trio. She started to move slowly without any intention to get dressed again, but it seemed she still enjoyed herself and her body this way. At some moment she came closer to the corner where a camera was supposed to hang. It isn't that she just stood under it for a minute. Not even several seconds. But she somehow walked close enough to a camera, and at some moment she directed her face almost toward its lens, and that gave an opportunity to see her facial features on the still. That is quite a face. Beautiful face of a woman filled with sensitivity. I think it is those big eyes possessing softness of female glance that make me feel so. Something tells me that I wouldn't forget this face too soon.

Nov, 28-29
from Dictaphone Record
by Martin

A recent interview with Susan left a specific feeling in me. I am afraid that I almost made some fault. It was supposed that I could ask anything, but actually, I am not sure that I should ask absolutely anything. And also I wonder whether Susan should really know how much I do know. When I asked her about strawberries, it seemed for a second like she understood what I was talking about. Then we both were confused and made expressions on faces like nothing happened. I actually meant whether it was strawberries in a movie I watched. She could know because she could ask someone directly. She could have the details from Jess.

This time I went rather far with Susan. I mean literally because I saw her home. I saw a place where she lives. At least, I saw a door. She almost made me in. She supposed we could drink something. I said it was late, and I should keep working, but I noted that next time I wouldn't refuse, of course. And I noted that it was very nice to ask me. She said OK, and it seems to me that there was something like a mild surprise on her face for a second at that moment. I just went home then.

Before going on with Susan's interviews, I should deal with one matter. This matter that worries me most of all is identifying the personality of the mysterious woman from a recent video. I want to interview Susan for one more time to make sure that I don't miss some important detail. Maybe it's so wrong that we developed some sort of friendship during these times. It isn't because there is something wrong with having a good feeling about a nice little blonde, but because it may be the reason why I miss something. Theoretically, that makes my opinion a more subjective one. I always try to avoid some personal feeling when dealing with one of the witnesses during the investigation. But possibly, that is only in theory.

And now I am obsessed with finding who the mysterious woman is. Previously I wanted to see faces of the video characters at least vaguely, despite the fact that at the same time I tried to drive such thoughts away because people at their private time have as much of right to be unrecognized as they would like to. If someone wants to stay unexposed, then journalist can't open identity of the source, except cases when it may hurt someone else. Mostly it is only in cases when a person is a certain criminal. And even in such cases, there may be something you can expose and still something you can't. And now when I finally saw a face that seems recognizable, I start to realize the truth. I start to feel that, no matter, it may prove to be difficult to find a person about whom you only know how her face looks like. I decided to use the entire resource I have. But what do I have in addition to myself? It is not a squad of secret service agents. All I could venture was asking Elise to help me somehow. There is an image search in some search engines like Google, and you can be lucky to find a face of a person by his photograph. No, I knew it hardly would do. I was not hoping for a lot. The engine doesn't recognize faces but searches for similar photographs. That means most probably you may have thousands of similar BW mug shots of other people. And so, all I could really do was asking Elise. And she surprised me somehow this time. It is not that she surprises me for the first time in a lifetime. She did it before. But that doesn't happen on a permanent basis. When I showed her a cropped still with a face of the woman zoomed in, she said she knows who it is. She said at least she knows one person who has a very similar face. As it was late and we were preparing to go home, she promised me to prepare a profile somewhere during next week. I asked her to do it as soon as she can.

Dec, 2
Susan's Interview Seven
from Dictaphone Record
by Martin and Elise

Martin: It's nice to see you again. How was your weekend?
Susan: Fine. What do you want to talk about, today?
M.: Actually, I feel like I want to ask you the same question. There are some things I would like to know about next affair, one similar to your first one. But also I would like you to tell me what you would like to tell. That can be anything about your time in the Agency we didn't previously talk about. You know, I just thought that we probably might miss something important. It can be something that doesn't seem to be so. That is why I would like you to talk freely without considering any frameworks or whether it seems important or not. It happens with many investigations that some little detail that was missed can become a crucial key to the entire matter.
Elise: What was the next affair? Why do you say it was like the first one?
M.: As I understand, there was a similar scenario in use. Right?
S.: Yes. I think I know what you mean. It was planned to be very similar. You know it is very

smart. I mean it is very rational to use the same thing again. But you know it was still fun because it was still a different experience because there was another object. There was another woman, and it made it all different. And that is why we changed something. I mean not the story, but just something. She was another person, and she was supposed to have some different preferences. And that is why we were supposed to do it another way. But the story was really the same.

E.: Do you mean you performed the same trick with spyglass? You watched others when they were lovemaking?

S.: Yes. But, actually, me, I wasn't watching, but Jane and that woman. They were watching. I was more concentrated on entertaining the object in another way. That was a general change in my role.

M.: You may say it wasn't very much different than it was for the first time?

S.: Well, I may say so. I think yes, it was pretty similar. But you know, this time a woman was different. And as it seemed, she enjoyed being nude with us.

E.: Do you mean she displayed some exhibitionist behavior?

S.: Yes, it was something like this.

M.: Did you notice something strange that time?

S.: No, I wouldn't say so. It was easy.

E.: And what about that woman? Did you ever see her before or then again?

S.: It seems like I did.

M.: What do you mean?

S.: I think I saw her at some presentation. It was weird because it seems like she worked for our company.

E.: You said - worked. You mean she doesn't work there now?

S.: Yes. Actually, as I know, she was fired. I don't know why exactly. Maybe it was her intention. Maybe she decided that the job was not for her.

M.: Are you sure that exactly this person worked for the same company as you?

S.: Well, I am not sure, but she seems to be the same woman. I mean if she has no an identical twin sister that should be her. I recognized both her voice and looks.

M.: And do you know what position she occupied and what her name is?

S.: Sure I know. Everyone knows. She was from high stuff. And her name is Helen. She is a very beautiful woman. You know, it was a surprise to me to know that such beautiful and sexy woman works as one of the top managers in our company. What a story! I thought she could be something like a fashion designer, model. Or maybe some countess. I even expected her to be a foreigner. But I couldn't expect this.

M.: That is the story indeed. And do you know anything else about her?

S.: Actually, I don't. I had some temptation to get more knowledge about her because, before that, I even didn't know her name. I only knew her as an object. I knew her preferences and all of that, but nothing else. But, you know, I decided that it could be improper somehow to try to find out. This game we played was her private story. And I think it can stay to be this. So actually, after we met this way, the main thing about her was the same to me. She is really hot.

E.: Excuse me. You mean... When you saw her for the first time, before all this agency thing, did you feel like you would like to have something with her? Like an affair or date?

S.: Well, most probably. I think – yes, I would.

E.: And... What about Jane?

S.: Jane? She was usually good that time.

E.: No. Please, would you tell me?.. Did you have something with her?

S.: Oh. With Jane? Yes, of course. She was so great I couldn't stand it.

M.: You mean you were great friends?

S.: I mean we were friends, and we had a lot of fun together. We were going places, we were enjoying each other, and we were talking much. And lovemaking with her was one of the best things I ever had in a lifetime.

M.: You mean you were lovers?

S.: Uh-huh.

E.: Well, but Susan, didn't you think that it was strange to have an affair with someone who belongs to the Agency?

S.: There is nothing strange. I don't know what you are talking about. And actually, we began before I knew about Agency. I just couldn't prevent falling in love.

M.: Did you like her that much?

S.: Yes, I adored her. She was such a great person.

M.: And did it last long? How much time did you spend together?

S.: It was our beautiful summer love. It began that summer and ended before summer was gone. It was a wonderful experience.

M.: Would you like to tell us something about your relations with her? And something about her that you think may be useful for us? If you want, you may tell only a few things. You shouldn't talk about something that you consider to be your private matter.

S.: There is no problem. I can tell anything you ask. And actually, I don't think I would tell anything really bad about Jane.

M.: True is that I don't know what to ask exactly.

S.: Really? [laughter]

M.: You may just tell what you want. Maybe there will be something useful.

S.: OK. What to begin with? Ah... Jane, she was an exceptional entertainer, if you know what I mean. She made me feel fine. She controlled my pleasure giving me no chance to escape it or to feel unsatisfied. We made it for the first time in the water closet on our level. It was after hours. It was the third day of our acquaintance. We just went there and made love. I still think we could go to my place because working hours were over and that could be more comfortable. I don't think that a water closet is the best place for such things. But with Jane, it's always sooo good. I think maybe we just couldn't wait. She was so passionate. And she knew lots of great games. She could pretend she didn't want me to touch her pussy and would do anything to prevent it as I tried to do so until she completely surrendered. Or of course, it could be me pretending this way. I also liked it very much when she made me lie and close my eyes. And she would tell me a story about myself walking by pure white sand of the ocean side. And she would tell me that I go there and here. She would also caress me at the same time. And she did it all slowly and very pleasantly. It was such a simple game, but I really enjoyed to be nude and horny and her to see it. Maybe that is just because it was Jane. Maybe that is because she was great about anything she was doing. While telling me about this place on the ocean side she kept caressing me. She touched me over my entire body with her soft hands and lips and with her tongue too. After telling me about sand and ocean, about nice breeze and palms, she would tell me that she was approaching me and then she would just do it. I felt like flying. And I felt like an orgasm was a soft, beautiful cloud that I embraced while flying.

M.: OK... Would you tell us what was unique about her except her... unlimited sex imagination?

S.: She was exceptional in everything. She was beautiful, smart and everything a great woman can be.

E.: How was it over then? When did you split and how did it happen?

S.: I don't know how to tell about it.

M.: If you don't want to tell you may keep it secret. It's OK.

S.: No, it's not this. I just don't know how to tell it. After this affair with the boss from our company, I waited to be called into the Agency again. Jess said she would call me again after some time if I would like to continue to collaborate with them. And of course, I said I would like to. And after this, I never saw Jane again. After a month I went to the mansion where we usually assembled, but it seemed to be absolutely empty and even abandoned. It looked like that there was nothing inside, and there was nothing around it. It felt so sad to see it. It was the fall. Maybe that was so sad because sky seemed to be so gray.

M.: That was how it was over? She never called you again?

S.: Yes. I don't know what has happened. Everything disappeared. I think something happened. But I don't know what. And then my life went into its usual way. Everything became like it was before. And sometimes I wonder whether I saw it into a dream or whether it was a true story.

Dec, 2-3

Private Audio Diary of Elise

by Elise

Yesterday we had an interview with Susan. We had it again. The more I know Susan, the more relaxed I feel about her. That should be due to the general effect. We are more conscious of things that we don't know. And now it seems I know something about Susan. And she doesn't seem as suspicious to me as at the beginning of this affair no matter that I now do know that we are two different girls indeed. Maybe from the very beginning, there was something that made me feel suspicious about her. I suppose that was her display of infantilism. She is not a bad person indeed. But on another side, such infantilism has dangers for a person and for those who are around this person. My opinion is that in depth of her soul she is probably not that childish. That should be something like a defensive mechanism. I am a little baby – don't treat me too tough. Isn't this position a comfortable one?

I don't know what danger she can mean to me, but still, it's not my favorite type of human being. Society is what it is. And you should grow older. The truth is that for many men such girls who behave like underdeveloped little ladies seem to be too attractive. Sometimes it seems that the men's ideal is a woman who is developed in quality of biological item having breasts and hips, but who is underdeveloped in social qualities. Such a bimbo girl. Such girls prefer to have as few responsibilities as possible. Maybe that is what makes them so attractive. Such girl won't ask to marry her on the spot and won't ask for kids as this would mean having responsibilities for them.

And no matter that now I tend to feel better and it's better to say more comfortable about Susan, there was one question itching in me, and I couldn't stand asking it. I thought about their relations with Jane. It seemed to me that Jane could somehow direct her. She could be a leader in their couple. And then how did she reach such influence over a little nice infantile blonde? Did they?.. Did they make love or something? I couldn't stand it. I was thinking how I could ask it correctly, but instead, I just shot it directly. I just asked her. And she answered almost without confusion. And I suppose that her little confusion was about the way I asked, but not about answering the question. She kinda thinks that she is some character in some TV reality and so, she is really glad to tell others anything about her most private life.

Yesterday was a day of Susan. I mean it was a lightheaded blonde's day. But today was a day of the blonde who is definitely a smart one. Martin gave me a task to make the file on this woman whose photograph he showed me. It was a strange photograph. He then told me that's because it is a still from the surveillance footage. But it was even stranger that this woman was one whom I recognize. She is this same woman involved in a sex scandal. She is this same top manager who according to one reporter was fired for having fun with call girls. That may explain everything. Or it may explain at least something. Or nothing. I made a profile. I was searching for everything I could find and gave it to Martin, and we even discussed things about her. What I still remember is that moment when Martin showed me the still and asked whether I could help him. I immediately said that I saw this face before. I recognized the woman. He made a strange grimace at that moment. It was something weird.

I am going to bed. End of line.

Dec, 2-6
from Dictaphone Record
by Martin

After we recorded a recent interview, I had a feeling that this could be the last one. If I will need to ask Susan something else I will call her. That is strange how my feelings to Susan changed in recent days. I don't feel desire for her that much anymore. At least not that kind of desire. I still know that she is attractive, but... Currently, all my thoughts are with another object. Who is that woman? And what is her role in the affair? I need to find her. If there is any possibility to find her, I should do it and ask her a couple of questions. I wonder whether I will find something about her in one of my magic envelopes. There is some information on her that I received from Elise. It's only some general available-to-everyone data, but it is better than nothing. Now I know how high she was in the corporation and what project it was under her control. In brief, I would say she was very high, and this project was the most important item in the investor folder for shareholders.

I think there is indeed a strong probability that I can find more in one of the envelopes provided by Mr. Shadow, but my idea is to ask her first. I want to know her version of the story, and only then I would like to open next envelope. Those envelopes are really magic, but they can wait because I don't think it is possible to finish this documentary before Xmas. Nor even to present some row version of it until end of the year. Such method should help me to have a more correct image of events. It is not that I am trying to cheat with Mr. Shadow, but I want to be accurate about things. If she has another truth, I may like to know her version first.

As it was not hard for Elise to find out what the woman's address was, at least one belonging to the place where she should be still resident, I thought I should go there and try. And if I won't be lucky, then I will try another way. Maybe when I open another envelope...

So, I went to her place. And what I saw was a modern, beautiful house. Very stylish. Place where she lives is gorgeous. I tried to find out whether there was someone inside. At least around there could be someone who knew her. For some time it seemed that there was no one and I almost went back home. But then I saw a woman wearing sunglasses. She went to the gates. What do you need? I started to explain that I would like to ask a couple of questions to her. I didn't lie but explained that I am a journalist. I told her that I would not reveal anything she didn't want to be revealed. I said that I would accept any requirements she would ask about. She denied that it was possible, but she didn't go away. And that somehow encouraged me. I kept insisting. She insisted too, but softly. You better leave. I have no mood to talk now. I said no matter I would know everything because I already have a source deep in the matter. I said she better tells me her side of the story. After that, she was silent for five or maybe more seconds, but it seemed to be an eternity. And then she agreed to meet me again and to talk. But she said I would be not able to refer to her as to a source. She said if I want to hear anything I should forget about things like Dictaphone or recorder. And she said no one should know we ever met. I am a person who prefers privacy. That's the sensitive matter to me. And then she removed her sunglasses. And I saw her eyes that were indeed that beautiful as I expected when looking at the still. And then she said that I should come there this time of day, maybe a week later. I assured her that she could trust my word and I even was on the verge of telling her that she is one of the most beautiful women I ever saw. I don't know why I felt so. But this soft melancholy in her eyes and her delicate beauty are something. And at the same time, she looked somehow strong to me. Even menacing. Possibly menacing. Maybe that is all that soft power she radiates around her. Soft but undeniable.

Seven days is a period long enough to open another envelope from Mr. Shadow, and thus I didn't yet decide whether I should open one before meeting her. And now there is something I should note about Mr. Shadow. He unexpectedly made another appearance. He called me out of the blue sky when I was in my apartment. Frankly, he didn't scare me that much this time, but I don't like that the bastard controls every my step. I almost forgot that he should do so. In his computer-changed voice, he informed me that I should follow the instructions no matter what. He said that I should not open the envelopes in wrong order. And only then for the first time I asked myself why I kept opening them in proper order. Yes, there were instructions, but... Maybe I just liked the story. I just almost like read an erotic adventure novel. And now there are only a few envelopes left. So, I think this call was just a reminder. Big Brother is watching you, dude.

I should say that some envelopes had music terms like Overture or Coda written on them like the short remarks. And now few are left unopened. And one that is supposed to be opened last has a word Finale written on it. I don't know why I am afraid of it, but I just feel like a scent of death replaces scent of sex in the most natural way. And maybe it's not a call of Mr. Shadow, but something else. When I was coming back home on my route to my apartment, I found myself in an elevator with a man who looked like Max von Sydow in Three Days of Condor. I know it is most stupid to be afraid that you will get killed by a pro killer in an elevator you used many times only because a person looks like a pro killer from some movie. But that was what I felt. I was afraid to die there, and I was afraid to breathe until I went out of the elevator at my level. And then when the man went out too, I saw that he looked indeed that much similar to Max von Sydow. Ouff. What a day I had! I indeed feel how scents are mixing. I feel the sex and death getting closer. And I am not sure what of these two elements of the life circle will be a reward to me when this affair comes to its culmination.

Some Notes on Sex and Death
from Dictaphone Record
by Martin

I always felt that these two things should be connected somehow. Sex and death are the two principle elements forming a circle of life. My opinion is that everything in the world has two sides opposing and complementing each other. And this interaction creates motions of the universe. There are light and dark, motion and stillness, cold and fire and many other things. We all exist in a variety of such diapasons which extremes create interactions. That is almost my religion. I would call it a binarism. For instance, there are man and woman. And sex is their interaction.

Why do we die? It seems like we would like to live forever. Many of us if receiving a magic drink providing the body with immortality would seize the opportunity. But then - why? Mother Nature doesn't love us that much? Or does she have some reasons for it? Or is she unable to keep life in a single biological unit for too long? The first thought that may come to a mind is an idea that we go away just to provide the next generations with some blank space. Sources are limited on Earth, and there can't be too many people. But then this thought seems to be doubtful because it seems quite evident that a struggle for dominance and survival between different kinds includes methods of increasing numbers of the population. And also once there were seven thousand people in the world, and now we are seven billion.

Some researchers use a populist saying when describing the reason for the existence of death. They say death is a payment for sex. That phrase may seem to be strange, but it has a point in it. Death and sex are indeed complementing one another in the process of evolution. One has no sense without the other. If people were immortal, that would mean that the evolution would stop, because genes of the previous generations would be mixing with genes of a current one. And that would mean that the process of genetic reformation would be stabilized. If there is a one-thousand-year-old man in his looks equal to a twenty-five-year-old man, he can marry a twenty-year-old woman, and they may have a kid who will have genes probably average of the current generation and of a generation that appeared on the stage of evolution a thousand years ago. Evolution would find itself permanently stuck in the middle. That would stop it. That is why we should admit that if there were no death, we would not exist because the evolution of animals using genetic recombination as a way of multiplying would not develop further than the single-cell creatures. Without death, genetic recombination could be not more efficient than mitosis. And animals who multiply themselves by a simple division into two don't need to die because they keep being similar after division. Without death, the only way for evolution in both cases would be a genetic mutation. And that would make genetic recombination less efficient than mitosis as first is a method with a more complicated process. And thus, one may indeed say that we pay with our death for our sex.

Actually, we may say that everything we do is motivated by one of these two major drives. One can't be without other. Or we try to survive, or we try to reproduce. That means every action taken is somehow deeply rooted to the sex or death. And what is the difference then? I have quite a theory for this. I suppose that the death drive stimulates everything that is calculable, short-planned, and more connected to material culture. That's because certain facts help you to survive. Money helps you to be a part of the society. Being a part of society is what subconsciously should be associated with survival. When you are part of the flock, your chances to survive increase. On another side, things continuous, incalculable, and connected to culture are more driven by the reproduction. For example, when a woman is young, she listens to Britney Spears, but when she gets pregnant, she may start preferring Mozart as Baroque music is good for the fruit of her womb. That is what magazines say. And that is why despite the fact that most of the people seem to prefer someone like Lady Gaga to classical pieces, a pregnant woman fifty years from now might listen to Mozart being unaware of any contemporary pop performer. Thus saying it rude, material culture is more connected to death, immaterial to sex.

Different emotions are stimulating us for actions. We need emotions to make us act because we don't know what the outcome will be. We only suggest it. Some emotions are quite negative. Others are pleasing. Those that are negative stimulate our survival. Things like stress and fear. The pleasing emotions are more connected to the reproduction. But that's a model thing because it is really hard to separate one from another as these two elements are deeply intertwined. The reason why we have these two sets of emotions is a matter of time. We can be stimulated to do something when we expect that this something will help us to avoid pain. But for nature, there is no other way to stimulate us to do things that are beyond our lifetime than with something pleasing. It should be something that we would like to experience right now, something extremely attractive. Like the endorphins.

And on another side, that means we need to involve into some reproduction-driven matter to be provided with the endorphins. We need to manifest our individuality, but it's not about earning too much money. Yes, to receive these endorphins we need to have some level of safety, some level of comfort. But still it doesn't mean more money – more happiness all the way. Many famous and rich people lived rather unhappy years when being rich and famous.

A problem of our society if regarded this way, is not that we act via the conventional motivations, but in fact that we have our death and sex motivations imbalanced. Our death drive exceeds our sex drive as our space for anything is limited. Our material culture exceeds our immaterial culture's ability to support it. We live in a time when in the western world there is an evident excess of the material culture. That's why we have so many problems with things like the ecology, education, and sex. Everything that has a strong immaterial side and needs long-term planning. If you look closely, our tower of Babel, despite looking like some organ from a distance, appears to be a giant electric vibrator. And it demands that we all or enjoy it or simulate that we enjoy it. Didn't you notice that everything that is shown on the TV including shows and commercials looks like an imitation of an orgasm?

One may try to escape the tower in search of Eden. And Eden is a position of balance in between sex and death.
The closeness of death and sex like the two principal elements of a life circle raises some interesting questions. Being closer to the death are we more motivated to fulfill our sexual destiny? Do we become eager for sex when we know there is danger around? It is possibly something like this. It is essential that the oxytocin produced during interaction into a human body is effective against aggression when endorphin works well against stress. And maybe there is something else. We know that many insects, for example, spiders, have a strong probability to be eaten after they have sex. Some females of insects may eat their males after the process is finished. Actually, one should not overestimate the risk of male as in such cases this insect has not a lot of time to live after his mission is fulfilled. The process of self-destruction is automatically switched on after a successful interaction. And thus it is not that important whether he will be eaten or not. But then it means that paradoxically such insect searches to finish his life cycle in order to begin another one.
And probably the human beings do keep this ability to search for fulfillment of their natural desires when even risking their lives. And that is also may explain

why man can be not that fearful to play the games with the dangerous but sexy woman like the lead character from the Basic Instinct movie. Of course, it is only the film and reality is different. But there should be at least a reason why so many men like such movies and such heroines. No matter how real the danger is, that may attract just if man or woman is on the way to fulfilling the sexual destiny prescribed by the Mother Nature.

Sex also in its workings helps nature to link us to her needs. We keep doing what nature wants from us no matter how far our civilization goes. It is no matter how high the Towers of Babel grow, nature is still able to stand higher just being in the basis for everything. In the ecstasy of love, on its top of excitement, we may feel to be immortal. Maybe it is only for an instant, but that happens. At this moment our sex drive overcomes the death drive, and we forget we can die. And thus we believe that we are somehow immortal. At least, in our kids. But the truth is that nature is immortal, and we are just people.

Dec, 13
from Dictaphone Record
by Martin

I will tell this record slowly, trying to remember every feeling and thought I had. Today was the day when I had an audience with an object I became obsessed with. I arrived at her home by taxi, and soon I was permitted to enter the internal area behind the fence. I still didn't feel that there was at least someone to care about security and I expected to meet her face-to-face. I expected us to have a private talk. It's a pity I could not record our talk like we did with Susan. I could only talk to her about things that she approved. She decided what we could talk about. But that is her right entirely. No one should disclose what she doesn't want to.

As I was approaching an entrance door of a house, I began to understand what a nice luxurious villa it was. I would not say that I saw something too big or grotesque, to the contrary, it was laconic and stylish. But I am sure that this is an expensive piece of architecture. I felt uncertainty when standing in front of the door. I still expected I could find myself in a trap. But I wanted this interview. And I wanted it now no matter what. Maybe this woman is able to make you feel her power. And I don't know whether it is her beauty or it is her smarts. And sometimes it seems to me that it is some sort of scent coming from her like a soft trace of her deep and complex individuality.

As I entered, I felt even more respect. Those things should belong to some stylish owner. Soon she appeared. She approached me and told me I could feel myself at home. And also she informed me that there was no one but two of us. I took off my coat, and we went to a room where we could talk. There was a lovely sofa. And the coffee was waiting for us. And there was one thing that almost hit me. In the middle of the wall, there was a photograph. I couldn't do anything but pay attention to it. Probably my gaze became fixed on it for a couple of seconds. And she undoubtedly noticed it, but for a while she made it seem like she didn't. I knew that there was plenty of questions I had to ask her. But the truth was that I didn't know how to start. And that was not because she made me feel uneasy or scared. She was completely different than Mr. Shadow. So, probably I couldn't begin, precisely because she was very nice to me. She radiated soft womanhood. There was something beautiful about a delicate melancholy in her eyes.

We started to talk about things that didn't have anything to do with the matter I wanted to discuss with her. I let it be. It is one thing to move fast when you know how to do things when the situation is a usual one, but this wasn't a usual talk. I decided that would be OK to talk about nothing to just break the ice. I thought I would wait and when feeling ready I would turn talk to the matter.

Surprisingly... we were talking about the geometrics among other things. We discussed the beauty and beautiful things. I didn't immediately notice that the time floated faster than I felt it. She was talking, and it was interesting to listen to her. She encouraged me to join a discussion and I at first started to make some notions and then I was talking more and more. Now I understand that she is not only a lovely talker but also a great listener. Now I know that I enjoyed telling her about my ideas on a subject. Probably that was sort of trap. She made a thing go in the direction I didn't plan to occur. Finally, she recognized my keen interest for a big photograph on the wall. She explained to me what was pictured there.

She said this still presented something like replica for a composition of Lady Godiva's image by John Collier. What I saw was a beautiful woman with quite a thin body sitting on the horse. And her long curled hairs were streaming over her back. I noticed that it had to be an expensive art piece. She said it is not expensive, but it is dear to her. She said she only paid to model because she actually made this photograph. She said she adores this image by John

Collier. In her opinion, it is probably one of the best erotic masterpieces ever. She noticed that even with that salary she had, it was impossible to buy anything like the actual Lady Godiva, but if even she had that money and picture would be on sale she would not like to buy it. Things like that should not be the property of a single person, but they should be available for all nations and for all ages as she explained it. Real art is more than just a property. It's the joy it brings. That was surprising to find an artist in this delicate woman who still made an impression of a strong person able to get what she wants when she wants something. She has certain charms taking such different forms.

When we finished our discussion of the photograph featuring a beautiful young woman on the horse, I still felt myself enjoying talking to her. I still couldn't find a comfortable possibility to get what I wanted from the very beginning. And then she decided to continue discussion of the beautiful and led me to another room to show me something. As I entered the room, I saw that there was another sofa similar to the one I saw in the previous room. Also, there were bookshelves which contents I didn't recognize immediately, and there was another artwork having a central place in the composition of the room. I wouldn't be surprised if it were a statue of a beautiful woman, but instead, it was a painting. It hung on the back surface of a bookcase. It was rather big and rectangular. And its shape was long. Its height was something like one and a half meter. The picture was not a usual one, and I didn't realize what it took for its model. Actually, I didn't realize it until she told me. What was painted there was a Playboy spread. It was nothing but the image of miss October 1993 by the name of Jenny McCarthy took from Playboy pages and painted with a very little difference from the actual spread. Jenny McCarthy is not that famous everywhere as she is in the States. But the fact that she is mostly a nationwide star doesn't mean you can fail to recognize her twenty-year-old looks that were photographed more than twenty years ago.

She explained to me that she ordered this painting because she likes this spread and because Jenny McCarthy is her favorite Playboy model ever. She is cool. And her legs are great. Do you agree? In the nineties, things were different than now, maybe because it was a time of changes. And there was the whole bunch of the shining blondes defining the image of epoch's sexuality. There were Silvstedt, Anderson, and others. And they were probably even a little more perfect than Jenny. But they were colder. And Jenny McCarthy was never that cold. No matter that many people feel like being colder makes you look cooler. McCarthy hadn't only the shine of her looks, but also an internal shine she expressed in her smile and in the way she did things. And also, Helen noted that though she never met her in person it seems like now at her age, miss October 1993 is still that kind of a great woman. Of course, she is older. And of course, the nineties would never be back. And as she underlined the epic meaning of the nineties with this phrase, melancholy in her eyes gave its soft sparkle of sensitivity. And then she also told me that despite the fact that many people dream of a time machine for very different purposes, the only thing worth to use it for her is to go back to 1992 and to make love to Jenny McCarthy.

I liked her recent saying as it seemed to me that it was a sort of mild joke and at the same time had some wisdom in it. I gave her my opinion on why people want to have a time machine in possession. I told her about reflection and other stuff. I said that we always want what we have not. And that is true that probably if we had a time machine, it wouldn't save us because then we would still want more. So, that is very smart indeed that all you can do is to get some pleasure and all other things are not that important. It seemed to me that she listened with interest when of course, I couldn't know what was going on in her head. And I also paid great attention to the picture of her favorite Playboy model in return. And it is indeed a beautiful image. It is one thing to say that it is a great masterpiece, and I am not saying, but it is beautiful.

For sure, it wasn't anything like what was painted by the Pre-Raphaelites or by the masters of Renaissance, but no matter that was something. The picture portrayed a young girl who wore her Catholic school uniforms offhandedly. And uniforms covered her back and didn't cover her breasts, belly, and long beautiful legs. Her long legs seemed so beautiful that even their knees seemed beautiful. She stood supporting herself with a vintage field-hockey stick, thus bending a little aside. Room on the picture was filled with some vintage sports equipment, and there was a lancet window in the background to complete the image of the traditional college. Model tried to smile, but instead of looking happy she looked a little shy. I noted to Helen that it is indeed an image of a young, beautiful woman who looks so natural somehow and that creates a great feeling about her. I also noted that this shy smile is probably the best thing in the picture. That was probably a crucial element of being natural. There is nothing surprising that the girl who looks a little shy may seem to be more natural than the one expressing as much joy as she only can. I even noted that the shyness by its meaning in the picture maybe is regarded as something similar to a gesture of delicate shame on the picture of Venus by Botticelli. Probably John

Collier's original featuring Lady Godiva bears something the same. Something that is also present in the photograph which I saw in another room. Of course, those pictures are epic and dramatic in a different way than the image of Jenny McCarthy, but still this shy smile of hers being part of human behavior makes some bound in between nature of flesh and human nature of the model similarly to great paintings of the past. Helen supported my opinion, and I told her that though I am not a great expert on the matter, I would choose Jenny McCarthy to be my favorite erotic model too. To this moment it seemed like we found a lot in common about us, together with many things that were different but that only made these different features of our personalities to be more interesting and attractive in each other. And only then I noticed what contents were on the shelves. I wouldn't say for all the books there, but for sure, there were a lot of sex manuals, books about sex, books about relations and tons of Playboy magazine issues including the vintage ones of the eighties and nineties together with rare collector's editions. I noted that she should've been sort of a... collector. And she said it is her little secret fun. It is nothing special but just a little joy for a busy woman. I just like the books with beautiful illustrations. I hardly even read them. You just buy one, then a little more. And one day you may find you got quite a collection. I felt a little petrified suddenly finding my own in the middle of someone's private space. But for her, this room probably wasn't that private as it seemed to me for a couple of seconds, despite the fact that this one had even more of erotic flavor than one that belonged to Lady Godiva. I thought that probably she was indeed a woman who could make love to another woman. And also it was clear that she could have some soft inclination to exhibitionism, but not that sort of exhibitionism as Susan's.

I needed her to reveal her secrets to me, and she hid them perfectly, giving me access to the intimate spaces of her life, what made me feel that she was open to me, decreasing my struggle to disclose her. We spent, at least, more than an hour talking about nothing. And that was pleasing, but that was not my aim there. Finally, I just needed to tell her. You know that I am here not to discuss the beauty of Jenny McCarthy. No matter that you are indeed the most beautiful companion, Helen. I don't know why I said beautiful because I could say interesting. Indeed that was what I meant. And I continued preparing myself to insist. You know that I would like to know what probably you would not like to tell too many people. I just want to note that I have a source that will give me any information on the matter and I am not here to know it. I am here to have your version of the events. I don't know how I managed to be even that tough with that woman. She made me like her. So smoothly. And I felt more and more of it with every next moment of what was supposed to be an interview. She went to a window and turned her back to me probably blankly staring through the glass, like performing a cliche element from some movie. She seemed uncertain whether she would talk about it and I insisted as softly as I could. She finally made me give my word that I would not retell the story to anybody else and of course, I agreed. I said that what we had previously agreed still mattered and I had no recording device with me and would not retell a single word from our talks in her house.

And then she confessed what could be hard to believe if I would not get used to unbelievable in a current of the whole matter. She told me that she used the services of the Agency on the advice of a friend. I then interrupted her, feeling that she should've known that I knew about it. I again told her that I already have a source deeper than those who just wanted to investigate a scandal probably connected to her removal from her high position. I felt it was fair for her to know that I knew more. No matter that I didn't disclose how much I knew. But I assured her that I would not mention her name dealing with Agency, despite the fact that I couldn't guarantee the same about connecting her to activities of the corporation. I underlined the fact that what I needed was the truth about corporation she worked for, but not peculiarities of a sex scandal. She listened to me and after giving a breath out told me the rest of her story and I was afraid to interrupt her as what she was telling me was something. It was almost as good as Jenny McCarthy if you want. She told me that it is possible to say that it was that sex session that caused her removal from the corporation and at the same time it was not that, but another reason. She was inaccurate enough to choose the city apartment that she employed for additional working hours outside her office as a fun spot. She explained that this apartment was a place she used to work at nights when it was necessary. And with this most important corporation's project, it was necessary. There she kept some of her documents. And after that night of fun, one of the folders disappeared. Information stored in it became available to a third party. She understands that it was her fault, but that was hard to expect. First of all, she said she believes that those who made it had someone inside the corporation. They somehow were able to know how the actual folder looked and what it contained. Nothing else but this most important folder keeping the secrets of the most important project was stolen. And also she is almost sure that it was one of the girls. And as she explained to me how this girl looked, I got that it was Jane. She said she was not able to prove anything, but she is sure that the Agency was used for a purpose. Or even, as she supposed, Agency could be a fake. It seems too difficult to manage it, but that was a smart way to get her. And all it happened just a couple of days before the council's planned meeting. And the most important shareholders somehow knew that their asset number one was going to be available for use to a third party. Maybe it will go to the internet, free to download for everyone. And that turned the project to dust. And she was a principal person responsible for the development of the project. She was fired on the spot without receiving a golden parachute as her contract gives a possibility to shareholders to refuse it in the case when actions of an employee caused the damage to the reputation of a company. And such formulation probably was what caused the rumors connecting the matter to the sex scandal.

After she finished her story, I insisted on seeing her again. I said that I would like her to make notes if my source gives information not matching her story. She said that it is very much possible that someone who organized the entire affair may try to fool me. For example, they can try to make me believe that the Agency was a real one. Such confusion may lead me to nowhere, to a clue that won't open a single door. Keep your eye sharp. Double-check everything. At that moment I thought - was it not too difficult to manage all this stuff for stealing just a little folder from a little apartment of a big boss? And there were all these things happening to Susan... Susan. Only then I started to gather her real part in the affair. Susan is just a cute little blonde whom you can expect to fantasize too much, who when attempting lying won't show the top skills. Such girl is not able to lie well because if she tries, she will be caught immediately. And that was her part. She was supposed to tell a True Story everyone would believe. All this was staged just for her, and all she was supposed to do was to tell how great it was. But wasn't it too complicated?

I then asked Helen to tell at least approximately what the possible cost of losing this folder was. She said its cost was a number consisting at least of nine digits. And that changes a lot. Nine digits. That wasn't that complicated a way to do it.

If I have some interesting facts about the story, we can meet again. She said, she will call me when she has time.

Some Notes on Importance of Geometrics from Dictaphone Record by Martin

It is an interesting question - why do we perceive some things as beautiful ones? What is the beauty? And what are her rules? These questions were raised by so many smarter people than me without achieving any great results. That's why I wouldn't exactly dare to challenge the secrets of the universe. But again I would try to find some sort of explanation in the field of our basic instincts. Of course, I could try to talk about beauty like about a transcendent value, but that is what I will do next time. For instance, in my younger and more vulnerable years, I would describe the beauty as a sensual manifestation of the highest reason in the universe. I would mean then that the beauty somehow has a form that is in reach of a human mind and the human senses when at the same time being part of something that a human being is unable to grasp due to an evident lack of cognitive capacity that is endlessly small when compared to the size of eternity. But I grew older and became more cynic and practical. And thus I would prefer to search for any reliable answers into an area of material sciences dealing with mathematics, human

behavior, and with sex in particular.
As we know the art is a sphere of human activity trying to deal with the laws of the beautiful. Art tries to grasp the beauty, and in opposition to a science, it uses methods of intuition, but not the empiric ones. And also we are taught by Freud that a masterpiece is a result of sublimation. And that behind it there is some sexual intention. And thus beauty in arts should have a connection to how we define beauty in a person who may theoretically become our sex partner. How does this fact influence the art?
When I look at the contemporary art, I sometimes wonder what people find in it. For instance, there can be a green stool with the label saying that it is indeed nothing but a green stool. And that is the thing that may be considered a masterpiece. That means that someone bought this stool in the IKEA store, then put a vast amount of green paint on it. And that is why a person should buy a ticket to New York and then, probably after spending time in queue, buy a ticket to something like the Guggenheim museum only to see a green stool. If this person were me, who then would I be? Maybe I exaggerate a little, but that is what the modern art seems to me sometimes. Something I can't feel. And art is what you should feel. Maybe I am so unique and don't see the obvious things, but I don't believe in the art based on concepts. I am not sure that the

concepts should be its primal element. Yes, I suppose for art, it is better to be a form of sexual manifestation. And there should be two parts of it. One part is more subjective, and another is more objective one. That means that artist manifests his internal impulse that somehow has almost absolute quality and on another side, the artist does it in a very personal way creating something unique. Without uniqueness, there is no sexual attractiveness, and thus there is no beauty in the art without it as we believe that the art is this sort of impulse.

That is why it is not natural to take concepts created by someone else for your art piece. It should be something indeed more like the intuition than math. But almost paradoxically, this intuition is one trying to read the transcendent mathematics of beauty. Maybe I am becoming irrational for an instant, but I would say that I have my intuitive ideal for the essence of beauty in arts. My opinion is that the nature of beauty in the art should tend to the art of beauty in nature. When of course, it is not the art completely, when it is a product of nature. And artist then should not go to another extreme. I mean art still should have its artificial element. On one side it should be based on nature, but on another, it should be the result of the human efforts and thus being able to reflect a human personality. And thus there should be two opposing elements forming a binary combination. And they are the objective element presenting the omnipotent power of nature and the subjective element representing an individuality of the artist. That is the major difference of human beauty - including the beauty of arts - from the beauty of nature. One can take a beautiful girl and make photographs of her as she enjoys the streams of a waterfall when being nude. That should be indeed very beautiful, but that is not the art because most of the merit will be on the side of nature which created this waterfall and this beautiful body of the girl. A photographer has to invent something not only unusual but also some aesthetic way of photo shooting to become an artist in this situation.

For example, there are two erotic images that evolve a strong feeling of contemplation in me. They both carry a great amount of the beautiful in my view. They are Lady Godiva by John Collier and Playboy October 1993 spread featuring Jenny McCarthy. But only one of these images is the piece of art in its essence. John Collier's work, featuring a delicate young woman sitting nude on a horse that seems to make a sharp contrast to her frailness with its massive figure. In this work, Collier pictured not only a frail, beautiful body but also the frail feelings that are his subjective view. There is a universal idea of the fragile quality of the beauty. In case of young

Jenny McCarthy, I may say that this girl has the beauty that is equal to the highest artistic aesthetics. But still most what we enjoy in this picture of hers is a creation of nature. That could be said that in this case, a photographer made certain effort to create an interesting environment placing this beautiful girl into a room that serves as some sports items store in a Catholic school. And that is true. This environment is better than usual Playboy's way to picture a girl on the bed in some motel, but it is not that enough. Miss October 1993 Jenny McCarthy of Chicago contains in her looks as much beauty as any great masterpiece. But she is not an artistic masterpiece because she is the natural one. And thus I would define two extreme kinds of masterpieces that are both not artworks in some meaning. They are the amazing creation of nature like a waterfall and pseudo-beautiful creation of the human concepts. First one is not art masterpiece because it has no any human influence and the second one is not an art masterpiece because it has no trace of nature. One isn't artificial, and another is too artificial to be an art piece. If we don't follow the trace of nature, we lose the presence of beauty. And that is why I despise a so-called modern art because I would prefer to spend fifty bucks to buy miss October 1993 spread than fifty thousand to buy a green stool no matter that both things are not exactly masterpieces. At least, beautiful woman is something like a natural masterpiece in case we see the Nature as a master. Today, artists create too much of abstractions, and that looks like that they found nothing and they know nothing about what they want to find themselves. Artists of previous ages mostly portrayed the women and foods. Of course, there was also some stuff like horses and countryside. But still, there were women both dressed and undressed together with clusters of grapes among other fruits. Those guys knew what they wanted. They recognized their natural intentions and didn't disguise them under cover of pretentious concepts. Beauty may be regarded as a subjective concept of humans as animals do not experience it, but on another side, it appears inside human when a human looks at nature. And it can't be another way. A human being can't beat the nature in the creation of beauty, exactly because human is able to create anything like this only when following the natural path. We would never create a masterpiece more beautiful than a beautiful woman. And true is that when we adore an art masterpiece, we adore its author, and we adore her sexuality that was transformed into this art masterpiece through the process of sublimation. No matter how conventional the artistic beauty seems, it still can't exist outside beauty of nature, because there is no beauty except beauty. Indeed it is not that

conventional as we taught sometimes.
In universities, they may teach that the beauty comes from human culture because human beings not only discovered but probably created its rules if we consider that the beauty is a conventional creation. But the beauty is not a conventional item to that extent only because it is not available for animals. For instance, there are birds that can fly and there are animals that can't fly, but that doesn't mean that the ability to fly is not natural for the birds. As our primary natural destination is the reproduction, then we should recognize the beauty when choosing sex partner, if we regard an issue from the standpoint of the evolutionary process.
And again as beauty in arts has a natural ground that may mean that the initial kind of beauty should have some similar aspects. For example, it also has two parts - subjective and objective. And thus an objective component of beauty is what should be common for entire kind. That should be something that affects anybody. And then, the subjective component should be something connected to the individuality of a person.
There was pretty interesting research performed by the Toronto University stuff. They tried to investigate a facial attractiveness of human being. They measured the facial proportions of Jessica Alba taking this actress as a model for a beautiful face and

then compared them to the average proportions of many other people's faces. Those people's digital photographs they put into a memory of the computer for processing. It happened that the average proportions of millions were similar to those of a beauty model. Thus it says that our subconscious perceives the median facial proportions as beauty. It is interesting that our subconsciousness is able to perform such intricate mathematical calculations comparing the proportions of any face we see with the median proportions of all humanity. Of course, we can't know the looks of all seven billion people of the world. And we can't consciously know how a human face can look in all variations of the genetic code. But probably our subconscious is able to find a golden ratio creating a central line across diapason of all possible genetic combinations. Or our mind draws the median using the images of all faces we saw in our life. Actually, of course, it should be something very difficult, but there is still a sense in it.

So, it is possible that many of us are wrong about nature in us. We are often taught that without culture given us by the society, we will become nothing but another stupid animal. That undoubtedly has a point in it, but such extreme valuing of culture and thus denying the value of nature comes from the opposition of society to nature. Society teaches us that without it we won't possess any kind of beauty.

Median proportions are the thing that tells us that a person possessing them is one who has a higher probability of having the better genes and thus is a probable mother or a father of healthier kids. And it is known thanks to the research that a human being reacts more to beautiful proportions of a face than those of a body. Maybe that is because in recent thousands of years we more often hide our bodies under cover of clothes when our face is usually open. Our subconsciousness tries to read genes of a probable sex partner via her or his looks. What advantage does a person have if having the median genes? A person with median genes is the result of a certain behavior of recent generations in his or her genetic line. When people don't travel too much to find their mate, then the similar genetic compositions start to dominate in their area. And they develop some certain peculiar elements in their looks and in their genes that are not at the median line. And that draws them out of the golden ratio. But if generations of people from one genetic line searched for mates that are different to them, that might be probably of another nationality or just somehow belong to another genetic group of humanity, they behaved like the strong searchers. And thus they behaved according to their strong

biological motivations. Group inclined to travel is in many cases a biologically stronger one than a static group. Remember about birds crossing miles in their annual migrations.
It is vital that a beautiful person is not just the one with a smaller chance of having kids with a genetic illness. For example, hemophilia that is the sex-determined illness. Such chance grows when people form couples with similar genes. But it is also vital that a beautiful person has a strong probability of being a result of the proper biological behavior of ancestors. Nature wants us to make the fusion mixes. That is because this way it grows a variety inside the confines of the kind. And sex as a way of reproduction is in general about variety. Wider variety increases chances to survive in case of the dramatic changes of environment and also it increases the speed of evolution giving to the kind the higher ability of adaptation.
If variety is that important for the kinds using genetic recombination as a way of multiplication, then it may bring the link to individuality and the subjective side of the beauty. Something objective may seem to be the result of combining the multiple subjective elements. Then subjectively humans are inclined to behave in such way that increases chances for healthier and more beautiful descendants.

It's interesting that for nature, individuality is absolutely necessary as an objective thing.

That is why we may like the people with exotic looks. We prefer to choose not only a beautiful person but also one who is very different from us. Differences in looks and behavior tell about a possible difference in genes. Nature would prefer us to form the unions with the biggest possible genetic difference. That is what should benefit the entire kind. Most probably a white European man may prefer a beautiful Asian woman to European woman of same beauty if motivated by his biology, but not by the advice of his mother. But that's only in a model situation.

Similarly, that approach may explain why gentlemen prefer blondes. On one side, European women choose to dye their hair so often that the blondes should not have a special status of uniqueness. But it is not a question of how many blonde women there are, but it is a question of how many blonde men exist in the population. The thing is that the blonde genes are rare and that is why for many who do not possess them they are attractive on a subconscious level. Twenty-five thousand years ago a group of humans went north showing an extreme motivation for the widening of areal. They most probably suffered massive losses as it was difficult to survive in Northern Europe that period of history. But they gained the specific features of their genetic code

including some genetic mutations together with their looks. Their genes were determined by the need to live in the area of cold air and limited sun radiation. And thus in reward for their effort for widening the human areal their descendants have a unique genetic code that differs even in the range of European ethnic groups.
And that is why the mass culture has chosen a blonde as hair color for many classic celebrities.

Dec, 14
from Dictaphone Record
by Martin

I opened one more envelope. And again I think about things that made me act in a way Mr. Shadow told me to do. Now I don't feel like I was afraid. Maybe indeed I liked the current of the story that much that I didn't want it to stop. And this envelope should not be the end of it, but it can be the door to the final act of this story. Will I feel pity if the story ends? Maybe that can happen if I will find the truth and at the same time, I will find it to be more trivial than I expected. Or maybe I will need to accept something that will not look good enough to be a real truth as truth for my documentary because I need to tell people something.

I expected that I might find something surprising again in this envelope. And what I found was indeed surprising. That is because I could not expect the envelope to prove Helen's doubts, her suggestions. She is indeed a brilliant woman and probably with some intuition too. But envelope told me that she was right in almost everything she suspected, and that's unusual. She said she felt that the entire Agency was a fake thing and I doubted that because that could be too difficult. On another side, I

doubted my own doubt - and that's quite normal to me - because in the affair with nine digits sum involved there can be almost nothing too tricky or too strange.
And what my source told me, carefully explaining every step of this extraordinary sex affair, is in general next few facts. First of all, there was no any Agency. Actually, I suspected something from the very beginning but couldn't catch the trail of fake. And as Susan told me more and more with all the enthusiasm she possesses, I was becoming surer that the most of it had to be true. I expected only some minor facts to be a result of Susan's fantasy and some sort of naive and unconscious exaggeration. That happens to many emotional storytellers who feel that their stories are interesting for their listeners. And Susan made me - and probably Elise too - listen with great interest. First of all, no matter true or not, these stories were at least peculiar, and at their best, they were definitely exciting with their sex element and intriguing with their unexpected turns. Susan seems to be a lovely naive girl with very moderate egocentrism, and I always couldn't guess what she would tell next time. That is true, but to suspect something you need to have a reason for it. You need to see some motive. When a billionaire husband dies, and all his properties go to his wife you may suspect her to be a murderer as she

benefited from event greatly. Of course, most wives are honest, and most of them have honest grieves, but at least you may suspect in depth of your mind. But how could I suspect that someone performed such difficult combinations only to please honest little Susan? And the truth is that indeed all that was done exactly with this aim - to please Susan. And that's an interesting point in the story. Someone hired a pack of professional escort girls to perform this entire contemporary play about sex school for a curious young lady unable to suspect there can be something wrong. Something can't be so wrong when it is so good. Or maybe, something can't be too wrong when it is too good. The whole trick could fail if there could be someone like me as an object. But maybe I exaggerate my rationality. But Susan is nothing like me, no matter. She would not suspect someone only because this someone pleased her in any possible way. And it looks like I am a different case of a suspicious person. I kept my hidden but strong sexual intentions toward Susan finally being able to keep my journalist ethics with me when not being seduced by her. And she was really nice to me without any doubt. And I feel another way about Helen. She who keeps being cold and defensive toward me personally, but who keeps being interesting and charming as much as possible in general, becomes a primal element of my night dreams easily replacing any wishes about Susan from my mind and my heart. Susan is a wonder, no doubt, but Helen is a sort of magician. And that promises that she can do wonders in lots.

And also she has a great amount of mystery around her. I remember how shadows were playing around her beautiful body on that video.

And now, returning to the question of sex academy that was indeed a show performed by a bunch of hired sex professionals, I would say that according to information provided by my generous source - on whose account I still have doubts too - center element of all this game was Jane. It is more correct to say that it was a girl who called herself that, as all of them hardly used their real names. And also all of them didn't know each other before all that began. I also would note that I called Susan today and asked her whether she could show me an agreement she signed with the Agency about which she once told me, and she said she would try to find it. She promised that she would deliver it to me as soon as possible, even most probably today. And she indeed came to my place today, and I almost got ready to get surprised, but instead, she explained that she couldn't find the paper anywhere. She said she remembered where it should've been, at least, in what area of her apartment, but she no matter failed to find it. And thus she only came to tell me this and to check whether I had any questions to ask. And all we did - we drank coffee and talked about nothing for an hour or more. That was quite pleasing, and I went to a point where I felt I could tell her that I would make love to her with great pleasure if she wanted it, but only when the job is over - as James Bond used to think about it. I just couldn't let myself try it now. I can't judge for Susan whether she would want it or not, but it looked like a possible thing at least. Maybe now I am more interested in Helen than in Susan. And that's all. That is why I needed to make her feel like I was busy with the documentary features. But it looks like I gave her a certain feeling that she can come to me to have a good time whenever she wants. Some other day. Yes, there are always so many other things you can do another day because another day is not today.

And today I think about Helen. I think how this smart woman with all her intuition could get into such a mess. Everyone can get unlucky. But at least she kept some of her money and this luxurious villa. Maybe she will soon sell it. What does she feel now? Being that tough and that smart, then she happens to be a scapegoat in someone's game. That should be... That shouldn't be pleasing. They fooled her, and they fooled Susan even more than her to make Sue tell the story that would lead anybody in the opposite direction from the truth. Probably we often believe

in what we want to believe ignoring the purest truth placed in front of our noses. And we want sex. That is so common for us.
Helen wanted little of fancy sex and some adventure. And same did Susan no matter that they are the two most different women I ever met. And then there is someone representing the corporation that is the major competitor of Helen's ex-employer and that I would call the Corporation B. And then this someone carefully prepares and gets what he wants in a first attempt getting into a sacred business apartment where Helen keeps some of her employer's secrets. And then - boom. As the secret project is not secret, then the Corporation A - that is how I would call Helen's employer - should shut the project, or should start the secret talks with Corporation B which in turn may probably lead to reshaping the spheres of market influences. Now I don't know why, but I can't think of anything, but this tennis game they made to impress Susan. This is it - game, set and match. And someone earned great money. That would be interesting to know how great a single payment for the modern corporate espionage expert can be. And again reviewing all the facts available I agree with Helen that there most probably was someone inside the Corporation A working for the competitor. She told me that she suspected that.
I can't wait to see her again as they say. I feel I really

need to see her again, at least, I should try to get more details about how it all happened and what she feels indeed about it all. I would like to know what her feelings are.

Dec, 17
Day
from Dictaphone Record
by Martin

She called me last night and told we could meet if I would have time for it. She said today it would be OK. I couldn't go to her place in the morning, just because I was busy. I needed to talk to people from one of our investors. You can't avoid such meetings and such talks. Those who give you money make you depend on them. But as soon as I was free, I called her. It was late in the day, and I thought she might change her plans. But she said that would be OK. She mentioned that she would be occupied with one of her hobbies, but I could come to see her.

She picked me up on one of the streets. She drove her cool red vintage car. I was quite impressed. Again. She said it's not a real vintage car, but only a replica of a classic model. It has cool vintage looks, but it's contemporary machine on the side of technology. And it has an electric drive engine. That's good for ecology. I enjoyed just being close to that woman. She has her delicate superiority around her. Some inner elegance that floats about everything she does.

We arrived at some place located far from the

business center. I wondered what she meant by this. She took a big black bag from a car's trunk. She said I could help her. If I don't mind, I can be her assistant today. I said yes, I don't mind. We entered an abandoned building. And in the area, there are many as it seems. Inside it felt clean and white. Surprisingly, there was an old-fashioned white bathtub. And there was water in it. Also, there were lights, white vertical surface, white stools, and white table.

I carried her bag inside. And as she started to unpack it, I saw how she got some several unexpected items out of it. There were a bathrobe, towel, white shirt, white female shoes, boxes with jewelry, camera. Shoes had high heels. Jewelry was Tiffany. Camera was a pro photo camera.

We then stood there silently. She put the things on the table. I didn't know what to ask. It seemed like she was going to make a photo shoot. I almost wanted to make a joke about a tub in the center of a big empty room. But I had no guts for anything as it looks. She said that jewelry, clothes, and bathrobe were not for her. She was waiting for a model. She should arrive soon. That's why we are waiting.

A couple of minutes passed, and we heard how a taxi parked close to the building. Someone slammed the door and was heading there. Soon a young woman came in. Beautiful woman. She looked like someone who could have a name like Frida or Elsa. She actually had the purely Scandinavian looks. Blue eyes and blonde hair. And a very cute face. She seemed to have a most delicate body. The looks of a deer from a northern fairy-tale. Actually, later Helen told me that indeed she came from Sweden. And now she tries to make a career in our country.

What was going on then, made me rather embarrassed. I didn't give too much help to Helen while she was photographing a beautiful Swedish model. The process appeared to be quite intimate as it felt to me. First of all, a lady took off her jeans, shirt, sneakers, and lingerie. Actually everything. And then she puts on only this white shirt with buttons and white shoes with high heels. And she did it right here, just leaning on the table's edge. She indeed seemed to be a pro. Undressed with no embarrassment. And that type of behavior when a person doesn't express any emotions. Like a pro.

I was only one who felt a little uneasy, despite the fact that a display was most elegant and softly erotic. Helen kept shooting the girl while she changed poses. And finally, Helen asked her to take off her still unbuttoned shirt. Then she made some more shots. And then, the model - following Helen's request - lied into a tub with her shoes on. She just had her legs over the tub. And the white shoes and the white heels were above everything.

When a photo shoot was over, I helped Helen to pack. She said I needed to call a taxi. She will drive a model home, not me. I said sure it's OK. And she drove off with the Swedish lady by her side. And I waited for a taxi.

I remember how this pro model started to dress up. She used a towel and then put on everything the same silent and regular pro way she undressed. That was the only minute when I was able to start a conversation with Helen about the matter. In general, I didn't really get anything new. Interesting is that she said she made her own little investigation. No details now. And she didn't find the major answers. But she has something interesting. Not a lot, but it's interesting. I asked - didn't she think it all was too complicated? She said people just underestimate the possibility of the things only imagined to become true. What someone imagines may become true. When even it seems quite impossible. Things like these no matter happen. You just need to be lucky enough to see them turn true, irregular as they are. Such things happen in their secret and fragile reality. Some places. Some times.

Dec, 19
from Dictaphone Record
by Martin

This time we met at an apartment. It was located in the prestigious area. And I didn't recognize what place it was. She called me last night. And we decided we might exchange some information. I collected some stuff I got. That includes some of the videos and my lists of people from corporate personnel. I suppose that whoever gave me videos he wouldn't mind me showing few of them just to build a communication with the principal witness. And no matter she is the one who received the blow in the case. And my lists consisted mostly of people who could be involved in the case. I just tried to figure out who could have an interest in the matter.
And well... I stood there in some apartment. There were shelves and books and stuff. Like furniture. And style was nice and laconic. I couldn't get why it all felt so familiar. And then I saw the spyglass on one of the shelves. And I got it then. It is that same apartment where the things happened. She kept it.
She said that this apartment she used to store all the stuff of her little investigation. She didn't get any real clues. But she has something that may lead somewhere. If we will have some luck. She said we

and I liked it. She said she knows me a little better now and maybe she feels she can trust me. That was why she would show me what she found.

That woman. She impressed me again. Her lists appeared not only to be longer. They were better developed. She found much of information about people who were high in the stuff in any of two corporations. She also collected some information about the top personnel belonging to another firm. Actually, on the market, there are three major players. I asked whether she really thinks a scheme could be even more complicated. Could this third corporation, Corporation C, to be another participant of events? She said it is possible. Who knows? You need to check everything you can check. She has no evidence, but she made a profile.

She said there are some facts to be taken into account. There is the rumor that the Corporation B received the folder by mail. And then they were not able to prove they were not linked to the matter. But those who really paid to the spies most probably kept only the copies. They probably will try to use the useful things from the folder little by little. And so, no one will be able to track their origin. And that's smart.

After she showed me all stuff about people from the elite of the industry, she also demonstrated me one more peculiar thing. She said she was able to track

that some girls who were with her in this apartment actually worked for the same business unit. Susan and Jane. She didn't try to meet them in person. For a reason. That's a wrong way. There is no need to appear in the stories again. I think you understand.
Sure I do.
She tried to find Jane through another person. She was careful. And then she bribed her and got some details. But Jane, it seems, knew only a part of the truth. And she knew nothing important. Someone behind the thing organized it all. Smoothly. Every performer knew her role, but nothing else. Almost all she gained from Jane was some several scenarios they used for their games. And that's not much. She tried to find any clues in these texts, but there were no any.
And about Susan. She found a video that shed some light on her past. Actually, it was Jane who pointed to it. A short movie was available at some web-platform selling the porn and softcore via subscription.
Well, to tell it shorter, she launched her laptop, and we both watched some extracts from it. She just clicked on some points of the timeline to make me see a picture in general. In this video, two girls were pretending to be superheroes as they wore some sort of cosplay suits. One of them was most probably a professional porn actress, and the another was... It

was Susan.
So, I asked Helen whether she thought it meant something. I said it probably meant that someone tried Susan for a thing like this to be sure then that she would manage. Helen agreed. Yes, most probably. But actually, it could be even easier. Maybe someone exactly involved her knowing that the girl had such an experience by her own will. In this video, you know, she doesn't naturally make love to another girl. But they make enough of caresses. That means she was OK with things like that.
At that moment, Susan's previously super sexy image started to vanish somehow. I didn't feel it for her anymore. Not that much. She became something like a regular softcore model to me. Not something so intriguing anymore. Softcore models are cool usually, but... I don't know. Actually, I thought that all these tennis-and-stars games were needed as some performance staged for Susan. And now it seems like they double-checked everything. And also they needed to make the thing as believable as possible. And Helen agreed. Yes, there was only one real object in all that performance.
Then I felt it was my turn. And I ventured to show her a piece of footage that was made in this apartment as I supposed. I played it on my phone as I still follow an agreement with my source. In

general. And I explained it to her. I need to follow the ethics. She said she understands. The deal is deal. I am glad you are showing me this. I couldn't stand looking at her legs then. Indeed, lovely legs she has. She noticed my glance I think, but she didn't show it.

She said then that she had to suspect it. They were much smarter. They had surveillance. Watching her every step. Probably her computer was hacked. I asked her about a so-called insight. Did she permit to do such thing? She said no. She wouldn't allow such thing. Who would?

I also asked her about where they could have a breach big enough that gave me a chance to be provided with all these files I got. My source is someone who used this breach. What could it be? She said that question is a very interesting one. She will think about it.

Finally, we drank some coffee before I left. We then chatted about random stuff. And she was most pleasing. Soft, charming, sophisticated. She is a very charming woman.

Dec, 20

Private Audio Diary of Elise

by Elise

Today I saw one more peculiar dream. I was looking through the window of some house. A window was big, and I could see a forest that stood close to the house. At some moment, a beautiful deer appeared from it. He stared at the house, stayed freeze for a while. And then the deer ran away. And then, snow fell. And then I woke up.

That was another day when I hadn't much to do about my job. I did in general what I was supposed to do for today and then decided I could leave earlier. That's because Martin wasn't there. He called me later and explained something about why he is not always there. He said these days he is occupied a little more and that's why.

Suddenly we also talked about some cultural stuff. Right on the phone. He asked me whether I knew who Lady Godiva was. I said yes, I know. Then he asked me what I thought of her story. How this story ends? She rides away for good? Or is it just an accidental ride? Sure, things must change after that. Is there a happy end? And also he was talking about Tom, one that was peeping. Is his end that bad? What version of the story is more probable? One where he dies or one where there is no damage to any possible spectators? Also, he said that when Lady leaves the tower, she also can end not that well. The tower may be charmed somehow. If it's Godiva – then she survives, but if it is Lady of Shalott, then she may die in the end. Godiva can lose her cloth and Lady of Shalott can't. I was like – What? Shallot? Some onion? But later I googled it, and now I know it was another legendary person. And then if there is Lancelot, the lady dies, the knight survives. And what if there's Cleopatra? Then Tom can be definitely executed by her. And also he said that Lolita most probably will manage rather well because her infantile state is close to some innocence. She is pretty and kinky, but that's somehow not her fault. But then in this story, Humbert should die. But he said he prefers most the original version of Lady Godiva's legend as it is simplest and purest somehow. But in it, there are many gaps. What happens then? Whom she meets then? And so on. He said that this version is showing the Lady to be very elegant and smart. And also Lancelot shouldn't die in it. He asked me what I thought about that. I didn't know what to answer. Martin seems to go really crazy sometimes.

All those characters are very interesting for some sort of cultural analysis. But what I didn't get was how all those people could be in a single story.

Some Notes on Passion and Love from Dictaphone Record by Martin

Passion and love are often understood as similar things or two elements of the whole feeling complementing each other. On the famous picture of Botticelli portraying Venus coming from waves of the sea, the author united Flora and Boreas in one sub-composition of the artwork. Unity of these two divinities symbolizes the unity of passion and love. But the reality is not always what we want it to be. Passion and love are indeed two elements that should complement each other in the process of evolution. But what happens in a life of human beings is not what able to fit any system perfectly.

Dividing a passion from love, I would call a passion that sort of the human emotion that moves us to another person through understanding this person's sexuality. And on another side, I would call love that emotion that makes us want to stay with a person who is our desired object. And again I would note that saying love I don't mean that kind of love portrayed in romantic movies and novels. I rather mean a biological phenomenon representing the chemical reaction including the production and consumption of endorphins and oxytocin. My opinion is that such love as in movies and books represents sort of sublimation of the original biological love and thus represents sort of an art piece by itself. That also means that the most of the people are not experiencing such kind of love as it needs a special sensitivity and ability to sublimate. Here I mean the love that is sung by poetry, the love when two contemplate each other and the feelings they have like two art masters would contemplate two art pieces. And actually, love in the art deals more with loneliness than with love itself.

But biological love is indeed more available as it represents a basic chemical reaction put into a human by nature. Why do two these different emotions exist then? My guess is that the human feelings are divided by the moment of love's consummation as that is what whole this stuff is about. Nature wants us to continue evolution on Earth. My idea is that the passion is what supposed to be before the moment when a woman gets pregnant, and love is what should happen then. One may say that you don't need to have kids or to want kids to fell in love. It is true, but we don't have kids every time we make love. And actually, according to nature, sex has only one primal aim. And this aim is a reproduction.

Passion is what should happen to attract two to create a sexual union. And love is what designed to make them stay together while female needs support of male during the pregnancy and then support during the first months of a child's life. Probably most correctly, according to nature's planning, love should make its sure entrance after three months of pregnancy as at this moment a woman starts to feel a big difference. Of course, she knows about her pregnancy before, but it's at this moment the hormone levels start to increase seriously. But that's only a theoretical model.

Both passion and love link to this particular moment when the process of genetic recombination happens. But they stand on the opposing sides of the timeline. Passion is what stands before, and love is what stands after. That is why passion is more selective for beauty and love is more careless about looks and in many cases about other features of the personality too. That is because love is designed to have no choice. When everything had happened, the parents are supposed to have no choice but to try proving that this result of their genetic interaction is good enough to be a chain in the evolution. And that it is not a dead end. Regarded from this standpoint the love is a post hoc feeling. When the passion is exactly that feeling making us make a choice. Passion is a desire for beauty, as beautiful looks and other signs of sexuality tell us that a person possessing them has lesser chances for some bad genes. The role of love may also explain why in most cases the love exists years but not eternity. Love exists as long as it is necessary for a woman to have assistance in breeding the kids as they are too little to be managed easily. And similarly, the role of passion explains why this feeling can exist only one day or one night. One night is enough to express the passion but is not enough to show all of your love.

And there is a great bunch of interesting questions about love that are hardly able to be answered. Is the love that great only because it gives you that much of endorphins? But what about aftershock? When you get used to endorphins, and then their production decreases you may feel certain abstinence. And also, the love can prove to be very dangerous, more dangerous than passion. When you have problems with a woman, you may be still motivated to fight for her probably only because she fits well to be a biological mother of your kids. Or she seems to have an ability to fulfill your dreams. Love produces strong oxytocin neuromodulation that makes you think differently when passion is more like an accidental one-instant endorphin drug. So, maybe love is just a form of a stronger passion. One so big that it even can move you to challenge the object of your desire itself. There is no surprise that the world history knew more crimes committed for love than crimes committed for a passion.

Dec, 21
Evening
from Dictaphone Record
by Martin

I called her. I wanted to see her. I said I got some new thoughts. Frankly, they are not that capital but may have some effect somehow. She said OK. We can meet. But not at her place. She is now in the business center. Could I meet her there? Yes, sure I could. To my surprise, she gave me an address of her former job office. Yes, of course, I knew where the tower is. I said I would find her there. I thought whether I could meet Susan there again. Hardly, I heard she left the job.

I arrived at the place, and I saw a familiar red car there. I called her and said I was there waiting for her. She asked a favor. Could I go to where her office was to help her carry some stuff? Sure I could. It appeared that she left some things at her former office and they wanted her to move them away. No trace of Helen is supposed to be there. I used an elevator and was there. She gave me one box to carry while she took another. And there I saw another woman who seemed to be a secretary. I wasn't surprised to find one more good-looking woman near Helen. Lady was impressive. No matter that she

wore quite a formal suit and rectangular glasses. Beautiful face and the finest body.
They chatted a little. Seems like Helen knew her well before. A lady secretary said she could drive Helen to her area. She finishes soon. She now no matter goes to a fitness center, and she can drive Helen home. As we were going down in the elevator, Helen explained to me that the lady was her secretary and now she is the secretary of a person who replaced her.
After we drove to her home and left the boxes there, she asked whether I would like to have some coffee. I proposed that we go somewhere out. She said yes, why not. She has a couple of hours. She said she needed to go to the bathroom for fifteen minutes. She wouldn't even change her dress. Actually, she was dressed in style. Casual but elegant. Black coat and black shoes. I said she looked great. You look like a modern lady, Helen. And by the way, would I like to see the photos of this Swedish model? Sure I wanted. I almost forgot about the model.
As we drove to the place, she said she didn't want to talk about investigations today. She was a little tired and needed to relax. But we will finish them. She said we would if we work together. She said that previously she worked in the entertainment industry. Something like an assistant product manager. But it was nothing like the art or something creative. So she changed to a better-paid

position in another company. And now she is so tired of them all. With all their requirements and all the limitations. She said she wanted to have her own company. In a way. As a joke, she called it the SpyCorp. Ha-ha. Now she will watch others and enjoy the action. It wouldn't be like it was before. They watched and controlled her too much before. Now that's enough. She will play her own games. Maybe that's a great thing about that little game in that apartment. To watch others, to stay in control. And she kept that apartment to make it the headquarters of her own company. In a way. There she collected so much data on them. It can't be in vain. There it all started. There it will end. That is where the story will end. She said this and touched my hand softly. She said I should remember. That is where the story ends. I will remember everything from this day. Or at least almost everything. A woman like this makes you remember. Today she was softer and seemed openhearted. She had all the elegance and the style about her, but that was different.

We sat at the table in a very nice place. We enjoyed the food and wine. She gave me a tablet, and I could watch her photo art that was downloaded on it. She was giving me comments. Swedish model and all this whiteness looked great. A little of jewelry and a little of clothes. There is the model still dressed in her T-shirt with a Pepsi legend on it. There, she is nude. And all the photos were good. She said she didn't buy a lot of jewelry. Though she uses her own Tiffany's stuff for the photo shoots. She isn't a real collector. She likes luxury, but not the... glut. You know. Those corporate leaders, that so-called elite taught her something in a way. The way they spend money and how snobbish and disrespectful they can be to the people. That's why she only affords herself something from Tiffany, sometimes. She wouldn't buy shoes that cost five thousand dollars. She has money, but she wouldn't. Jewelry, it's different. It is a real thing, you know. And she doesn't buy too much. And it's essential that you always should be able to drop the option. Only then it's a real luxury. You should have money. It's another thing when money has you. Those people from the high stuff there. They don't know how to be truly luxurious. You should always have some negligence about it. Like you don't care. Beautiful woman with style always should respect herself more than any dresses she wears. And same about jewels. You should wear them like you don't really care. And those people. They always care about things. They care too much. That's why they don't know about it. There's the difference between fashion and style. People just don't see it. Society now wants more. Always more. And that's trouble. The style isn't about more. It's more about the balance. She said that's why she likes Scandinavian things. Like the Scandinavian style, Bergman's movies and many other things. You know, their stylish minimalism about everything. People who survived thousand years in such cold should develop something minimal, strong and efficient. Just to survive. And fjords are magic. She never was there. But she wants to go to fjords. Previously she was so occupied with her job, but now she can go. I said I like Bergman and Fjords too.

Her photo shoots were cool. Elegant and sexy. I said she could be a pro photographer. She could make great money. Magazines would like it. She said yes. Maybe. But. You know I am not a girl who is so modest. But I do it not for money or fame. I really like it. That's all. That's the reason enough. I said she is a real artist. Oh, thanks. She was pleased.

I noticed there were some cool photo shoots with models dressed like the superwomen. There were Catwoman, Lara Croft. Something like a comic-con thing. She said yes. In the beginning, it was more of sexy stuff with some cosplay and things like this. But then she developed a more sophisticated and elegant style. And it is very sexy too but in a subtle way. But maybe she will do something close to this again. Maybe there will be some photo shoot with badass sexuality in it. Maybe some cool lady with tattoos, nude on a motorbike. I said that it could be something like Lady Godiva and Superwoman mixed. Yes, something like this. She began with a superwoman theme. And then changed. She once was at the comic-con event. It's for kids, yes, but... She tries things once sometimes to know what it is like. And at the event, she met a girl who was dressed like Lara Croft. Sexy Girl. And they dated then for a while. That's when she started to make the superheroes photo art. No, it isn't that girl in the photo. It's some model. She said she likes Catwoman and Lara. Powerful women with style. You know they are close to the danger. And so sexy at the same time. She said that some scientists say that we pay for the sex with death. But those simpler creatures that don't use genetic recombination when multiplying, they die too. We more like pay with the fear and complexity of our lives. On the emotional side. And comics heroes like Lara and Selina, you know... there is some kind of childhood experience. And they go through the dangerous adventures so smoothly. That's really sexy about them. And that girl, they had no future together. She understood it after a few weeks with her. But at that moment, she was so cool in her Lady Croft outfit. Pretty face like this. And a body of a true comics heroine. She was a dream kid. Oh, by the way, doesn't she talk too much about the private things? Maybe just wine is so nice here. I said no. It's OK. I may tell her about my dates too. Really? She would like to hear. And I told her about some girls I dated.

She told me actually she didn't really date too many people indeed. She dated some women and some men. It was just those photo shoots. They actually started it all. She said people at the board didn't like her erotic artworks. Gosh, she didn't sleep with every model. Maybe it was once or twice. But that's all. But high stuff people. They don't like you when you are not like them. At school, would you believe it or not, she was a good girl. Always got the top scores. She even played chess. A perfect student and everything. I said sure I believe. I saw her school time awards on the shelves. She said she knew I had a sharp eye. I said I am on her side. The modern woman has a right to her private life. She said that's all she asked for, but they don't see it this way. Those rumors. She doesn't know who started them. But why do people trust the rumors so easily? And why are rumors enough to make such troubles? She said that all it started long before that video was filmed at her apartment. Why couldn't she have her private time as she wanted it? She made her career. Honestly. Just worked hard and had some luck to be the youngest woman in the corporation to be promoted that high. She didn't sleep with anybody from her job or something.

But Helen, you know. All this stuff at your place,

everything around Jenny McCarthy, it looks unusual a little. No, I am on your side. It's your private thing. But you know what people are. She said yes. That's what matters. They don't accept anything irregular. And no matter soon I will burn this all. That McCarthy library will be destroyed. I am going another country. And I will need to destroy all these collections. They are just too big to be carried. But there is no problem with my photo art. I have it in the digital form, of course. I can't really leave this all to anybody in town. It's all too private. And the only person whom I trust is my former secretary. And she no matter also leaves for another place soon.
Didn't she have something with this pretty secretary lady? Oh, sorry. I felt I was asking about private things. Maybe wine too. She said no, it's OK. We are friends now. She said she didn't date her secretary. But they were friends. Close friends. But it wasn't a job that made them close. They became friends visiting the same gym. She does some fitness too. But her friend is much more obsessed with it.
It was a great night. I really enjoyed her company, her elegance, beauty, and smarts. Time floated smoothly, and we were talking and talking. I don't remember having a date that great in my entire life.
But time after time I felt uneasy. Could I be so close? Do I really know who was indeed behind this all? I remembered all those lists of people from high

corporate stuff she made. How deeply she investigated everybody. That made a sense. And I felt uneasy because there was one particular detail I couldn't get rid of.

This office lady stuck in my memory. She seemed familiar somehow. Not her entire figure exactly. But somehow it was a back of her neck I felt to be familiar.

Dec, 21

Day

Private Audio Diary of Elise

by Elise

Today I arrived at the studio just a little later. And I still felt quite sleepy. Actually, I felt so for a couple of hours on. Martin wasn't there. He actually didn't appear today at all. Instead, he sent me a peculiar voicemail. Something like a voicemail. I received it late at night. He said that he knows who was behind all these games. He said he would risk encountering this person. He will try to challenge and turn the tables, no matter how crazy it seems. He said it might be dangerous, but I shouldn't worry no matter. Now it is only his matter. Oh, boys! They always play superheroes, you know. He said that probably we wouldn't see each other again. No, he said - most probably. What a way to end with a person with whom you worked for quite a long time. Oh. He also said that he would pay me double money for this month. Actually, I kinda keep on working, finishing all the stuff, for another couple of weeks and then I am kinda fired. I kinda need to find another job. Like it is easy to do!

I now should go to Martin's apartment and pick up the files dealing with all the stuff we did recently. But

I still can't get what I should do with it.
And later in the day, one of the most irregular things happened. The Woman. She came to the studio. Just opened the door and stood there. I even didn't notice her immediately. I didn't know how long she already stood there before I was conscious of it. She had a red coat and red shoes on. What a choice! Like she wanted me to remember her for a long time. She was queenly appareled.
I kinda said hi in a low and silent voice. And she only answered me with the movement of her pupils. That was enough. Very expressive. She walked around the place like some cat. In slow steps. She took one of the things, one of the books and regarded it like she was interested in everything there. I remember that Martin once proposed a strange theory. He said that in general every woman who is attractive, sexy et cetera can be described as one of the two types. Either she is a cat or a bird. I suppose that in his terms she is a very attractive woman. And sexy. Actually, I suppose that if I were a man, I would be horny about her. Actually, if I were a more ambitious girl, I probably would want to be her. Most probably. I remember how Martin noted that she has something he called the inner elegance. Don't remember he said something like that about me. I am not jealous.
We then even kinda talked a little. She told me that

previously she also worked in the entertainment industry. She was something like a product manager. I asked her about the usual stuff - what plans she has and so on. She answered politely without much of detail. Then she took one of the books from the shelf again and regarded it. It was something about peoples, nations, and society in general. Holding it, she made a little speech. Maybe we don't know too much about society in fact. How can we know when we don't know those whom we meet every day. And those we meet accidentally. We almost never know the single person for sure. How can we know? Most probably society is just built on lies. In a way. And on prostitution, I suppose. All those lies. All those games. In games like these, if you want to win the hearts right, you need to hold the balls tight. And for a while she was silent. You know what? I hope you won't need my advice, but I wanna give one. If any bitch, then the super bitch. I mean - if you prostitute yourself. In a way. And she smiled. Then, make them pay as much as they can. Just if other kids don't want you to play the games they play, invent your own games and play them as you want, honey. And she released a long breath out. Isn't it peculiar?

And then she went out. And I didn't notice again when she did it. Strangely enough, I soon discovered the key on the table. I didn't see it before, but I knew what it was then. It was a key to Martin's apartment.

And one more strange thing for today's record. When I was going home, I saw Martin and Helen at some cafe having food and talk. Or at least, it seemed like that. It flashed, and there was some distance, but maybe they really sat close to cafe's window having talk and food and drink, and I don't know what else. Maybe I am just a little tired. No matter what I feel about Martin after he left this way, I am a bit worried about him. I didn't see him for some days in a row, what seems unusual. Hope he is really well. Going to bed. End of line.

Some Notes on Bad Girl Attractiveness from Dictaphone Record by Martin

Some people believe that the women coined by society as bad girls in many cases seem to be more attractive to others than those who are considered to be the good ones. Is it only an accidental believe? Or does it have some kind of ground for it? Undoubtedly a bad girl does not mean a sexy girl necessarily. It is known that many people would call their mate a bad girl during foreplay just to increase excitement. In rare cases, a woman can call herself a bitch or a bad girl to show her partner that she is horny. Maybe that explains something. People may subconsciously believe that the bad girls are hornier and readier for sex. Such suggestion may lead to a simple explanation. The responsibility of being good to others is what belongs to the Superego part of a mentality that is opposite in its influence on Ego to Id responsible for an initial impulse of sexual manifestations that include signs of being horny and signs of sexual desire. Or telling it another way, it is the society that wants a girl to be good, but her sexual desire is what placed on her animal side of personality.

But that is too simple to look sufficient. There can be

something else at least. Or at least, a more extensive kind of explanation regarding the question from multiple standpoints and thus representing more acceptable reasoning for the matter. The simplest and most obvious path I may choose is to compare an attractive bad girl presentation in the media and relation of the question to the major theories regarding the human nature from the basis of psychology and biology. Media industries like television and cinema reflect many archetypal views of the broad audiences. The movie business has widely used the image of a smart, beautiful and extremely dangerous lady playing tricks with men. And these men almost consciously understand how dangerous the matter is, but still cannot stand temptation and go crazy about the sexy bad girl risking their careers, fortunes and lives entirely. Sexy bad girl image like this is seen in a classic character by Sharon Stone in the Basic Instinct. Of course, it is not the only example, but just one of brightest examples. List of attractive bad girls is long one and, for instance, includes Jamie Presley in Poison Ivy series and James Bond rivals like Pussy Galor from the legendary 1964 Goldfinger movie. In such stories, male characters are attracted to the sexuality of woman no matter what dangers it means. Thus these stories manifest prevailing importance of sexuality over anything else. Sex is so important that nothing can get in its way. And the women skillful and sexy enough can play great tricks of manipulation using natural desires of others to reach their aims. And thus men may like women whom society doesn't like at all.

Otherwise, the good girls are those girls who should be adored by parents at home and by teachers at school. Freud suggested in his works that normally the infantile attractiveness, that is quality mostly adored in a girl by parents, should transform into mature sexuality adored by men. And in cases when such transformation does not appear that may happen to be pleasing to parents, but not to a husband of such woman as she makes a cold wife. And as great Austrian analyst explained it, she is not able to fulfill her wife's duties. Parents usually give kids the elements of Superego to be integrated into their mind when instructing them how to behave in society correctly, but do not support the development of sexuality. On another side, according to same Freud, it is a parental love that naturally stimulates future sexual intentions in a person.

Actually if to take in account the fact that the sexuality is a biological item, then good and evil as they presented in society may be understood like not having a link to how sexy a person is. If sexuality, as our subconsciousness perceives it, is the complex of manifestations showing the quality of health and essence of the genetic code of a person, then it does not matter whether this person behaves according to the society's rules or not. Regarded from this point the rules of society can be seen as something rather conventionally shaped. But then there may be something that still presents the good girls like the less sexy creatures. Of course, it is so if we still believe that the bad girls seem to be more attractive in most cases.

Maybe the core of a question can be found if we will try to understand what the evil really is. I suppose that the evil has some rather artificial shape into society. The truth is that the society will always defend most of it no matter what. That is why all things that the most of the people do are always coined with the term - normal. And democracy is not a reason for it. Such understanding about the essence of what is good and what is bad existed in previous political formations of society. There is the difference in between democracy and the power of mass. In 1930s Germany most people accepted that to repress minorities is a normal thing and that was absolutely OK for most of the population in the country. They just let it be. Democracy doesn't mean liquidation of minorities by majorities. Instead, it means a guarantee of basic rights for all. But once in Germany, the opposite was normal only because most of the people accepted this as a social norm.

That is why we are always taught that there are evil minorities that corrupt society. Some criminals and perverts. They just hide somewhere, and government cannot find them all. But what if we all contribute to currents of evil existing in the world? The thought seems to be crazy. But what if there is a point in it? Are majorities that perfect or they just possess some power to grant themselves with any excuses?

An ancient legend about exile from Eden gives a suggestion on origins of the evil. What was the essence of the original sin? Being unconscious of evil and being not able to recognize it, Adam and Eve were blessed. And then they tried the forbidden fruit. They then recognized themselves to be a separated part of nature. And when a human understood own pains consciously together with the fact that she is a single unit of the universe, at the same moment a human understood that any another human similar to her has similar abilities to be hurt. Thus she recognized the evil and let it exist in her mind. Animals kept eating and fighting each other but stayed inside of Eden as they did not recognize the evil because they did not recognize themselves to be separated from nature. Church says that the animals and kids are blessed as they do not recognize the evil. As soon as you start to recognize the evil, it makes you responsible for it. Evil thus in most cases does not appear because someone really wants it to happen. It is only a few people definitely suffering the mental problems who receive any sort of satisfaction from doing evil to others on purpose. And they are the smallest minority.

As soon as a human being found himself out of Eden, he kept acting according to his natural intentions like those god's creatures that stayed inside. But the difference was that now as one god's son being able to distinguish the evil from the good he should act with more responsibility. But he did not, and Cain killed Abel as one animal kills other when being not able to find another way to overcome a competitor. Through ages, people kept competing for the power and sex partners using any methods they had available. And thus evil in most cases is not a result of a conscious wish for creating it but just the conflict in between Id of one person and Ego of another. We may try to get what our nature wants to get including sex, power or any sort of dominance without considering how it may hurt others. And that is why most of us are somehow suffering a trauma received from own parents. Society would not admit it as it believes that everything having mass existence is normal. And what is normal is not always good. For example, people typically die at the end of life, but that usually doesn't make anybody happy. For society, it is too hard to admit that the kids are born due to a biologic program of parents, and they simply can't know all elements of future conflict in between their natural intentions and needs of a kid's personality. And many people who claim they want to have kids, in future when it comes, dramatically hurt their kids causing some serious psychological problems.

Many bad girls are just these kids that subconsciously display a protest against their parents' inability to treat them like personality, like a special person instead performing the regular parents-to-kids program. Evil happens because we regard ourselves as special beings and others like usual ones. Most of the parents would tell you that their kids are special. But they do consider their kids to be special because those kids have special parents, but not because they would be special no matter who their parents would be. And thus Id of parents only wants to proceed a programmed reproduction cycle, when Ego of kids has a need to be recognized as unique one. The truth is that the parents, when treating a teenage kid, mostly try to make their kid learn the rules of society. They want their child to integrate into society because that is their parental project and thus it will be their success if such integration will be achieved. But wishes of a child can be definitely more specific than this.

Kid faces a society trying to put his or her unique personality into a proper format. And the institution that plays a prominent role in this process is the school. A problem of contemporary mass education is that it spends a considerable amount of its strength for formatting students, but not for creating conditions for the development of creativity in a person. School teaches us to act a role that may be standing opposite to our basic intentions. And thus, that may also explain why bad girls look so sexy sometimes. Good girls are those who act the role, and bad girls may seem to be more individual. Too much acting of a role may be what leads to neurosis. There is such film with Kathleen Turner called the Crimes of Passion. A story is about a woman who has a well-paid job but pretends to be a hooker just to lead a more diverse sexual life. Probably it is her social role that motivates her to do so. Such spicy things are not part of it, and she searches for them creating another self. Of course, a movie is a rather grotesque one, but there is some point in it.

At school when a good girl receives the mark that is not so good as her usual top result, she may face a teacher explaining to her that it isn't good for her to put her level down. But when some bad girl receives the same mark but which is better than her usual bad marks, she can be even praised for it. Isn't it some differentiated approach? School is what can be regarded as a perfect model of society repressing person's individuality. In later years of human life, similar things happen. Did you notice that the biggest sex scandals happen only with persons occupying high posts? A porn star is never a principal element of such dirty stories. There is nothing a porn star can do to break society's expectations. If someone tries to express a negative opinion on usual famous porn star's activities, this person won't have society's support, but most probably will be claimed to be a sexist and chauvinist. But what if a woman who holds a high position in the political system or the big corporation will be found performing less wild sex actions, something not in a regular way, for example, participating the BDSM club, group orgy, hiring an escort or just having an often change of partners? That may be a scandal. Society won't support her side in general. Many people would consider that she deserves to be blamed. No one really blames the porn stars, but the good girls could be blamed for less activity than that. That's an interesting point.

In economics there is such term - demand discrimination. That means that the company sells a similar product at different prices to different buyers. If a person is ready to pay more, he does. Thus the unified price of equilibrium does not exist. That is what society does to people since the school years. Society is about making people bear some responsibilities. That is the difference in between society and the Coca-Cola company. Coca-Cola company sells drinks at the unified prices, and society sells responsibilities. More correctly a society sells the roles and statuses and responsibilities are the coins of exchange. A certain amount of responsibilities is the price for a particular role in society. But actually it isn't that important what you would call a price and what you would call the product, there is this sort of link in between role and responsibilities. The more a person shows readiness to get responsibilities the more he receives. That is why some good girls wearing the proper business suits face problems when being sexy. And not only during the school years.

If society is an author of the play, then it searches for actors who fit in specific roles. And most probably you should choose among those roles offered. But what if your role is more a choice of society than your choice? And it does not fit you that well? People usually go schizo when their personality splits into two parts. One still serves to the society and another to the basic biological intentions. That is how maniacs are made. And that is why maniacs may seem to be so good and so law-abiding before their full activity is revealed.

There are indeed two parts of personality, and when they do not work well, it breaks the human being from inside. It is again an essential question of the evil. The question of a bad girl's sexuality is not about being bad but about the manifestation of individuality. The external problem happens in between society and this individuality, and the internal one happens in between these two sides themselves. There is such saying from a movie. People say that the evil wins when good is silent. But true is twice shorter. Evil wins. It is indeed true that the evil is inexhaustible in human society. And there is a reason for it. To prevent evil in a person, to prevent conflict in between Id of one person and Ego of another, a human being needs to balance his biological individuality and his social one. Biological individuality is a permanent unit. It has a hundred percent level no matter what because this is guaranteed by the genetic code. But social individuality is not permanent. Thus it has the quality of a double possibility. It may be present, and it may be not present in the human. And it is evident that in an average human it may happen to be around fifty percent level. Hundred percent of biology and only fifty percent of humanity – an apparent imbalance. Evil wins.

The truth is that to be really good a person needs to have personality. That is how in theory a strong biological personality may benefit to goodness in a person. But actually, same way conformism may be prescribed by the biological behavior as a result of evolution proceeding in groups. Thus biology does not supply the good qualities in a person because good and bad are items of society, not biology and they exist like the social qualities. The individuality of social kind is necessary for a good human because this sort of individuality serves as the shell where human qualities can be kept. If a person has this, he will always act according to his own principles. If he doesn't, he will conform to the general rules no matter what these rules are.

Asher's experiments proved that the most of the people conform and there is a minority acting according to their own principles no matter what others say. Maybe that is what also prescribed by evolution. The social group doesn't need everyone to be a reformer. It is enough to have few who will develop the possible options. And then, when society would find itself in a state of crisis, most of the people would like to change something, but they wouldn't know what exactly to do. And at this moment they would use those options. On one side, the idea doesn't need too many minds to be born, and on the other side, conformism is what keeps a society strongly united no matter what. Society needs heroes who will risk trying to change it. That is why we are able to stay conformists, but at the same time to adore those who challenge the society. Why are movies about serial maniacs like the Silence of

Lambs are so popular no matter that its leading character is one doing such harm to society? People may almost subconsciously like Hannibal Lecter only because he challenges an entire society having no fear about it. An even more evident example is shown by superheroes who always wear masks and don't follow the rules. And do you remember who was the very first superhero in the very first book of our civilization? Some guy with superpowers who stood against the Empire, fighting for all the good people.

In the Bible, Jesus Christ was given the cross when being already famous and adored by the people of Palestine. That means that the entire mass of his followers let him be crucified by a few Roman soldiers without an attempt to prevent it. And that is why people may like those who challenge the society. They take an entire risk of the revolutionary affair on them. And rest of people may remain spectators. People like Jesus Christ and Giordano Bruno revolutionized society and paid with their lives for that. Christ was killed by Roman Empire and Bruno by Christ's church that replaced Roman Empire in medieval times, occupying the Eternal city of Rome and taking power over the minds of European people. Time after time, society comes to a crisis, to its break-point moment and thus it asks for heroes ready to sacrifice their lives for the sake of others.

Partly, something like this may be true about those whom we call the bad girls. They don't play by standard rules, and we may suspect that they may present some different principles. Ask yourself how many films you watched featuring a protagonist challenging the society. Such films are hundreds. And Hollywood makes them through decades because we still like them. We like the heroes in them. In recent years there are more of films about dystopia and the hero standing against it. That possibly says that the western society feels itself a little stagnated and now we love heroes even more. We would like an action character who stands against the whole army. We would like an artist challenging the industry. And it is no surprise we would like the bad girls sometimes. We may just like a woman who challenges the industry giant in her fight for the right to choose what she likes.

Society just needs a few guys with some badass complex to be able to change. Another good example is arts. Arts are a very existentialist thing. They need an understanding of evil through the experience of evil because art can't exist morally without it. Artists are always rebellious. They aim for changes. They are passionate. And big passion may have some destruction in it. The thing is that this badass should be the proper one to make a person an artist, but not some murderer. For example, Hitler tried to enlist in art academy, but he didn't become an artist. Hitler was a destroyer. And Rothko, Picasso, and Dali were destroyers too. The difference is that the Nazi leaders were destroying the human lives, and the great masters of creation were destroying the art. Thus they reinvented it and gave it an influx of new life. Art is about destiny. It happens when there is no choice other. Artist can't survive the other way. And also art is a form of emotional exhibitionism.

And that is what makes me think about Lady Godiva. I think she runs away from the Tower where her abstract husband strictly rules. Being a good girl would mean to stay and to obey him no matter what. And their conflict is not about power over the city exactly. It is more about freedom and respect. Her husband insists that she has nothing of her own inside the tower. She thus lives in it thanks to the fact that she sleeps with him. That makes her a prostitute of a kind. She has only her beautiful body and her physical sexuality to be valued inside the tower. But that's not enough for her. She needs her personality and her sexuality to be regarded as a more complex thing. She can't accept such position. That is what some less complex and more infantile creature can do as such creature won't see trouble about it. But she loses her cloth that is an artifact of material culture. Cloth saves from cold. It may provide with status, but hides much of the truth. She thus becomes closer to a state of Eve in Eden. In the beginning, she uses the only thing that she can use inside the tower – her sexuality. But as she goes away from its shade, she develops a more sophisticated way to exist. She is in the saddle, and her horse is strong as nature in the human should be. In the eyes of a society, the Lady is a bad girl. And she is still here. Sexy and powerful. Riding like this, she is a mystery. She is an enchantress. And true beauty is always a mystery unfolded. I suppose that now she should be riding the highways having some cool motorcycle under her, dressed in some black clothes with the aviator sunglasses on. Though, her dress and her road can be something else. But no matter. She definitely visits the places where we live. Our cities. Our ways. And if we have an eye sharp enough, we can see that she has survived and that she is sexy.

Dec, 21
Night
from Dictaphone Record
by Martin

All, what happened in these few months is not so easy to comprehend. But I think I can try. Now when I think I know what it was, I can see it clear. Finally. All these days I was like in some tunnel having a limited vision of the situation. In depth of the story, it all began because there was some corporation that didn't see a problem in using prohibited methods of competition. And also there was a person who was smart and courageous. And this person made up a plan that was risky and complicated. And this person was finally able to fool everybody including me.

And this person was sure smart enough to use some dark strangers to communicate with everybody involved. Just the accidental amateur actors were used as connections. They were delivering the messages and wraps.

It happened that the Corporation C appeared ready to cheat two its opponents – Corporations A and B. One of them should lose its principal project, and another one should be blamed for that. This way C should stay out of all connections to the matter. Someone probably in a gray hat and a gray coat gave them a reason to think that they may have the Lost Folder if they pay enough. It was said that the folder with the data on the Principal Project was lost at some apartment. But who could believe in such simple thing? True was that simplicity made this turn a genius one. To justify it the creator of the master-plan simply added a scent of sex in the plot. Everyone knows that the passion can make anybody go crazy when even it is president of the state himself. Everyone can lose prudence.

Initially, it was planned to collect enough of files and the data proving that the story was like this. It also meant involving some people that would prove that by believing it to be true. One peculiar girl with interest for sex adventures went through several amusements that were so entertaining that she believed everything to be as pure as her pleasure was. She wasn't a true actress, but she was better than this. She was unconscious actress what made her performance most brilliant. And most believable. On another side an author of serious documentary films, having an evident interest in actions of business as a journalist and having evident interest for pretty women as a man, was involved to be a reliable media source.

Also, it is possible that the Corporation C will not have an advantage. Simply because they don't know that the folder, itself is nothing but another toy in the game. Everything was the game.

Now the story was fabricated and performed. And soon it will generate the damage for corporations that were chosen as targets. The creator of the story receives an ovation in addition to a generous amount of money.

Now I don't know what I can do except doing something what creator is not exactly expecting. I just will encounter her for one more time. This time we will both know what the truth is.

Dec, 24 and After
Private Audio Diary of Elise
by Elise

Many things changed since things happened. I am moving soon. I was proposed to occupy a position in another city. I will be working for one of the nationwide TV channels. That won't be a major TV show in prime time, but at least one of the major channels. And most important - I will have much bigger salary than before. And telling something about other participants of recent events, I don't know much. I heard Susan also moves to another city to become a celebrity. She is going to participate one of the reality shows. She also participated one more photo shoot for some magazine and even appeared on the cover.

The story wasn't revealed to the broad audience, but still, it was shaped sharp enough to cut deep into the minds of corporate leaders. Corporations of the industry suffered some blow but were not crushed. They will soon rebuild their towers. Lady has escaped. She did it with the help of some humble knight she charmed. One corporation lost the project, another one lost its reputation, being blamed for espionage, the third one paid for all the game and got the false data. All three suffered some damage and got no advantage from the situation. All the ABC of them was hit. They were given the story that seemed true. And they paid a lot just to see this story happen. And the lady vanished, riding away from the shadow of their might. She just exchanged her cloth for her own little kingdom.

And about Helen, I didn't hope to find where she went to. But I tried to find something about her past. I didn't get much. It all looked like I saw all those things in a dream. Place where Helen, as I know, lived is empty. And I couldn't find anybody like a realty agent or anybody else who could at least confirm that he knew about her. Like I kinda invented her! I seemed to be the only person who knew about her existence. And the same thing with the house. One where there was the Agency. Empty and no one knows what I am talking about. Everybody says it was unoccupied for a couple of years. No hint, no traces of what there was as we thought. Just another big empty house stuffed with luxury. Like there was some mist that came one morning, and all the strange and elegant ladies were moved away by it.

One morning there was the mist actually. Though, it stood only early in the morning. It was the day when I headed to the apartment of Martin to pick up the records he had.

That night I saw some peculiar dream. I dreamed I

am a woman dressed in the Supergirl outfit. I mean a comics character actually. Then I came to the mirror and undressed in front of it. And then I just stared in the mirror at my own self, entirely naked and unprotected.

There, in the apartment, I found the records and documents that after hours of examination would give me the situation clear. On a pile of folders, there was an open envelope. At first, it seemed to contain only a blank page. But then I noticed that there was the writing. That is where the story ends. Now I kinda know what happened. I mean in general. I actually never was in this apartment before. It was most unexpected to me that we won't make any doc film based on all this stuff. Now I think if you can't make a documentary, maybe you can make a fiction feature. Maybe I will send it to some novelist, and maybe I will have a nice share of sales.

But before I was in, there was a thing that made me delay a visit to the apartment. I drove in my old little car to the area where Martin lived. And when I started to park my vehicle, I saw something. That was another time when I was conscious of my dream state. A very sharp image of the red sports car flashed in my eyes. And it wasn't all. I also felt like I knew a man and a woman who sat in it. I thought maybe I went crazy or something. But it did seem to me that I saw Martin and Helen. The Superwoman of the story was always a mystery to me.

I followed them. Those two people who could probably be ones I know. And it happened that they were going to the airport. I kept following them when they were outside the car. I kept some distance, of course. Then I was sure who they were. I kept a distance, but I saw enough to be sure. Them indeed - Martin and Helen. And what was even stranger they just walked. And at one moment they suddenly kissed. On the lips.

Now when I know how the things really stood, I can feel easy about it. But that was weird to me when I saw them like that. After all those events they were together like that.

Now they were something different. Martin would hardly make any new journalist investigations. And she now took off her superwoman's outfit. She was now another beautiful and elegant woman. She lost her steel-made skin, her artificial cloth and revealed the lady under it. And they left together. Now they should be enjoying themselves somewhere in the Bahamas living under false names. But actually, it can be something like Norway or Iceland. Something with fjords. I will remember this day. And they left on the big airplane with the beautiful silver wings.

Life is so much brighter when you know the things like this can happen. A beautiful mystery, crossing your life like a shooting star in the sky... Some

places. Some times.
And as I remember they wore some regular clothes, nothing so special. She didn't wear something so impressive like that red coat. I am positive that Martin noticed me. At some moment he gave me a long glance to make sure. About her, I can't be so sure, but I think she knew too. When she was going away, at the moment I saw her for the last time, she lifted her hand with the beautiful red nails and kinda waved. I was staring at her back, and she didn't see me. But I think she knew I was watching and gave me the sign.

Some Notes on How to Entertain from Dictaphone Record by Helen

Entertainment our days becomes one of the major industries. Markets expand, and the audiences grow wider and wider every year. But the art of entertaining audiences is still a complicated and undiscovered matter. It is one thing to entertain someone particular, and the other is to entertain some broad segment of the nationwide audience...

Can we give to our audience something so universal but efficient that it will suit the tastes of many different people? Question is a tough one.

But in the beginning, there are primal questions of the creation. How to come with a genuine and stunning idea for the show? Hardly that is answerable. Some people believe that the hardworking is always giving the results. But my own experience is that you need to have some revelations or glimpses in the process. At least that is how I do it.

Keep thinking about what you want to achieve in effect. And maybe your subconscious will give you something. Collect this flashes and try to organize them. And then go on with hardworking. That may work indeed.

Mass entertainment has its differences compared to the classic art. It requires the happy endings and many other things too. But at least it may mean more money. Try to find the advantages. It may work too.

And no matter don't make your audience feel that you think they are stupid people. If even you are critical about the mass audience, just think about those people who are smart and intelligent. And work for them in a way. Add some hints of intellectualism and the elite vision.

I think first of all think about where you start and where you want to finish. What should your audience feel at the start and what feelings they should have when they go a full circle. And then turn on the evolution. Create steps in between point A and B. They should not know everything from the start because they want to be fooled, in a way.

Also, it is very efficient to put yourself in the chair of your audience. Think what you would like to see if it can be anything you want. Maybe for the author, it is just really great to find an audience with the similar taste. That's why it can be very useful to investigate the audiences and maybe you will find one that fits you.

But also remember that it is important to cast the proper performers for your team. They will be those who will talk to your audience. They should be able to communicate to it with all possible originality. Should be able to be genuine.

Create all the pattern for your audience to follow. They should feel free inside it, but at the same time, you need to maintain the control over the thing. And that's one of the tasks. Remember if they really like it they won't feel chained. People never know what all the truth is, but they always like the cool stories. Also, create the little gaps in which they will be able to put their own experiences and perceptions.

Seduce them and make them love your show. You should do it before they got it. Seduce them before they know they are seduced. Don't forget that your show should be a long one. Only longtime success has the great esteem today. To achieve it, create the small culminations located on the way. They should be bright, and they should develop your story a little every time. That is how it can be, at least.

Uh. What else? It all looks like some mess of the words. Maybe it's hard to have a general concept of the matter. Just I hope someday I will have some really great ideas. And maybe, then...

And then finally make it happen. Give it all. Don't cheat and make your audience as satisfied as possible.

The rest is improvisation.

To the Beautiful Rule-breakers.

CPSIA information can be obtained
at www.ICGtesting.com
Printed in the USA
BVHW031342160120
569727BV00001B/7